Falcon's Egg

Falcon's Egg

EDWARD WILLETT

SHADOWPAW
PRESS

FALCON'S EGG

Published by
Shadowpaw Press
Regina, Saskatchewan, Canada
www.shadowpawpress.com

Second edition
First published 2015 by Bundoran Press

Copyright © 2015
by Edward Willett
All rights reserved

All characters and events in this book are fictitious.
Any resemblance to persons living or dead is coincidental.

No part of this book may be reproduced in any form or by any electronic or
mechanical means, including information storage and retrieval systems, without
written permission from the author, except for the use of brief quotations in a
book review.

Print ISBN: 978-1-989398-23-4
Ebook ISBN: 978-1-989398-24-1

Cover illustration by Dan O'Driscoll
Created with Vellum

This book is dedicated to the town of Butler, Missouri, birthplace of two important people: Robert A. Heinlein, and my mother.

Chapter One

NO SMOKE ROSE from the ramshackle cabin.

There should be smoke, Lorn Kymbal thought.

He lay in the snow atop a ridge overlooking the clearing, his winter field uniform making him little more than one white lump among many in the snow-drenched landscape, peering through binoculars powerful enough he could zoom in on individual nail holes in the cabin's rough wood planking. But the windows were shuttered, the door was closed, the snow lay as thick and crisp and even as even Good King Wenceslas could have liked, and there was no smoke.

There should be smoke.

Lorn checked his watch. Two minutes until he was supposed to approach the cabin and meet with the man who had lived there for as long as he could remember...the man who had never asked to meet with him before, or shown the slightest interest in him, despite his long relationship with Lorn's parents.

He dearly wanted to unsling the multirifle he carried on his back, but one thing he knew very well about Javik, the man in the cabin—if he *was* there—was that approaching him with a weapon was a very bad idea. Even if he was the one who had asked for the meeting.

Lorn wasn't even sure why he was so nervous about this whole set-up. The only threats he normally faced in this part of the frontier—where, after all, he had grown up—were winter-starved longtooths and the occasional poacher. The dead-enders of the Skywatchers cult had been cleared out of this region long since. Lorn had cleared out a few of them himself a few months ago and had a jagged red scar on his thigh to show for it, from a slug which had come within centimetres of taking out his femoral artery, and him with it.Things had generally been quiet here.

But now it's too quiet, he thought. As they like to say in the holoadventures.

He scanned the surrounding woods. Nothing moved, and maybe that was why it seemed too quiet. Not a bird, not a barkrat, not a biterbunny. As though everything had gone into hiding.

As though something had scared them off.

Probably just a big predator, Lorn thought. Longtooth, maybe—or a pack of meathawks. Nasty, but nothing I can't handle.

Though he'd be surer of that with a weapon in his hand.

His watch vibrated. *Time to see what's what at last.* He got to his feet and headed down the snow-covered slope.

The door stayed closed. The windows stayed shuttered. The only sound was the crunch of his booted feet in the snow.

On the porch, he took one last look round at the dark, brooding woods, then put his hand on the latch. It lifted easily, and he stepped inside.

From the outside, the cabin had looked like the thrown-together-out-of-odds-and-ends shelter of some sort of bearded mountain man. On the inside, as he had suspected it would—though the man who lived there had never before, to his knowledge, allowed anyone to enter it—it looked like the nerve center of a global intelligence gathering operation...which, in a way, it was.

But Javik was not seated at the rough wooden table, above which flickered the restless lightning of holographic data displays. Instead, he lay on the bed in the corner, as rough a piece of furniture as the table, made of unpeeled branches. His eyes were closed, but his eyelids twitched, and his lips with them, though he made no sound. The green blanket beneath him was stained, and the smell rising from it made Lorn blink hard and swallow. Javik had never been one for personal hygiene, but from the look and smell of things he'd not only not bathed in weeks, he hadn't moved from the bed for days.

Maybe he's sick, Lorn thought. He stepped closer to the bed and cleared his throat. Javik didn't respond. "Javik," Lorn said. "It's Lorn Kymbal. I'm here."

Javik's eyes jerked open. "Anomalies," he said, his voice a croak. "Anomalies!" His right hand, which had been lying out of Lorn's sight on the far side of the bed, suddenly rose. In it, he held a small rectangular object, black and featureless—a netlink. "Take it!"

Lorn reached for it. The moment the netlink, still warm from Javik's hand, was in his grasp, Javik's hand dropped, and he dug under the blankets for something else Lorn couldn't see. His head turned toward Lorn, his pupils wide black pools. "Now go. Into the woods. Get out of sight."

Lorn felt the familiar surge of the anger that these days always lay close to the surface. "Like hell! You hauled me all the way out into the middle of nowhere for this! I don't care how secretive you like to be, you're damn well going to tell me—"

"Get out!" Javik snarled. His right hand came up again. Now it held a pistol, a massive, ancient slug-thrower of a design Lorn had never seen outside of a museum. The end of the barrel gaped at him like a screaming mouth. "Now!"

Lorn's hand twitched as though feeling for the familiar-but-missing weight of his own sidearm. Fuming, he backed slowly away, never taking his narrowed eyes from the reeking hulk of the man in the bed. The pistol tracked him to the door.

"Into the woods," Javik said. Now his voice held a note of pleading. "Into the woods, boy...Lorn. Out of sight. Fast!"

Lorn hesitated. "Javik—"

The pistol flashed and roared, and Lorn ducked instinctively but uselessly as a large chunk of the doorframe disintegrated, showering him with splinters. "Damn it, Javik!"

"Out!" Javik said, the sound a howl. "Out! Hide! Now! Time's up!"

Furious, Lorn turned and slammed out through the door. He ploughed through the deep snow and into the woods, then turned and glared back at the cabin. *The man's finally gone crazy*, he thought.

Crazier, he amended. Javik hadn't exactly been right in the head since the day he'd installed a permanent link to the planetary 'Net in his own brain and whatever bizarre software-to-wetware translation algorithm he'd come up with to make the interface possible. *Why does he even* need *those holodisplays?* he wondered. He snorted. *Because he can't get an upgrade, that's why. Technology's leaving him behind. Maybe he's—*

His thought broke off as he heard a faint sound, the rustle of something small moving through the snow. *So not every-thing's been scared away.* He glanced through the screen of branches toward the noise. *Probably a barkrat. Too bad I can't shoot at it without Javik emptying his pistol at me. Make a good supper—*

He froze. The thing moving through the snow wasn't a barkrat. In fact, it wasn't any animal he'd ever seen before.

What it *looked* like was a giant black spider, but no such creature existed on Peregrine to his knowledge—certainly not in these familiar mountains, though who knew what dwelt in the uncharted jungles of Margaret's Land, across the sea...

Then he realized what it *really* was, and he tried to stop breathing. Because he had seen something like it before...*but not on Peregrine*. He had seen it in *Mayflower II*, the ancient starship in orbit above the planet, whose near-disastrous arrival seven years before had nearly led to the planet's destruction—not to mention his own: he'd almost died there as a teenager.

It was a robot, kin to the maintenance robots aboard that ship—maintenance robots that could also be programmed to kill.

Though this one was much smaller, little bigger than the barkrat he'd first thought it. It scuttled across the snow on eight flickering black legs. It scaled the wall of the cabin. It dashed across the tree-branch roof and dropped down the fieldstone chimney.

Javik's pistol boomed once, making Lorn flinch and sending snow sliding from the roof.

And then the cabin exploded.

The blast and a wave of searing heat hurled Lorn onto his back, burying him in the snow, while bits of wood and metal and stone tore through the tree branches above him in a deadly hurricane. Bark and leaves and branches dropped all around him. He could hear debris pattering the ground for several seconds.

Lorn hauled himself to his feet, coughing on the acrid smoke drifting past him. He stared at the shattered hulk of the cabin, nothing left but a few blackened support timbers, splintered and splayed out from the few hearth stones left standing like the petals of some strange charcoal-colored flower.

He didn't bother looking for Javik's remains; he knew he wouldn't find them.

Shit, he thought. *Shit shit shit.* The crazy man with the built-in netlink had always just been here, part of the background of his life as long as he could remember. And now, just like that, he was gone.

He lifted the netlink in his hand and examined it. Blank and black, it told him nothing. He'd have to activate it if he wanted to learn anything. Which at the moment seemed like a really bad idea.

Javik knew that thing was coming. He knew it was coming, and he wanted me to see it...and to have this. But why?

Why me?

He hadn't been close to Javik. The only person who could make any claim to have been close to Javik was his mother. And now I'll have to be the one to tell her he's dead. Damn fool. What the hell did he get himself mixed up in? What is he trying to mix me up in?

"Anomalies," he growled. He pocketed the netlink, turned, and climbed back up to where he had left his pack and his snowshoes, unshipping his multirifle as he toiled up the slope. He didn't figure he'd be putting it down soon because whoever had sent that robot likely hadn't wanted any witnesses. He had to get out of there. "Damn snow," he muttered as he trudged along the ridgeline toward his camp, a kilometer distant. "How am I supposed to hide my tracks in this?"

The answer was, of course, that he wasn't. All he could do was keep an eye on his back trail and hope that if those black spider-robots moved in pairs, they didn't have enough autonomy to follow trails in the snow—even really obvious trails like the one he was leaving.

But he couldn't keep looking behind *all* the time. An hour later, he was struggling up a particularly steep and slippery bit of slope toward the rocky outcropping he had chosen as a landmark to mark the route down to his camp, just a couple of hundred metres away on the far side of the ridge. The climb had required him to sling his multirifle again and use both hands to take advantage of the handholds provided by the undergrowth. He knew how vulnerable he was during those four or five minutes, and that made him hyperaware of the sounds in the snow-shrouded woods all around him—otherwise, he might never have heard the soft slithering sound of something behind him.

He threw himself to the side. The multirifle was out of the question, but his sidearm was in his hand even before he raised himself up again, facing back down his trail—just in time to see the black spiderbot, twin to the one that had skittered down Javik's chimney, gathering its metal legs under it. It jumped, and he fired at the same time.

The pistol, like the multirifle, could fire a laser, a slug, or an explosive shell. He'd set it to default to the slug, and the bullet caught the spiderbot in mid-air. A single pistol shot, as he knew from bloody experience, couldn't transfer enough energy to an onrushing human attacker to stop his forward momentum, but the spiderbot massed far less than a human: it wasn't hurled back, but it *was* stopped in mid-jump. It dropped into the snow, legs splaying out as it fell. It immediately scuttled forward again, but the momentary pause had given Lorn enough time to thumb his sidearm from slug to laser. He pulled the trigger. A flash of light, and the spiderbot simply...stopped. There was a neat round hole through its center, the edges glowing red but already darkening. Lorn rolled over again and frantically scrambled on up the slope.

He'd just crested the ridge when the spiderbot exploded.

The blast sent him tumbling down the slope in a welter of snow. Ten metres downhill, he slammed into a tree trunk. Groaning, clutching his bruised side, he pulled himself upright and looked at the cloud of smoke dissipating overhead. "If Javik wasn't already dead, I'd kill him myself," he said out loud. He shook his head. His ears rang. "And I really should stop talking to myself." Then he snorted. His therapist had said something like that. "Which is reason enough to keep right on doing it!" he said. Then he clamped his mouth shut because *that* had just sounded crazy.

He could see the bright blue of his tent just a few more metres downslope through the trees. With relief, he struggled to his feet and stumbled down to it.

Hoping the spiderbots didn't travel in *threes*, he set to work striking camp. He wanted to be kilometres away before dark... and before he looked at the netlink. He had everything in his backpack and was heading down the slope into the next valley over from the one the unfortunate Javik had called home within ten minutes. He continued to keep a close watch on his back trail, but nothing moved, and as he plunged through the snow, he heard birdcalls resuming in the trees around him—a reasonably good indication, he hoped, that no strange black spiders were stalking him through the trees.

At the bottom of the valley, a stream burbled over rocks, flowing to his right—south—eventually emptying into the Green Falls River, the biggest river in this part of the Peregrine wilderness, and a relatively heavily populated region, though the scattered farms and villages along it were still considered remote from the heartland on the other side of the mountains rising behind him. If he set out straight ahead, over progressively lower ridges, he would relatively soon emerge into the vast desert that dominated the eastern half of the continent, stretching all the way to the ocean. It was out there that he and his father had seen an aircraft crash seven years ago, when he was just fifteen, and had rescued from the wreckage Art Stoddard, whose arrival on the planet from *Mayflower II* had triggered so much change.

Not enough change, Lorn thought, not for the first time.

His boots were waterproof and heated; he stepped into the stream without hesitation and began picking his way downstream. Running water was still the best way to throw anything off a trail, whether human, animal, or—he hoped—robot. The going would be slow and the footing treacherous, but it was more important to cover his tracks than to traverse large distances. Distance would mean nothing to something like those spiderbots.

As he cautiously made his way along the streambed, checking behind him at regular intervals, he tried to figure out where they had come from. They clearly weren't of Peregrine design. That pointed directly at *Mayflower II*.

Could they have been smuggled down from the ship? There were dead-enders on board—Art Stoddard's parents, for example—who refused to descend to the surface, living aboard the starship as though nothing had changed (though he suspected even the Stoddards weren't averse to eating the fresh food shipped up to *Mayflower II* by shuttle).

But the only way to get anything down to the surface from the ship was via that same shuttle, and knowing what he knew of the security procedures in place, he had a hard time picturing how that could happen. If the devices weren't found during the initial screening on the ship, they would surely be found during the careful examination on the planet. The Peregrine authorities weren't about to trust the good intentions of anyone who had chosen to remain aboard the ship that had once threatened to bombard the planet with matter/antimatter missiles.

That didn't mean, though, that the designs hadn't been smuggled down, and the spiderbots constructed in some hidden microfactory. Pretty much anything could be made by one of those, given the right programming and raw materials. So that could explain how they had been constructed. The bigger question was why—and without looking at the netlink, it was a question he couldn't even begin to answer.

One thing was clear. Javik, the man hardwired into the planetary 'Net who had been the first person outside the government to know about the approach of *Mayflower II* all those years ago, had also known the spiderbot—or something—was coming for him. Which meant not only that he had discovered something someone desperately wanted to remain secret, but also that those same someones knew their secret had been discovered.

The uncomfortable question from Lorn's point of view, then, was: did they also know Javik had summoned *him*?

If they did, they knew his name. They couldn't know where he lived, since he had no fixed address, but they could well know where his parents lived, with his little sister, Melissa, now a teenager; they would know his friends—though there were few enough of those. They could threaten him in all sorts of ways.

And if that second spiderbot had had visual capability and someone had been monitoring its usage, they could be sending more—or something worse—after him right now.

"Thanks a bunch, Javik," Lorn muttered. "I love you, too."

He glanced up at the sky. He had hours more daylight. He intended to make the most of them.

Chapter Two

SIX HOURS LATER, Lorn sat cross-legged on his sleeping bag, tucked inside his tent, which in turn was tucked beneath an overhanging cliff face, hidden from the unfriendly gaze of any passing aircraft or satellites. The heated frame had warmed the interior to the point he had taken off his white winter outerwear and was comfortable in his regulation State Security Intelligence Network black T-shirt and pants. He held the netlink in his right hand, regarding it warily.

It was currently powered down, which was supposed to mean that it was untraceable...although Lorn knew full well that commercially sold netlinks in fact contained secret hardware and code to enable the government to track them anywhere, anytime, powered down or not. But this didn't look like a commercial netlink: it looked like a black market version, neither company logo nor serial number marring its black matte finish. *Come on*, Lorn chided himself, *this is Javik we're talking about. There's no way he handed you something that could be traced.*

But...if he turned it on, would it link to the 'Net? And *then* could he be traced?

He had another option, of course. He could simply throw it in the snow and hike away without ever looking at it. Javik was crazy. Even his Mom had said as much. Getting mixed up in whatever had killed Javik would make him equally crazy.

On the other hand, that bloody robot had tried to kill him.

He thumbed the power button.

The netlink's screen lit instantly. He saw at once that it was not connected to anything, which was a relief. That made it nothing more than a data storage device...but what data?

The device answered that question almost as he thought it.

"Lorn Kymbal," said Javik's voice, though the screen displayed nothing but the usual status icons against a blue background. "I have chosen to give this to you for two reasons. One, as a part of this planet's security apparatus, you have the necessary knowledge and training to potentially investigate the information contained herein, with at least some possibility of surviving that investigation."

"Hello to you, too," Lorn muttered.

"Two," Javik's voice continued, "although you are part of the security apparatus, you also have connections to Art Stoddard, the young woman known as Shadow, and the former revolutionary Avara Morali. These connections could serve you well, depending on how you choose to deal with this data."

This is sounding more ominous by the minute, Lorn thought.

"If you are hearing this, I am dead," Javik said. "I signed my death warrant the moment I downloaded this data. I thought it a reasonable exchange. My life has meant very little to me for years. I trust my death may be more meaningful." His voice stopped.

And I guess that's your epitaph. I've heard worse.

A new voice spoke: a generic voice, a computer voice. "To unlock this device, please press your thumb against the screen."

Biometric lock, Lorn thought. Not perfect, but way better than a password. Then he frowned. How could Javik have my thumbprint?

No answer to that, and no one he could ask. He pressed his right thumb to the screen.

The device beeped. "Identity confirmed. Corporal Lorn Kymbal, State Security Intelligence Network, you are authorized to view the data on this device. Have a nice day."

A new icon appeared on the screen, a green circle. Lorn thumbed it. Javik's voice began speaking again. "The first anomaly to impinge on my consciousness was an encrypted message transmitted by satellite to a strangely indeterminate address that resolves to one of the secure servers of the planetary government. The encryption was of a type I have never seen before and unbreakable with any of my usual tools.

"My netlink algorithm has deteriorated over the years, and there could well be new military-grade encryption schemes with which I am unfamiliar. However, what heightened the anomalous nature of the message was its point of origin. It came, the transmitting satellite insisted, from the far side of the planet: specifically, from deep within the jungles of Margaret's Land."

Lorn touched the pause button and stared at the netlink. Margaret's Land (named, the story went, after the back-on-Terra girlfriend of the scout who had originally identified Peregrine as habitable) was the sole continent on the far side of the world. There *were* only two continents, in fact, although there were a number of significant island chains, mostly uninhabited, scattered around the planet.

Margaret's Land had only a few permanent settlements, all clinging to the more temperate southern coastline, where the temperature and humidity were sauna-like for only eight months of the year instead of all twelve. Aside from some fishing and a modicum of agriculture, needed simply to support the population, the settlements' sole business was catering to the wilderness adventurers who liked to test their mettle against the jungle. A distressingly high percentage of the time, the jungle won. But the fact hundreds of adventurers had vanished without a trace into the continent's interior over the past few decades seemed only to encourage more to mount their own expeditions. The driving force for such suicidal foolishness was a single sentence in the original recorded-audio scouting report, which conspiracy theorists had ever since been claiming indicated an alien city had been seen in the jungle, a city which supposedly vanished between one orbital pass and the next.

In the transcript, the sentence in question read more like gibberish than anything else—"City sighted...beamslice matter forget I can't...buildup ruins/not?" was the most coherent version of it Lorn had seen—but of course, every official attempt to point out that the sentence was almost certainly nothing more than the product of a solar-flare-garbled transmission, or a slightly tipsy scout celebrating his first habitable planet, was simply more grist for the conspiracy-theorist mill. No one who had ever emerged from the jungle alive had produced any evidence that there was anything in the tangled wilderness other than thorny undergrowth, twisted trees, and wildlife armed with a truly alarming variety of natural defenses of the claws/teeth/spines/deadly poison variety. Those who had *not* emerged alive hadn't produced any evidence either, of course, but somehow the mere fact they had vanished was taken as proof there must be something to the tale—especially since the government had long ago made clear it would not make the slightest effort to rescue anyone foolish enough to risk the jungle.

Now Javik claimed he had detected a strange signal emanating from the middle of Margaret's Land? It was enough to make a conspiracist hyperventilate...or, in the case of some of the more excitable ones, orgasm.

But those spiderbots were nothing alien. They were too similar to the maintenance robots on *Mayflower II* to be anything other than human-made.

Which raised an even more disturbing possibility. Someone was up to no good in Margaret's Land...and on a planet that had just recently narrowly escaped both all-out civil war and bombardment from orbit, "no good" could be very no good indeed.

"Shit," Lorn said. It was becoming the theme of his day. He resumed the playback.

An hour later, he was no happier. In fact, he was so much less happy that his initial trepidation might well have been mistaken for jumping for joy. Because although the messages coming out of the jungles of Margaret's Land were encrypted in a way Javik had never been able to break, the messages going the other way used SSIN military encryption...and Javik knew how to get through *that*.

Someone with access to the highest levels of the Peregrine government, and an extensive clandestine network within the government, seemed to be doing nothing less than laying plans for a coup. And the timeline was frighteningly ambitious: the trigger would be pulled in less than six months.

That much was clear. But the details of the plan were presumably hidden in the unbreakably encrypted messages from Margaret's Land. Certainly, the quantity of data in those messages was enormously greater than that in the terse acknowledgements from the government servers.

The question was, what was he going to do about it?

As a corporal in the State Security Intelligence Network, his duty was clear. He should immediately hand over the netlink to his immediate superior, Lieutenant Stanford Molitor.

Lorn snorted. Like *that* was going to happen. Lorn was currently on leave because of Molitor, a by-the-book academy-trained martinet with all the imagination and people skills of a rock. A very *dense* rock.

Their latest falling out had occurred after a Molitor-organized raid on a handful of diehard Skywatchers holed up in an abandoned factory on the edge of Stepperville, a nondescript city of about 20,000 people where nothing interesting had ever happened before.

The raid had been a disaster. Twenty-seven Skywatchers, including six women—two of them pregnant—and eight children, had died, some in the crossfire, most when the building caught fire and the ceiling collapsed on them. Six SSIN agents had also died. And two civilians had been killed and eleven wounded when an old fuel tank had exploded, hurling shrapnel through a crowd of onlookers Molitor had failed to keep at a safe distance.

Sickened and furious by what he had seen—and done—Lorn had confronted Molitor in full view of witnesses. He'd been arrested for it. Locked up for a while. Finally released but kept on "stress leave," required to report every day for two hours of "therapy" with a soft-voiced noncommissioned nincompoop who was supposed to be helping him deal with his "issues" and instead had only made him angrier.

Javik's summons had seemed like a lifeline, something real to do, a reason to blow off Molitor and the therapist and the whole stupid rigamarole. He'd left a message that he was taking his saved-up leave. He'd earned some time off, after all. Maybe he hadn't exactly followed Standard Operating Procedure to have it granted, but he'd told them where he was going and when he'd be back. So he wasn't AWOL...exactly.

Anyway, that was one reason he had no desire to hand over the explosive data Javik had bequeathed him to the next-highest link in the chain of command. The other was more sinister. The messages had made one thing clear: the SSIN itself was compromised. *Compromised again*, Lorn thought bitterly. His own father had been cashiered out of the SSIN years ago because he had recognized the growing influence of the Skywatcher cult as a threat and had said the wrong thing to the wrong person. Lorn had no way of knowing who was or wasn't part of this new conspiracy, and this time around, it seemed clear, both from the messages and from the deadly spiderbots, revealing his knowledge to the wrong person wouldn't just get him kicked off the force, it would get him killed.

But there was *someone* he could give the information to: Art Stoddard. The erstwhile Conqueror of Time and Space must still have trusted channels through which he could pass along something like this. The government had given him the Starred Cross of Honor, after all, and tasked him with the important—Lorn supposed, though it sounded deadly dull to him—work of helping to integrate the former passengers and crew of *Mayflower II* into Peregrine society.

What Lorn found hard to swallow about Art, though, was that he simply wasn't the man he used to be.

Or maybe, honesty forced him to add, he aas never the man Lorn had built him up to be.

Truth was, no one could have lived up to the level of admiration his teenage self had felt for Art Stoddard. Art had arrived from outer space, had offered excitement—a little more excitement than Lorn had bargained for, culminating in his being shot and then blowing out an airlock to save Art and his companions from the Crew out to kill them—and a chance to do something that *mattered.* But Art, for all his good qualities, and all he had accomplished, had turned out to be just an ordinary man after all. Once the extraordinary circumstances that had made him great had faded into the past, he had resumed being an ordinary man, doing ordinary work, much of it in cooperation—and occasional conflict—with the woman who still called herself Shadow but whose real name was Cynthia Nikos. The daughter of the Captain of *Mayflower II,* Shadow had led the young Crawlspacer rebels who had seized control of the ship and helped prevent all-out war.

Art's wife, Avara Morali, once a Colonel in the SSIN, now hosted a current-events-and-entertainment talk show on the 'Net (Lorn couldn't stand to watch it). They also had a four-year-old daughter, Melissa (named after his sister and, he had to admit, pretty much the cutest thing to ever toddle around on two legs since *his* Melissa had been that age), a cat, a dog, a substantial home in a wealthy suburb of Bagnell, and a very nice holiday property in the mountains. In short, they were settled and respectable, their adventuring days of derring-do behind them.

But he wasn't asking for any derring-do. He just wanted to wash his hands of Javik's "anomalies," let someone else worry about it, and get back to...

...to what?

He shook his head. He didn't have an answer. He didn't know what he was trying to get "back" to. Serving the SSIN? After that last raid, he wasn't sure he wanted to serve the SSIN.

But he didn't want anything to do with *this.* He thumbed off the netlink.

Of course, deciding to dump the problem on Art was easier than actually doing it. He obviously couldn't risk transmitting the information. That meant hand-delivering the netlink, and it was a three-day hike to where he had left his ground vehicle and then more than a full day's drive from the mountains to Bagnell. It could be the better part of a *week* before he could even arrange to see Art.

So, I'd better get started, he thought. *In the morning.*

Mind made up, he tucked the netlink into a pocket of his backpack, turned off the light, and stretched out in the sleeping bag. He hoped sleep would come quickly.

It didn't. In fact, it didn't come at all.

With nothing else to think about, his mind went back to the moment when the cabin had exploded. One second, it had been there, and Javik with it. The next...

He rolled onto his side. He tried to put it out of his mind. But all that did was call up the other memories, the ones that had been keeping him from sleeping well for weeks. The burning factory. Some of the Skywatchers had run for it, dark figures silhouetted against the flames inside the building. The SSIN had shot them as they emerged. Then the women and children had started screaming. Molitor had ordered the SSIN to stay back, told them it was too dangerous. Lorn had listened to the screams. He'd disobeyed orders. He's started forward...

That was when the roof had collapsed. The screams had stopped.

The firefighters had extinguished the flames. When they could get close enough, the SSIN had examined the bodies of those who had been shot fleeing the fire.

They weren't all fighters. Two of them were pregnant women.

One of them, Lorn was pretty sure, he'd shot himself.

Dammit. He rolled over onto his back, stared up into the

darkness. No light penetrated the tent: it didn't matter if his eyes were open or closed. But just because it was pitch black didn't mean he wasn't seeing anything. He could still see the woman, eyes open, hands cradled across the ragged hole in her swollen abdomen, blood soaking the ground, her blood, her unborn infant's blood...

That was when he'd lost it. That was when he'd confronted Molitor.

It wasn't my fault. It was his. He gave the orders. I just followed them. That's my job: follow orders.

He closed his eyes, but his heart was pounding too hard to let him relax, much less sleep. He opened them again. He clenched his fists.

And then he heard the sound.

He probably wouldn't have noticed it if his body hadn't already fired itself up to full fight-or-flight mode. It was just a crack, the breaking of a twig somewhere in the surrounding forest. It could have come from an animal. It had *probably* come from an animal.

But just in case it hadn't...

Moving as quietly as he could, he shoved his feet into his boots, grabbed his coat and backpack, and then, multirifle in hand, slipped out of the tent, closing it behind him. Keeping to the shadow of the rock overhang, he crept away from the camp toward a large boulder he had made note of earlier. He rounded it, crouched down behind it, and then raised up slowly and lifted the multirifle's scope to his right eye. He thumbed it to nightvision and waited.

He expected to see an animal, or, at worst, another spider-bot. What he saw instead made him grin with relief: a man in the same SSIN winter gear he wore. The multirifle scope had already pinged the man's ID tag, identifying him as Corporal Semyon Zheglov, someone Lorn knew by name and had met once at some official reception or other. He was about to step out from hiding and announce his presence when it occurred to him to wonder just what Zheglev was doing there.

Lorn had hidden his own ID tag in a public campground fifty kilometres from where he'd parked his vehicle before hiking in. He hadn't wanted anyone connecting Corporal Lorn Kymbal of the SSIN to Javik. That meant that as far as the SSIN's tracking systems were concerned, he was camping out some three days' hike from here.

So how had Zheglev found him?

It was just possible, Lorn thought, that the twin explosions of the spiderbots had been detected by some sensor or other, but he would have been willing to bet against the possibility. The SSIN barely had resources to cover the cities. It wasn't much concerned with what went on out here, which was why those who didn't much care for the SSIN tended to *come* out here. That was why Lorn had grown up in the Wild, after all.

That left another, far more disturbing possibility: Zheglev had been actively monitoring the spiderbots—maybe even controlling them. And that meant, whatever mysterious plot was afoot, he was mixed up in it.

Which meant this was definitely *not* a social call.

He couldn't have known Lorn would be not just alert, but hyper-alert, wound up like an old-fashioned watch spring: the faint crack of the twig must have seemed unimportant. Which meant Zheglev probably thought Lorn was still asleep in his—

Zheglev stopped at the edge of the camp, raised his multirifle, and without giving any warning at all, fired a grenade into the tent.

The blast echoed from the high walls of the overhanging cliff. The blue shelter vanished in a ball of orange flame and greasy black smoke that gave way to a puddle of fire as the groundsheet merrily burned, his sleeping bag a blackened lump in the middle of it. From a distance, it almost looked like a corpse. But of course, Zheglev had to be sure. He walked cautiously toward the tent. He'd slung his rifle, but he had his sidearm in hand—

—the same hand that blew apart in a gout of blood and smoke as Lorn's first bullet smashed through it. Zheglev, screaming, turned in that direction, and Lorn's second shot, laser this time, burned through the back of his left knee. Instantly crippled, he thudded to the ground, still screaming.

Lorn rounded the boulder and strode toward the other corporal, who was trying futilely to pull his multirifle off his back with his left hand, though how he intended to fire it, Lorn didn't know. He put a second laser shot through the man's left hand to discourage him. Another scream echoed from the cliff.

By the glimmering orange light of the burning groundsheet, Lorn looked down at Zheglev. "If you'd told me you were coming," he said, "I'd have made tea."

Zheglev had rolled on his back. Eyes wide and white, he stared up at Lorn. "Kymbal, you've got to believe me, it's not personal," he said frantically, breath coming in short gasps of terror and pain. "What the hell were you doing at that cabin? They saw you through the bots' eyes, they couldn't let you get away, they ordered me to stop you." Blood was spreading around him, staining the snow, from his shattered hand and wrist. He took a shuddering breath. "Kymbal...Lorn...I'm bleeding to death. You have to..."

Lorn stepped over him and drove his booted foot down on the man's ruined arm. Zheglev screamed again, but the blood stopped. "I can bandage it and tourniquet it," Lorn said. "*If* you tell me who gave me your orders."

"I don't know!" Zheglev groaned. "Please, you have to believe me. It's just a voice. Over a comm unit. In my pack. I was to deliver the robots to the area, then stand by. The first one did the trick. The second was just a backup."

"And are 'they' monitoring you?"

"They're waiting for my report."

Lorn grunted. "Don't move." He released Zheglev's wrist and pulled him to a sitting position. Zheglev gasped as the bleeding resumed. Lorn opened Zheglev's backpack and took out the standard-issue SSIN first aid kit he found there—and an extremely *non*-standard-issue comm unit, a shiny black oval showing three green lights. He let Zheglev flop back again, opened the first aid kit, and with practiced skill applied a tourniquet and bandaged the wrist. Then he held out the communications device. "Use it," he said. "Tell them mission accomplished. Tell them I'm dead."

Zheglev nodded eagerly. He could still use his left hand, after a fashion, the laser having bored a neat, cauterized hole right through it. He raised the black oval. "Zheglev," he croaked.

"Identity confirmed," the ovoid said. Lorn frowned. The computerized voice had an odd accent—odd, but familiar, though he couldn't quite put his finger on why. "Begin transmission."

"Mission accomplished," Zheglev said, never taking his eyes off Lorn's face. "Lorn Kymbal is dead. I've got all his belongings. Nothing that looks like a data storage device."

"Transmission sent," the ovoid said. It fell silent for a moment, then beeped. "Message received. Stand by for final instructions."

Lorn blinked. *Final...?* "Uh-oh," he muttered. He turned and sprinted away from Zheglev, back toward the protective boulder.

"What are you doing?" Zheglev cried after him. "You can't leave me out here. I'll freeze to—"

His words ended in an ear-splitting blast that knocked Lorn to his knees. He felt something warm and sticky on the back of his neck and touched the place. His hand came away red with blood. It wasn't his. Red also flecked the boulder he hadn't quite reached in time.

He looked back. Very little was left of Zheglev at the place where he had left him, although he saw bits of him everywhere else he looked. "What the *hell* am I dealing with here?" he muttered. "Who *are* these people?"

He looked down at his bloodstained hand. It was shaking. He stared at it. He'd known Zheglev. They hadn't been close friends, but he'd liked him well enough. And yet Zheglev had just tried to kill him. *And I shot and tortured* him. He clenched his hand to try to stop the shaking, but the tremors simply moved up his arm. *I wasn't going to kill him. I didn't mean for him to die. That wasn't my doing. It wasn't my fault.*

Just like that Skywatcher woman wasn't my fault.

He clenched his fist tighter and then shoved it down by his side, out of sight. The groundsheet had just about burned itself out, taking the last of the light with it. But when he looked west, out from under the overhanging rock, he could see the stars bright in the sky. One particularly bright star moved steadily across the firmament. *Mayflower II*, he thought.

Between the stars and the snow cover, he had plenty of light to put a few more kilometres behind him before morning. But not in the direction he'd been intending.

There was no way he was handing this off to Art Stoddard and washing his hands of the whole thing, not after *this*. The rot went further than he'd imagined, if Zheglev, an ordinary SSIN corporal like himself, could be ordered to kill a compatriot—and was willing to do it.

That made it kind of personal—and that meant he wanted to look into it *personally*.

What he needed more than anything else was more information. He had to know what was hiding in the jungles of Margaret's Land, and he could think of only one way to find out. He would have to go there himself, reconnoiter, gather more information. Then he could decide what to do with it. Maybe then he'd give it to Stoddard. Maybe he'd do something else. He'd figure it out once he knew more.

So he wouldn't be returning to his vehicle. He would hike the other way, toward the ocean. In that direction, it was about two days to Abstraction Bay. The fishing village was too small to offer many transportation opportunities, but at least he could catch one of the ferries that nosed in from settlement to settlement along the coast and ride it to the relatively large city of New Vancouver, the closest center with an airport. A sub-orbital hop halfway around the globe, and he'd be in Ceora, the only town of any size in Margaret's Land, within a few hours. Allow another day or two to gather supplies...

He shook his head. It would still be a week before he could enter the jungle in search of the messages' source. And all the time, the plot hinted at in the netlink—and highlighted by Zheglev's attack—would be advancing. Still, there was nothing he could do about it.

Well, there was *one* thing. As soon as he got to Abstraction Bay, he could buy a datachip, copy the data from the netlink, and arrange for it to be delivered to Art Stoddard, with a letter explaining what he was doing, if he did not return and reclaim it within a certain amount of time. *A month*, he thought. *If I'm not back in a month, I'm not coming back.*

At least that way *someone* would know where he was.

Just in case he didn't come back. Because one thing was for certain: whoever was behind whatever was going on was playing for keeps.

Zheglev's grenade had at least saved him the time he would

have had to spend packing up his camping equipment: the only equipment he had left was on his person.

He shrugged. He had a knife, a coat, boots, weapons, the contents of his backpack. He didn't really need anything else.

Slinging his multirifle on his back, he plunged into the forest.

____

Chapter Three

FOUR DAYS LATER, Lorn settled into his seat for the two-hour suborbital flight to Margaret's Land. Paranoia had been his hiking companion every step of the way to Abstraction Bay, where the first thing he'd done had been to exchange his SSIN uniform for civvies and buy a large suitcase in which to stash it, his weapons, and his ammo. He probably could have carried the weapons openly on the boat from Abstraction Bay, this being the frontier, and he could certainly carry them openly in Margaret's Land, but he was equally certain he could *not* carry them onto the suborbital shuttle.

He felt jittery and naked without any sort of weapon at hand, and that exposed feeling kept his attention sharply focused on each of the passengers who boarded after him. There weren't that many of them—Margaret's Land wasn't exactly one of Peregrine's most popular destinations—and none of them paid him any attention.

Which didn't mean anything, of course. He'd keep an even closer watch on them *after* they disembarked.

The barebones shuttle offered neither inflight food service

nor entertainment. It was strictly utilitarian, and the accelera-tion that shortly pressed Lorn back into his insufficiently padded seat was far higher than most civilian transports employed.

Lorn didn't mind. He'd experienced far less comfortable flights during his stint in the SSIN. They'd be at their destina-tion that much sooner—that was all that mattered.

The sky darkened to star-studded night. Below, the curving planet showed only blue: the vast ocean covering most of the eastern hemisphere. Lorn stared down at it, remembering his first view of Peregrine from space, on his way home from *Mayflower II* after an extended period of recovery in its hospi-tal. He'd missed the view on the way up, what with being semi-conscious at the time due to having been shot in the back with a laser while boarding the scoutship Art Stoddard and Avara Morali had stolen during the Skywatcher uprising.

It had been breathtaking, that first glimpse of his home-world's blue-green sphere—everything he'd dreamed of as a boy. Escape from their rural life, adventure...he'd gotten it all at age fifteen. And the taste for it had lingered. He hadn't really imagined doing anything else after that but joining the SSIN. Like many others, he'd thought everything would be different after the uprising, after the arrival of *Mayflower II*. The influx of new people and new ideas, the narrowly averted takeover of the government by an apocalyptic cult, all of this was bound to loosen the authoritarian strictures on Peregrine society.

And for a while, it had seemed as if that was exactly what would happen. There had been a constitutional conference, grand talk about the importance of individual liberty, a freer economy, freedom of speech...

But talk was all it had proved to be. The old ways had clung. The constitutional conference, seven years later, ground on with little to show for it. It issued communiqués once a year lauding its progress, but the authoritarian impulse had not been quashed: there were still restrictions on speech and travel, endless red tape choking every attempt at innovation in everything from business to science to the arts. The SSIN, which Lorn had somehow thought, in his idealistic youth, would help to enhance and preserve the new freedoms of the new age, instead continued to be the government's heavy controlling hand.

His father had tried to warn him. Driven out of the SSIN himself when he had tried to alert his superiors to the growing influence of the Skywatcher cult, he had had no faith at all in anything much changing despite the near-cataclysmic events in the wake of the *Mayflower II*'s arrival. "The only place a man can be free on Peregrine is on the frontier, son," he'd said. "You're not escaping anything by going back to 'civilization.' Stay out of it."

But Lorn, as teenagers tended to do, had been convinced he knew better than his old man.

Now he stared out the window and wondered how he could have been so naïve.

It was all part and parcel of his youthful idolatry of Art Stoddard. He'd thought Art was a great man. Now that great man was just another bureaucrat. Avara had been a goddess to him. Now she was a talk-show host. His parents seemed content to live in a cabin in the woods, hunting and fishing and having as little to do with the wider world as possible. He'd thought that was a kind of prison when he was a kid. Now he realized the whole *planet* was a prison. Even if, for now, the frontier offered some semblance of escape, there could never be any real escape as long as all of them were trapped on Peregrine. And since Earth had kept the secrets of interstellar travel from its colonies right up until interstellar travel had stopped, and technology had pretty much stagnated since, it seemed they would all remain trapped on Peregrine forever.

He sighed, turned away from the window, and closed his eyes. *Maybe I won't want to stop these coup-plotters once I find out what they're hoping to accomplish,* he thought. *Maybe I'll want to join them.*

But they'll have to stop trying to kill me first.

He smiled slightly and slept.

He woke to the announcement that landing in Ceora was imminent. He stared out the window as they crossed the coastline and banked over a ramshackle-looking city boasting no buildings taller than four stories and, from the amount of vegetation, apparently fighting a losing battle with the encroaching jungle, which stretched as far as he could see inland to green-draped distant hills.

Once the spaceplane had taxied to a halt, he delayed getting out so he could watch everyone else disembark, following the last person—a rather large woman wearing an improbable hat made from a banded treejumper, complete with dangling flat furred tail and two curving black horns—out the door and down the steps onto the pavement.

The heat hit him like a blow. The woman ahead of him gasped and immediately pulled off her ridiculous hat. Behind him, the spaceplane pinged and popped, though he wouldn't have wanted to wager whether the sounds came from metal cooling down or heating up. He'd never felt a combination of heat and humidity like this, even at the height of summer in the smoggy environs of Bagnell. He found his mouth gaping like a landed fish's and snapped it shut, then headed grimly across the black expanse of the landing field for the modest terminal building, hoping it would be air-conditioned.

It was. But that wouldn't do him any good once he set off into the interior. As he crossed the terminal's open central expanse, whose sole decoration consisted of a badly stuffed and slightly mangy-looking dragonbear rearing up on its hind legs, snarling with yellowing sabre-teeth at the arriving passengers, he drastically revised his mental estimate of how much water he would need to carry. The key would be to get transport as close to his final destination as possible—which wouldn't be very close; he'd already looked it up. The nearest settlement to his target coordinates was a place that barely showed up as a dot on the map and went by the rather grim name of Carcass Creek.

First things first. He retrieved his luggage, glad to have his weapons closer at hand even if he couldn't pull them out right there and then, and then went in search of the ticket counters, hoping he'd find a local air company that flew to Carcass Creek.

He found exactly *one* ticket counter, for the same company that operated the suborbital spaceplane. A young woman emerged from a door at the back of the little booth as he approached. "Hello!" she said, flashing a bright smile. "How may we at Adventure Air help you today?"

He found himself smiling back. *She's kind of cute*, he thought. "I need to get to Carcass Creek. Do you fly there?"

Her smile faded. "No, sir, I'm so sorry, we don't." She looked so crestfallen at having to impart such bad news that he wanted to pat her hand and tell her it was okay.

"Does *anyone* fly there?" he said.

She looked around cautiously before speaking, as though afraid of being overheard. Lorn followed the gesture. The terminal was deserted, but still, she leaned forward and whispered, "Yes. But I'm not supposed to tell you. They're a competitor."

Lorn lowered his voice, too. "But I don't see a ticket counter anywhere."

She shook her head, violently. "Oh, no, they don't fly out of here. We own this terminal." She pulled a pad of paper from under the counter and scribbled on it. "Here's the address. I'll call you a taxi."

Feeling as though he'd fallen into a bad mystery novel, Lorn reached out and covered her hand and the piece of paper with his own. "Thank you," he whispered.

She blushed prettily but didn't move her hand. "You're welcome."

Lorn drew back the piece of paper, pocketed it, gave her a wink, and then picked up his luggage and headed for the door; behind him, the girl spoke into a communicator. The cab, a mud-spattered blue groundcar bearing the words Ceora Cabs in orange letters on its side, must have just pulled away from the terminal; its tires squealed on the hot pavement as it U-turned and came back down the road, bordered on one side by the terminal and on the other side by a high chain-link fence beyond which a wall of greenery blocked his view of anything else.

The cab jerked to a halt. He strode over to it as the driver, a fat man in a sweat-stained blue uniform, got out. "I'll open the trunk," he grunted, and went to the back of the car. Lorn shoved his suitcase into it, then got into the passenger compartment, separated from the driver's cockpit by a scuffed transparent wall.

It was hot as an oven.

"Sorry, air conditioning's broke," the driver said as he settled himself into the cockpit and pulled the gull-wing door closed. He gripped the joystick. "Where to?"

Panting a little, Lorn unfolded the piece of paper the girl at the ticket counter had given him. "Snake River Air," he said. "888 West Hopkinson."

"Know it," the driver said. "Surprised this lot told you about it, though." He pushed the stick forward. The car jerked into motion. Lorn, still looking at the paper, saw that the girl had written something else on it—a communicator code. *Call me,* she'd scribbled beside it, along with a name: *Rika.*

Lorn wondered what it said about Ceora that a girl was desperate enough to give a complete stranger her number just because he was a fresh face. Nothing good, he decided. "Sorry, Rika," he murmured. "Little preoccupied right now. Maybe when I come back."

If he came back.

If he didn't die of heatstroke before this cab ride was over.

Fortunately, Ceora wasn't very big and wasn't very busy. They rolled down streets with only a modicum of ground traffic and very few pedestrians. "Place looks almost deserted," he said to the driver.

"Would you be out in this heat if you didn't have to?" the driver said.

They drove for about ten minutes, then pulled up in front of a nondescript one-story building made of corrugated iron, from which hung a badly weathered wooden sign painted with SNAKE RIVER AIR in faded red letters. Behind the building, an open expanse held a couple of small aircraft, one fixed-wing, the other a helicopter. Nothing moved.

"Snake River Air," the driver said. "Twenty-nine bancor."

Lorn blinked. "For ten minutes? That's ridiculous!"

The driver moved his hand, and the doors of the oven-hot passenger compartment clicked locked. "Twenty-nine bancor."

Lorn thought longingly of his weapons in the trunk, but he pulled out his wallet and slid the bills into the payment slot behind the driver's seat. He'd had plenty of cash with him when he'd set off for Javik's; debitchips were useless in a lot of places on the frontier and unwelcome in even more—people trying to keep a low profile from the government generally having a poor view of anything that might be traced by that government. The ticket to Ceora had been expensive, and he was definitely getting low. And he still had to buy passage to Carcass Creek.

"Thank you for your patronage," the taxi driver said. "Enjoy your stay in Ceora." Lorn heard the doors and the trunk unlock. The driver, discretion obviously being the greater part of his valour, stayed in the cockpit this time with his own door locked until Lorn had retrieved his suitcase. Then he sped off, the trunk lid still closing even after he was in motion.

Lorn looked up at the weathered sign, sighed, and lugged his suitcase up the wooden steps to the red metal door, half-expecting it to be locked. But it wasn't, and he stepped into an interior that was blessedly cool, though otherwise no more finely appointed than the exterior.

No cute girl waited behind the single desk, the room's only furnishing except for a half-dozen rather uncomfortable looking red-upholstered chairs clustered around a brochure-strewn coffee table in one corner. This time he was greeted by a bearded middle-aged man, who gave him a squinty glare. "Yeah?"

Lorn put the suitcase down on the bare wooden floor. "I need to get to Carcass Creek," he said. "You fly there?"

"Carcass Creek?" The man looked him up and down. "Why would you want to go to that shithole?"

"That's my business, not yours."

"Might be my business, you planning to do something illegal while you're there."

"Just going for a hike," Lorn said. "Into the interior."

The man snorted. "Might have known. Looking for the Lost City, right?"

"Something like that."

"Got a new theory, prob'ly. Think everyone else's been

looking in the wrong place all these years. Gonna make a name for yourself. Gonna make your fortune."

"Do you fly to Carcass Creek or not?" Lorn said evenly.

The man leaned forward again. "Yeah, we fly there. Charter flight, though. No regular service. Gonna cost."

Lorn gritted his teeth. "How much?"

"Two thousand."

Lorn felt like he'd been punched. "That's twice what it cost to fly suborbital here from Abstraction Bay!"

"Then fly back again and save yourself a thousand. You want to charter one of my planes to Carcass Creek, gonna cost you two thousand. Take it or leave it."

Lorn glared at him.

The man smiled. He had bad teeth. "Well?"

"Give me a minute," Lorn grated. He knelt on the floor, put his suitcase flat, unlocked it, and opened it. He took out his sidearm. The man stiffened as he stood up, holding the pistol in one hand.

"Are you crazy?"

"Probably," Lorn said. He turned the weapon around and held it out. "SSIN issue. I'll give you three hundred bancor and this. What's it worth on the black market out here, d'you think?"

The man stared at the gun, then at Lorn. "How'd you get a SSIN-issue sidearm?"

"Are you going to take this deal, or do I turn this thing around and point the business end at you instead?"

The man licked his lips. "Make it five, and I'll take it," he said.

He reached for the gun, but Lorn pulled it back. "Four," he said. "And we leave *now*."

"My pilot isn't—"

"Aren't you a pilot?"

"Yeah, but—"

Lorn turned the pistol around and gripped it in his right hand. He held it pointed at the ground. "But?"

"All right. All right! Four hundred. And we leave now."

"Good. One second." Lorn knelt behind the open suitcase again. When he stood up, he was holding the multirifle. The man's shock at seeing the pistol was nothing compared to the way his jaw dropped when he saw the larger weapon. "Just in case you get any ideas, I'll be keeping this handy." With practiced ease, Lorn popped the battery and ammo cartridges out of the handgun. Only then did he hand it to the man. "I suggest you leave that here. I'll give you the battery and ammo once we land in Carcass Creek."

"You're SSIN," the man said.

"Am I?" Lorn said.

The man swallowed. "All right," he said. "Let's go."

"About time." Lorn closed and latched the suitcase, empty now except for his discarded uniform and winter coat—which it seemed unlikely he'd be needing out here. "I presume I can buy supplies in Carcass Creek."

The man nodded. "Only reason it exists, catering to fools who...um, people like you, wanting to go into the interior. Get anything you want survival-equipment-wise there. If you can pay for it."

"Fortunately," Lorn said, "I got a good deal on my flight. So I should have the cash. Lead on."

Chapter Four

<hr>

LORN WAS HOPING they'd be boarding the fixed-wing aircraft. Instead, the man (who gave his name as Piotr Franzen) led him to the helicopter, a rather battered-looking example of a pretty standard four-passenger model that Lorn had flown in a hundred times in training and on missions.

Including that last mission.

He could feel his heart pounding. "I get airsick in helicopters," he lied to Franzen. "Why can't we take the plane?"

"No runway in Carcass Creek," Franzen said. "No roads to it, either. You helicopter in, or you walk in. Feel free to walk." He gave Lorn a hopeful look. "I'll refund you your money. And your gun."

"Nice try," Lorn said. He tried to ignore the fluttering in his chest. "Get in."

A few minutes later, they were in the air. Lorn clenched the edge of his seat. *This is ridiculous*, he thought, as his stomach churned. *I've ridden in a hundred helicopters. This one is no different...*

...no different from the last one he'd ridden in.

He fumbled for the airsickness bag in a pouch on the door and threw up into it. Franzen gave him a disgusted look. "Helicopters," Lorn mumbled. "Fine in anything else. Even zero-G."

"Yeah. Sure."

Lorn didn't elaborate. He pulled a bottle of water from his pack to rinse out his mouth. "How long will we be flying?"

"About four hours," Franzen said sourly. "Which puts us there at sunset. Which means I gotta spend a night there."

"There's a hotel?"

"Great hotel. Too rich for my blood, though. Unless you're planning to sell your rifle, I'd guess it's too rich for yours, too."

Lorn eyed him warily. "So, what's the other option?"

"Place called the Jumpdown Turnaround. Mainly it's a bar, but it's got a few rooms to let. Just a word of advice. Sleep with your clothes on, one eye open, and your hand on your weapon."

"Sounds like my kind of place," Lorn said. Frenzen grunted.

They pounded on. Lorn's strange shakiness passed, and he shoved it to the back of his mind, refusing to think about what it meant. He spent the rest of the flight, due west toward the sinking sun, staring down at the endless jungle. He'd grown up in the mountains, and he was used to forests, but nothing like that sea of green. For the first time, he began to wonder if he'd bitten off more than he could chew.

He had a mental image of where his target coordinates were in relation to Carcass Creek on the map. In his own mountains, he would have said it was a two-day hike. But out here...he had no way to judge. It might take twice as long. Or three times. If he survived. Plenty of city people hiked into *his* mountains and managed to get themselves killed because they knew nothing about what it took to survive there. For all his experience, he was in the exact same position hiking into this strange jungle. In fact, it was probably worse. What he *thought* he knew could get him killed.

He remembered the stuffed dragonbear in the air terminal. There were even *worse* predators in these jungles—he recalled that well enough from long-ago planetary geography lessons taught by his mother—not to mention various venomous vermin and a plethora of poisonous plants.

I'm going to need a guide, he thought.

They flew on, over the hills he had seen from the space-plane as it came in for a landing, then over more hills beyond that and more beyond that, range after range of low, rounded, green-shrouded hills through which poked the occasional outcropping of black rock. Ahead, the sun sank below yet another range of hills, so much taller than the ones they had already passed that Lorn decided they could almost qualify as mountains. In the shadows of those mini-mountains, they descended at last, toward a cluster of lights on the shore of a broad river that snaked its way through the jungle. They set down on the beaten earth of a clearing, and the shuddering noise of the rotors finally ceased as Frenzen killed the engines. "Welcome to Carcass Creek," he said. "Pay up."

Lorn handed over four 100-bancor bills, plus the ammo and battery pack for his departed pistol, then got out, hauling his suitcase out after himself. "This Jumpdown Turnaround place," he said. "Would I be able to find a guide there?"

"Pretty much the *only* place you'll find one," Frenzen said. "Most guides I know drink away the money they earn. Got nothing else to spend it on."

"Any of them drink on the trail?"

"Doubt it," Frenzen said. "Ones who do are the ones who don't come back." He sighed. "Much as I'd love to be rid of you," he said, "guess I'd better show you where the place is. Come on."

Lorn followed him away from the clearing and into the town. He expected the streets, like the landing field, to be unpaved, but in fact, as soon as they reached the nearest buildings, they also moved from dirt to smooth black pavement. Lorn stared around as Frenzen trudged along. Far from being the run-down shantytown he'd expected, Carcass Creek looked prosperous—more prosperous than what he'd seen of Ceora, to tell the truth. They passed a sidewalk café where two men and two women, dressed in the latest Bagnell fashions (brightly-colored form-fitting suits and buttoned up black shirts for the men, mini-skirts and sequined midriff-baring tops for the women, plus lots of dangly jewelry), sat at a table sipping wine and laughing over something one of the men had said. Lorn stared at them as he passed, earning a cold look from one of the men, which he ignored, and a slight smile from one of the women, which he returned. He looked back at Frenzen. "Not what I expected from your description."

Frenzen shrugged. "This is the tourist town," he said. "Part of the hotel complex. Anybody you see in here is either a guest or a hotel employee. You try to go into one of these eateries for dinner, they'll very graciously refuse to serve you until you've checked in."

"And a night in the hotel would cost...?"

"Got a thousand on you?" Frenzen said.

Lorn winced.

Frenzen was right; the prosperous-looking portion of Carcass Creek was only four blocks wide. In the middle of it they crossed a broad boulevard that led, to their right, to the hotel: not very big, but grand in a quietly ostentatious sort of way, all white pillars and glittering glass, with a fountain, lit from below by colored, ever-shifting lights, plashing quietly in front. "Why would rich tourists come out *here*?"

"Same reason as you," Frenzen said. "Only they're not

stupid enough to plunge into the jungle to try to find the Lost City. They're on a package tour. Boat excursion up to Dead Man's Falls. Bus excursion to Bally's Folly. For the more adventurous ones, a half-day guided hike to Rabid Weasel Flats. Lots of food and wine in between." He spat on the smooth pavement. "Damn company has its own helicopters—and their own fully equipped helipad out back. I don't get a lick of business out of it, so I say to hell with it."

Lorn said nothing, but he gave the hotel a last regretful look before it vanished from sight and they left the touristy version of Carcass Creek behind.

The *real* version was much more like he had anticipated and in tune with the bare-bones landing field. Gravel streets. One- or occasionally two-story wooden buildings, the yellow light glowing through the windows indicating more reliance on biomass for illumination than electricity. The few wired for power also seemed to have their own generators or solar panels.

Lorn heard the Jumpdown Turnaround before he saw it: raucous music blasting through the still, muggy night along with the desperately hearty laughter of well-marinated men and women. Then they rounded a corner, and he got his first look at the place: two stories, with a wooden façade from which extended a broad pillared porch crowded with people talking, laughing, drinking, and smoking. Bright light—there was definitely power *here*—spilled out through the open doors and the high windows along with the noise. "You're on your own from here," Franzen said, and strode off without a backward look.

Lorn was still carrying his multi-rifle slung on his back. He took a minute to unsling it and put it back into his suitcase, then followed.

He got a few curious looks from the clientele as he climbed the wooden steps of the Turnaround and made his way inside the lobby, but clearly, strangers came and went here all the time: nobody paid him much mind. But he found himself gripped by a strange anxiety all the same. His weapon was out of reach. If someone attacked...

He pushed down his sudden nervousness and made his way through the crowd to the bar, staffed by two men and a woman. One of the men came over to meet him. "What'll it be?"

"Pint of Nilsson's Dark," Lorn said, "and a room for the night."

"I can get you the beer," the bartender said. "You'll have to talk to the boss about the room." He turned his head. "Boss!" he called. "Hotel customer."

The woman, about fifty years old, Lorn guessed, with graying hair in a careless pile held in place by three silver hair-clips, came over to him, rubbing her hands on her dark-green apron, while the bartender pulled a glass from under the counter and filled it with dark-brown foaming liquid from one of the taps at the back. He set it down in front of Lorn as the woman said, "Looking for a room?"

Lorn nodded.

"How long?"

"Not sure," Lorn said. "I'm heading inland. Need to get supplies, need to find a guide." He glanced around the room. "I heard they're mostly in here. Anyone you can recommend?"

The woman looked at him thoughtfully. "From the look of you, you know your way around the Wild."

"Not on this continent. That's why I need a guide."

The woman smiled. "But you *don't* need someone to hold your hand. Which means..." She peered around the room. "Ah. There. By the fireplace."

Lorn followed her gaze and saw a big black man with a bald head and a graying beard standing by a fireplace in which flickered strange blue flames. "Fireplace? In this climate?"

The woman laughed. "Cold flames. Draw energy from the surrounding air. Coolest place in here is by the fireplace." Lorn didn't doubt it. The Jumpdown Turnaround was air-conditioned, but the system was clearly laboring to keep up.

The man by the fireplace had a glass of something golden in one hand. As Lorn watched, he tossed it back. "You won't even have to go over there," the woman said. "He'll be coming here for a refill."

"What's his name?" Lorn said, watching the man thread his way through the crowd with the careful gait of someone who's had too much to drink but still thinks he can conceal it.

"Ekwensi," the woman said. "Jon Ekwensi. I'll introduce you." She regarded him curiously. "What's *your* name?"

"Lorn," Lorn said. "Lorn Kymbal." He saw no reason to lie.

She nodded, then waited as Ekwensi made his way up to the bar. He held out his glass. "It seems to be empty, Abby," he said, his voice a basso rumble. "This cannot stand."

"I'll fix that for you," Abby said. "Jon, this Lorn Kymbal. He's looking for a guide."

Ekwensi turned to Lorn. He was a head taller and about half again as wide. "A guide. To where?"

"Inland," Lorn said. "Specific coordinates."

"*Specific* coordinates." One of Ekwensi's bushy eyebrows lifted. "And what do you expect to find there?"

"I don't know," Lorn said. "That's why I have to go there."

The eyebrow came down, knitted with the other into a frown. "The Lost City?" he growled.

"I don't know," Lorn said again.

Ekwensi regarded him. His eyes flicked down and up again. "You look fit," he said. "Are you?"

"Fit enough."

"Military training."

Lorn felt his own eyebrow rise. "It shows?"

"It shows." Ekwensi regarded him for another moment, then shrugged. "All right. I'll guide you. Got any supplies?"

"Got a weapon."

"Weapon is a good start. The rest I can provide...for a fee. So." He smiled for the first time, showing startlingly white teeth. "The most important question of all. Got any money?"

The fee wasn't quite as high as Lorn feared; he was able to agree to it and still had enough—barely—for one of Abby's spartan rooms. Since the noise from downstairs didn't abate until shortly before the light returned the next morning, and he had a few suspicious itchy red spots when he rose that suggested he had been sharing his bed with unseen companions, Lorn thought one night in the Jumpdown Turnaround was all he could stand to enjoy anyway.

He'd arranged to meet Ekwansi on the far side of the bridge that spanned the sluggish green river. Beyond that, the jungle began in earnest, and he and Ekwansi weren't the only guide/guidee duo—or, in one case, guide/guidee/guidee/guidee quartet—checking packs and weapons. He eyed the others, wondering if any of them were traveling in the same direction, which might indicate they were part of whatever was going on out there in the jungle, but they all went off along the river, following a well-marked trail. "Where does that go?" he asked Ekwansi.

"Juggernaut Cataract," Ekwansi said. "Nice little teahouse down there for the tourists." He grinned. "Want to check it out? Hell of a lot easier than where you're trying to get to. And there's way-overpriced tea at the end of it."

"No, thanks," Lorn said. "I prefer my destination."

"Even though you don't know what's there."

"Even so."

"Suit yourself. Pack comfy?"

Lorn shrugged his shoulders. "Good enough."

"Then let's go." He'd leaned his rifle against a rock, next to Lorn's multirifle. Now he picked it up. "Keep your weapon out. Likely need it before the end of the day." He nodded at Lorn's rifle. "Nice piece, by the way. Not going to ask how you got it."

"Good," Lorn said. He picked up the multirifle. "No machetes?" Lorn asked. He'd been wondering about their absence from the supplies.

Ekwansi snorted. "You been watching holodramas set on Earth, haven't you? I may look African, and I guess my ancestors were, but this isn't Africa or any other Earth jungle, and it isn't a safe northern forest, either. Plants here don't take kindly to being slashed. Got ways to deal with it. You follow me, do what I do, you'll be okay. But don't trust your instincts. They'll get you killed."

"Not always," Lorn said. "Instinct told me to get a guide."

Ekwansi flashed a grin at that. "The exception that proves the rule."

He led Lorn to the edge of the clearing, where at first glance the trees seemed to form an impenetrable green wall, towering twenty metres or more. But a second glance showed Lorn an opening in that verdant fence. "A trail?"

Ekwansi nodded. "Leads to a cave complex some tourists like to see. But we won't take it that far. It curves south. We've got to get up and over the mountains." He set off along the path, rifle in one hand.

Lorn had thought it was hot in the town. Maybe the temperature wasn't any different in the jungle, but in the open, there had been a breeze, however slight. In here, between the towering trees which formed a thick canopy overhead and whose trunks were hung with thick black vines with broad green leaves, not the slightest breath of air could penetrate. Lorn found himself panting like a dog. He already longed for a cold drink, but he fought the urge to reach for his canteen.

They were carrying what had seemed like an extraordinary—and extraordinarily heavy—amount of water, but he knew well enough why, and he knew there would come a time when he would need it far more than he did this early in the hike.

Along the trail, the going was easy enough, although it became somewhat harder after about an hour when the landscape began to slope up. A couple of hours after that, the trail took a sharp turn to the right, along the bottom of the slope, and there Ekwansi called a halt. "Water break," he said. The sweat running down his face glistened in the green-tinged light filtering through the canopy. He took his canteen from his belt and drank deeply. Lorn followed suit. Water had rarely tasted more wonderful. He wiped his mouth and looked up the slope, and his eyes narrowed.

"That tree is blazed," he said.

"Sharp eyes," Ekwansi said approvingly.

"We're not the first to go this way."

"Never said we were." Ekwansi returned the canteen to his belt. "Figured you knew it. Surprised you don't. Not the first time I've seen those coordinates you gave me."

Lorn's eyes narrowed. "Why didn't you say so?"

"Just did, didn't I?" Ekwansi studied him. "You really don't know what's out there, do you?"

"Said so, didn't I?"

"Sure you did, but I didn't believe you. Lots of close-mouthed people out here who don't say all they know."

"Do *you* know what's out there, then?"

Ekwansi shook his head. "Never been there myself. Knew a guide who made the trek, though. Name of Trumak."

"What did he see?"

"He didn't say."

"Why not?"

"He didn't come back." Ekwansi grinned. "Okay, didn't

rightly know him. I...inherited some of his supplies when he was declared missing. Including a very nice GPS tracker. This one." He touched a black case attached to his belt. "Twin to the one he was carrying. Fancy system some of the guides use. You give one to your client, keep the other one yourself, so you always know where the tourist is, in case he wanders off and you have to collect the remains. But he wasn't guiding. He went out there alone—said he'd seen something interesting but wouldn't say anything else. Seemed convinced he'd make his fortune from whatever it was. I figure he thought he'd found the Lost City at last.

"Anyway, he left the second tracker unit in his room at the Turnaround to save weight in his pack. When he didn't come back, Abby cleaned out his room and gave me his stuff."

"Why?"

"Services rendered, and none of your business beyond that." Ekwansi squinted up the slope. "Tracker showed his path —same one we're following. He reached these coordinates of yours, and then his tracker quit tracking him. And that was that."

"Wait a minute." Lorn stared at him. "You knew where he'd gone and that he hadn't come back...and nobody tried to rescue him?"

"Rescue?" Ekwansi laughed. "Son, there's no rescue out here. You disappear, nobody's coming after you, unless you got family that cares enough. And Trumak didn't."

"What about you?" Lorn said. "Would anyone come after you? Abby, maybe?"

"That debt's paid," Ekwansi said shortly. "No, don't expect anyone would come after me, either." He regarded Lorn. "What about *you*?"

Lorn said nothing for a moment. Art Stoddard would shortly know where he'd gone. If he simply vanished, would

Stoddard follow up? Once Lorn would have been sure he would. Not any longer. "Maybe," he said at last.

"Well, let's hope you don't have to find out." Ekwansi regarded him another moment. "You want to tell me now what you really expect to find out there?"

"I told you, I don't know," Lorn said.

"The Lost City?"

"I don't believe in the Lost City."

"Well, that's refreshing." Ekwansi paused. "How about something called the 'Falcon's Egg?'"

Lorn blinked. "'Falcon's Egg?' What's that?"

"If you don't know, I sure as hell don't. It's what Trumak called this spot on the map we're heading to."

"I've never heard of it."

"Uh-huh." Ekwansi shrugged. "Whatever, son. You paid, I guide." He pointed up the slope at the blazed tree. "Looks like we've got a bit of break from the canopy. We're lucky, we'll be mostly in the open up to the top of the ridge. Valley on the other side is likely to be different." He readjusted his pack and set off up the slope, Lorn trailing.

What had Trumak seen or heard that had sent him hiking out to these coordinates? Lorn had a hard time imagining a two-bit guide hanging out in Carcass Creek had somehow managed to intercept the same messages that plugged-directly-into-the-'Net Javik had barely noticed. *He must have seen something while he was out in the jungle. But what? And why did he call it "Falcon's Egg"?*

And what happened to him when he went looking in earnest?

Actually, Lorn had a pretty good idea about *that*. He looked back into the thick jungle. The spiderbots had been hard enough to deal with in his own familiar forest. Out here, they—

or something like them—could be on top of him and Ekwansi with no warning at all.

Gripping his rifle a little tighter, he followed Ekwansi up the slope.

They passed the blazed tree a few minutes later and immediately saw another one after that...and another one after that. Back home, the climb wouldn't have been much. In this heat, it was harder, but Lorn set his jaw and climbed without complaint. He'd climbed mountains in temperatures that could freeze exposed flesh in minutes. The heat was uncomfortable, but all in all, he thought he preferred it.

It took them about three-quarters of an hour to reach the top of the ridge. The canopy reasserted itself just the other side, so there was no view to be seen of the valley below. Nor were there any more blazed trees. "Blazes don't last long in the thick jungle," Ekwansi told Lorn when he asked about that. "The trees heal fast." He studied the trees in front of them for a long time, then turned to Lorn. "Okay, here's what you need to know about the Peregrine jungle. Just assume that everything you see is dangerous in some fashion. If we're lucky, we won't see any big wildlife. We don't smell right, so the predators don't think we're edible, and the herbivores assume we think they *are*. But some of the smaller animals are just as dangerous and less cautious. The plants are mostly poisonous in some fashion or other. You wondered why we don't have machetes? You chop through some of those vines," he pointed at a purplish dangling bit of rope-like vegetation, "and get some of the sap on you, and you'll be paralyzed before you've finished the swing and dead twenty minutes later. If you wonder why we're zigzagging instead of travelling straight, that's why. I'm going to repeat what I said when we started out. Stay close behind me. It was important down there on the trail. It's *really* important now we're bushwhacking. I know what's relatively safe and what can kill us. You don't, and in this jungle, appearances are deceiving. You go off on your own and disappear, I won't come after you. Understand?"

Lorn nodded.

"Well, then. 'Once more unto the breach, dear friends, once more.'"

Lorn blinked. "Shakespeare?"

"What, I don't look like an educated man to you?" Ekwansi said. He struck a regal pose and said in sonorous tones, "In peace, there's nothing so becomes a man as modest stillness and humility: but when the blast of war blows in our ears, then imitate the action of the tiger." He relaxed and grinned. "I just told you appearances are deceiving in this jungle. That applies to more than just the plants and animals. Come on."

As the afternoon progressed, Lorn had the wisdom of his decision to hire a guide—and *this* guide in particular—rein-forced several times. Ekwansi did not force his way through the jungle; he *oozed* through it, slipping between this pair of trees rather than that pair ("poisonous bark," he explained, pointing to the faint green shimmer of sap on the trees he had avoided), ducking under vines Lorn would have simply brushed aside ("they trigger a burst of poisonous vapor from bladders higher up the tree,"), and once simply calling a halt with a sudden lift of his hand. "No talking, no moving," he said, and so they stood, completely still. Lorn listened to the sounds of the jungle: the harsh cries of the flying lizards, the chirping of unseen insects in the forest litter, the constant creaking of shifting trees. Then he heard what Ekwansi must have already registered, a strange susurration in the undergrowth, growing louder.

Just in front of them, there was a slight gully, perhaps ten metres wide, a dip in the landscape that was oddly free of any vegetation taller than about fifteen centimetres, all of which had the vivid green look of new growth. The strange sound was coming from their right. Something silvery glinted through the undergrowth. He thought at first it was the leading edge of a wave, that the sound came from a flash flood tearing through the gully, but then it swept by right in front of them, and he swallowed.

The silvery glint came from the shining carapaced backs of countless...well, he guessed they were insects, but since each was about twenty centimetres long, "insect" didn't seem quite the right word. Arthropod, maybe. The sound he heard was made both by their chitinous legs, in constant motion, and the snapping of their enormous mouthparts, stripping the young vegetation along their path. The wave of creatures took a full minute to pass, and when it did, the gully held nothing but bare red dirt.

Ekwansi kept his hand raised for another three minutes, then finally relaxed. "Pillage beetles," he told Lorn. "Mostly, they keep to a winding network of tracks, dozens of kilometres in length, long enough that the undergrowth reasserts itself just before they make another pass. But attract their attention, and they'll make a new path—right over you. Strip you to bones in seconds and eat those too, minutes later."

"Just another wonder of nature," Lorn said. "Tourists ever get a look at those?"

"Usually only briefly," Ekwansi said. "Very briefly. Come on, safe enough now." He stepped out into the gully and looked to his left. "In fact, I think we'll follow this for a while. It curves around in our direction a little further on."

"Um...okay." Despite Ekwansi's assurances, he stepped onto the bare dirt with some trepidation. But for as long as the track trended roughly in their direction, they made good time. Ekwansi called a halt with a couple of hours of daylight still left, as the beetle track curved back on itself around an outcropping of rock.

"Good place to camp," Ekwansi said. "Always better to be on rock than on the forest floor. Less chance of unwanted visitors in the night."

Thinking of the beetles, Lorn had no complaints about that.

Despite the heat and humidity, Ekwansi made a fire in a hollow in the rock. "Just for company," he said. "Something about a fire makes the night more friendly." Something screamed like a dying child in the middle-distance, making Lorn jerk and clutch at his multirifle, resting close at hand. His heart raced. He took a couple of deep breaths, trying to calm it, and turned back toward the fire to see Ekwansi looking at him. "You've had some unfriendly nights recently, I'm guessing."

"It's nothing," Lorn muttered. But he had to work to convince his fingers to release the multirifle.

Ekwansi, though his face glistened with heat in the light of the flames, poked at the fire so that a shower of sparks rose into the night sky. "Wish you could make one of Abby's cold fires out here, but you need a wall full of equipment to pull off that trick," he said. He leaned back again. "Military training, and you've seen action, probably recently," he mused. "So I'm figuring you're SSIN. But you're either undercover or AWOL."

Lorn resisted the urge to reach for his rifle again. "It's none of your business," he growled.

"Just making conversation," Ekwansi said. "Used to be SSIN myself. I kind of...disappeared during the Skywatcher uprising."

"Why?" Lorn said.

"Could say, 'None of your business,'" Ekwansi pointed out, but without heat. "But truth is, I found out something about myself. Found out I couldn't kill people I knew, and I knew a lot of people on both sides. *Did* kill somebody I didn't know, just to save my own hide, and found out I didn't much like that, either. Seemed likely if I stayed in SSIN I'd be killing more. So

I left. Probably I'm presumed dead by now. Never tried to find out, since that seemed a sure way to draw attention to the fact I'm not."

Lorn said nothing, staring at the fire. When he'd first joined SSIN in the heat of youthful certitude, he would have arrested someone like Ekwansi on the spot, marched him to the nearest transportation, guarded him all the way back to Bagnell, and handed him over personally to be court-martialed. But now...

Now, he was effectively as AWOL as Ekwansi, the thin fiction of his simply taking accumulated leave without going through proper channels certainly providing insufficient cover for what he was up to now. And he was AWOL for the same reason. Too much killing. He'd been killing bad guys since he was fifteen and opened an airlock on the *Mayflower II* to save Art Stoddard and Shadow and the Crawlspacers with them from their armed pursuers. He'd killed a lot of "bad guys" since. But that last attack...

The image of the dead pregnant woman flashed into his head again, her eyes wide, glazing, hand pressed to her swollen stomach, the blood pooling with amniotic fluid...

He found himself standing without any memory of doing so, multirifle clutched in his hand again, staring at Ekwansi—who had a handgun aimed at his abdomen. "Settle down, boy," Ekwansi said. "Put down your rifle."

Lorn looked down at the rifle. "Sorry," he muttered. "Sorry. I didn't mean..." He sank cross-legged to the ground again and released the rifle. "I don't..."

"I do understand, Lorn," Ekwansi said. Lorn thought it was the first time the big man had used his name. "Don't blame you. But not going to let you shoot me, either."

"I wouldn't have," Lorn said.

"Probably not," Ekwansi agreed amiably. "But you'll forgive

me for wanting to make damn sure." He holstered his weapon. "Hungry?"

They ate in silence. Ekwansi didn't talk anymore, and Lorn, still shaken, didn't have anything else to say anyway. In his tent, lying on his sleeping bag, not in it, because of the heat, he stared up into the darkness. *What's happening to me?*

Post-Traumatic Stress Disorder, the therapist had told him, in that cloying, sentimental, patronizing voice he'd hated so much. He'd heard of it long before that, of course. They'd had courses on it in training. The recruits *joked* about it. He'd rejected the therapist's diagnosis. PTSD was something other people suffered from, weak people, lesser people. Not him.

Yet it *was* happening to him. He couldn't deny it. But why? He hadn't had a problem after any of the other operations he'd been on as a member of SSIN. What had changed?

It was the damn woman, of course. She'd only been a dark shadow when she'd appeared in the doorway of that burning building in the Skywatcher compound: just another Skywatcher, just another target. But he'd seen where she'd fallen, and as they'd gone into the compound to clean up, he'd glanced at her, just a casual glance, and seen what he'd done, seen what the casual tightening of his trigger finger had done, and something had broken inside him, some dam that had held back years of...

...of weakness, he thought. He felt a wave of self-loathing. He couldn't imagine his father suddenly going weak like this. Even Art Stoddard had been stronger. And Shadow? No way. It wasn't his fault the woman had died. She shouldn't have come out of the doorway like that when she knew the SSIN agents were out there. She shouldn't have even been in the compound. She shouldn't have been a Skywatcher to begin with. It wasn't his fault. It was *hers.* It was *her* fault he felt like this; *her* fault his mind and body were betraying him.

I'll show her, he thought then. *One dead Skywatcher woman won't stop me from doing what I have to do. Like Art. Like Shadow. I'll do what I have to do and find out what's going on in this jungle. I'm going to fucking save the world, just like they did, or die trying, and I'll kill anyone to do it, too.*

But in his dreams, once he fell into fitful sleep, the woman still waited.

Ekwansi didn't ask him again about his experiences in the SSIN or talk about his own. They barely talked at all the next day, aside from the communication necessary to stay alive in the jungle—dodging deadly plant life and once dodging a dragonbear, twice the size of the one in the air terminal, but fortunately busy tearing apart some kind of insect mound upwind of them, so they were able to creep by without attracting its attention. That night Lorn ate quickly and silently. Ekwansi studied him across the fire but left him alone. *As he should*, Lorn thought as he lay down. *He's my employee, not my friend or mentor.*

Another night of poor sleep, followed by the hottest morning yet, left Lorn feeling more miserably uncomfortable than he could remember ever being in his life. He wished he could get upwind of *himself*. That afternoon, though, they climbed out of the broad valley they had spent most of two days crossing and into thinner vegetation on the ridge beyond. The air grew marginally cooler, slightly dryer, and most of all, *moved*, in a light breeze that dried sweat and rejuvenated Lorn's body, even if it didn't do much for his mood. He found himself relieved that the journey hadn't been worse than it was.

Of course, it might well be the destination—Trumak's mysterious "Falcon's Egg"—was where the *real* danger lay.

They saw no blazes in the thin forest of the eastern valley slope, but that was hardly surprising: even if Trumak had left any, it would have been pure luck for them to begin the climb at the same spot he had.

At the very top of the ridge, the vegetation vanished entirely, so that they toiled up black rocks, almost too hot to touch in the late afternoon sun, the breeze doing them little good in the face of that furnace-like blast of reflected heat. Lorn eyed the bare ridge uneasily, and before they crested it, called, "Ekwansi. Stop."

Ekwansi glanced back at him, his face glistening. "Not the best place to rest. We'll fry like eggs."

"I'm not stopping to rest." Lorn swiped his sleeve across his own forehead to clear the sweat trying to run into his eyes, then gestured up-slope. "The coordinates are in the next valley, correct?"

Ekwansi nodded.

"We're going to be completely exposed when we reach the ridge-top."

"You expect there to be someone to see us?"

"I don't know what to expect," Lorn half-lied, remembering black exploding spiders in the snowy northern hills. "I told you, I don't know what this 'Falcon's Egg' is. But if it's not just a ruin, and if what got Trumak wasn't just a wild animal or poisonous plant, but an unfriendly human..."

Ekwansi looked up at the exposed basalt's jagged edge. "You're thinking we should wait until dark?"

"Yes." Sweat ran into Lorn's eyes again, stinging. He licked dry lips. "But not here!"

"You're the client." Ekwansi pointed off to their right. "That outcropping there has shade beneath it. We'll rest there until it is too dark for us to be seen, then crest the ridge." He set off again, now angling across the slope. A few minutes later, they had their packs off and were sitting side by side in the rather skimpy shade of a large boulder, the sun sinking somewhere behind it, while they faced bare black rocks and bright blue sky. Lorn drank deeply of his water. They'd been able to refill their supplies a couple of times along the trek—the canteen's built-in purification system ensuring the water was safe to drink—and so there was no need to skimp.

Ekwansi drank just as deeply as he did. "Don't suppose you want to tell me what you suspect is on the other side of that ridge," the guide said after wiping his mouth. "You've gone really quiet since that little incident by the fire, and I've left you to it, but if you think I'm about to get shot at..."

Lorn stared up at the ridge. "I told you the truth," he said. "I don't know for sure what's on the other side of that ridge. Well," he added with a slight smile, "I'm pretty sure it's not the 'Lost City.'"

"Pretty sure of that myself," Ekwansi said dryly.

"What I do know," Lorn said, "is that whoever is over there has already killed two men, remotely, on the other side of the world. And took a good shot at me. Which is why I'm here. One of the men they killed was a...family friend."

Ekwansi raised an eyebrow. "You're here to get revenge? All by yourself against someone who has the resources to have people killed half a planet away?" He chuckled. "You really do watch too many holodramas."

Lorn felt a surge of anger but clamped down on it. After all, Ekwansi had a point. "No, I'm not here for revenge," he said. "I just want to know what's over there. Then I'll go back and get help." *Like a good SSIN agent*, he thought.

Ekwansi's eyes narrowed, and his hand went to his sidearm. "You telling me you're not AWOL, you're undercover?" he growled. "So what *else* will you report?"

"Nothing about you," Lorn said. "I don't care. Doubt anybody else would care either. And I'm not undercover. I *am* AWOL...sort of."

"Sort of?"

Lorn shrugged. "I had lots of leave coming. I just took it without...going through proper channels."

Ekwansi laughed and released his sidearm.

"I said I was going to report what I find," Lorn continued. "I didn't say I'm going to report it to the SSIN." He sighed. "I think SSIN has been infiltrated. Again."

"Skywatchers?"

"Skywatchers are practically gone," Lorn said. *Exterminated, you mean.* He pushed that thought aside. "No, this is something new."

"What?"

"That's what I'm here to find out."

Ekwansi released his sidearm and reached for the canteen again. "So I might get shot at."

"Might," Lorn said. "But I hope not. Plan is not to be seen."

Ekwansi grunted. "Probably Trumak's plan, too. Ever think of that?" He took a swig of water.

Lorn shrugged. "You can wait here. I didn't hire you to fight, if it comes to that. Just to guide me here and back...if I go back."

Ekwansi capped the canteen and returned it to his pack. "I'm not afraid to get shot at," he said. "I've been shot at before. I will see what is on the other side of that ridge."

Lorn just nodded. After that, the conversation died. Ekwansi closed his eyes and appeared to fall asleep. Lots of military men had the knack of snatching sleep whenever they had a few minutes' downtime. Unfortunately, Lorn had never learned the trick. *Probably sick the day they covered it in training,* he thought grumpily. There was no way he was going to be sleeping, so instead, he stared at the ridge and wondered what they would find on the other side of it.

Bad weather, for one thing, he figured: as the afternoon

wore away, gray clouds began to stream across the sky above the ridge, hiding the blue. It must have been chasing the sun, sinking out of sight behind the boulder that sheltered them, and just about sunset, it must have caught it, for there was only a brief blaze of orange against the ridge-top rocks before dusk descended, as suddenly as if someone had flipped a switch.

As the darkness deepened, Ekwansi finally stirred. He sat up and stiffened when he saw what Lorn had been staring at for several minutes.

"What's that?"

"I don't know," Lorn said. "But presumably, it's coming from 'Falcon's Egg.'"

The clouds above them were glowing.

Chapter Five

"THERE ARE no settlements this far inland," Ekwansi said. "And it would take a large settlement to emit that much light."

"Whatever 'Falcon's Egg' is, it isn't concerned about being seen from orbit," Lorn said, staring at the glowing clouds. "That's...worrisome." He glanced at Ekwansi. "Still want to take a look?"

"More than ever," Ekwansi said. "Margaret's Land is my home, and the people who live here are my friends and neighbours. If there is something across that ridge that poses a threat to the settlements, I need to know...and warn them."

Lorn stared at him, surprised by how sincere he sounded. But he didn't question it: truth was, he'd be glad to have someone at his side. "So let's go find out what's waiting for us, shall we?"

"By all means."

They gathered their packs and started up the slope. The glow in the clouds burned steadily, only shifting in intensity because of the movement of the wrack, not because of any flicker in the source of illumination. Which meant it was artificial.

He'd been discounting the notion of the Lost City ever since he first heard of it. He couldn't imagine an entire city populated with aliens could vanish at will just to evade encroaching humans. The whole thing sounded to him like nothing more than an elaborate façade hung on the flimsiest of mysteries, the meaning of the garbled scout message.

But it did cross his mind as he climbed the slope that he might be wrong, that the resemblance between the spiderbots and the maintenance robots aboard *Mayflower II* might be mere coincidence. And when at last they reached the top of the ridge and carefully crawled through the rocks, not trusting in darkness alone to hide them from any sentries, and he saw what lay in the valley beyond, for just a moment he thought the aliens were real...until he saw why Trumak had called it "Falcon's Egg."

In a vast clearing at the bottom of the valley stood an enormous ovoid shape, resting on four stubby metallic legs extruded from the bottom. The glow in the clouds came from powerful lights erected around it, illuminating it but raising no answering reflection from it, so that it looked disquietingly two-dimensional, like a black oval hole cut out of the world. Nothing marred its smooth black surface...

...nothing except for crisp white letters: *UESS Falcon's Egg*.

There was movement around the ovoid, but not human movement: the movement came from autonomic machines. Some rolled on wheels; some skittered around on legs.

Robots, Lorn thought.

"What the hell...?" Ekwansi said.

Lorn rolled over on his back, breathing hard. He'd never expected *this*. He'd thought he might find a camp of disaffected SSIN troops, possibly allied with the dead-enders of *Mayflower*

II and using their robot technology. But robots like those he saw below did not exist on *Mayflower II*, and they certainly didn't exist on Peregrine. They were one of the technologies deliberately withheld from the original colonists by a paranoid Earth government. The only robots they had on Peregrine were clumsy multi-legged cargo-carriers like automated mules.

The one place those kinds of robots might still exist was on Earth or on other worlds of the sundered Earth empire. And that made perfect sense to Lorn, because he recognized that black ovoid crouching in the middle of the jungle from old images.

It was a starship. An actual faster-than-light starship, of the kind that hadn't landed on Peregrine for some two centuries now. *UESS Falcon's Egg.* UESS: United Earth Star Ship. After two hundred years, one had finally turned up. *Running a little late, aren't you?* Lorn thought.

He might have thought the ship entirely crewed by robots if not for what else he had seen down there: several low buildings ranged in a circle around the starship, all with a prefabricated look, lights glowing behind windows, shadows moving within. Robots didn't need buildings. Robots didn't even need lights, come to that. No, there were definitely people down there. But who were they? Where had they come from? And what did they want?

As a kid, he'd dreamed that someday the starships would return, that he might actually be able to leave Peregrine and travel to other worlds. But he'd never imagined the dream playing out like this. A starship in Margaret's Land, sending transmissions coordinating a plan to seize control of the planet —and dispatching killer robots to ensure that plan remained secret—was more the stuff of nightmares.

"I need to get closer," he said to Ekwansi. "But you don't.

It's dangerous here. You've done what I hired you to do. You've seen what's here. You should just head back."

Ekwansi stared at him. "Back?" he said. "Are you joking? That thing down there...that's a starship."

Lorn was momentarily surprised, then realized he shouldn't have been. A man who knew Shakespeare had probably paid more attention to history than Lorn ever had. "Yes."

"A *starship*. But...after all these decades? *Why?*"

"That's what I have to find out." Lorn got up on one elbow to look at him. "Ekwansi, please, head back. The people in that ship have already tried to kill me twice, on the other side of the planet. But they don't know you exist. Go back to Ceora, tell people what you've seen—"

"They'll put me down as just another Lost City nutter suffering from jungle brain," Ekwansi said bluntly. "I'm not going anywhere until I understand exactly what's going on. Only then will I have a chance of convincing anyone else there's a threat."

Lorn gave up. "Well, I'll be glad of backup," he said honestly. He rolled over and raised up to look down at the camp again. "The trouble is, I don't know how good their security—shit!" He scrambled to his feet. "Run!"

It was far too late for that, of course. Even as he leaped up, and before Ekwansi had really had time to react at all, the spiderbot, several times the size of the ones he had seen at Javik's cabin, crested the ridge.

Light flashed, accompanied by pain. Lorn's muscles spasmed, pulling him into a tight ball as he crashed to the rocks. Lying there, he heard Ekwansi swear and saw him swing his weapon around. The rifle roared. The bullets whined off the robot's black shell. Light flashed again, but the attack must have triggered an automatically stronger response.

Like Lorn, Ekwansi toppled to the rocks. Unlike Lorn, he was missing his head.

Lorn's last sight before unconsciousness claimed him was of blood pooling around his erstwhile guide's decapitated body.

———

"UNGH." Lorn woke and groaned at the same time. His muscles were under his control again, but every inch of him ached, as though he'd been beaten. Trying not to move any more than he had to, he opened his eyes.

He lay on a nondescript gray bed in a nondescript gray room, lit by a single glowtube, caged in steel, directly overhead. He saw a high, narrow window, but it admitted no light, and from the bed, he couldn't see through it. There were two doors, each painted dark blue. One stood open, showing a tiny cupboard of a bathroom, with a toilet and a sink. The other door, which had a more substantial look, was opposite the window and, he was pretty sure even without trying it, would be locked. It seemed clear he was in prison.

He looked at his watch, wincing as his arm muscles complained, but it had stopped—at a guess, at the same moment he had been stunned by the robot. No way to know how long he had been unconscious.

At least the robot had *only* stunned him instead of detonating...or blowing his head off, like poor Ekwansi. Lorn wished he'd passed out before he'd seen that. "I told him he should go back," he muttered to himself. "He should have listened."

As an attempt to ameliorate his guilt, it was remarkably ineffective.

Groaning again, he got to his feet, a slow, step-by-step process interspersed with long periods of rest during which he gulped air and waited for his muscles to stop screaming. The pain eased off as he kept moving, though, and eventually, he made it to his feet. Now he could see through the window, but that was little help: all it revealed were clouds, aglow with light from below. Whether it was the same night he had been stunned or the next, he had no way to tell. He stumbled into the tiny toilet to relieve himself and then splash cold water on his face. When he stepped out into the cell again, feeling slightly more human, he was no longer alone.

Three men now stood in the room, two large enough to loom, the other a mite smaller than Lorn—which still made him a large man by Peregrine standards. "Who are you?" said the smaller man without preamble.

Lorn said nothing for a moment, still drying his hands on the rough white towel he had found in the bathroom. He would have known the three men were military even if they hadn't been wearing green camouflage uniforms, but he didn't recognize the insignia—they certainly had nothing to do with SSIN ranks. The man who had spoken, who was dark-skinned—though not as dark as Ekwansi—had a nametag. MALIK.

"Pleased to meet you, too," Lorn said.

Malik's lips tightened. "Answer the question."

Lorn shrugged. "No reason not to. My name's Sylvan Prester." He hadn't exactly pulled the name out of thin air; Sylvan Prester was the boy-wizard hero of a series of fantasy tales he'd enjoyed as a child.

"And why are you here?"

"Same reason everyone comes to Margaret's Land. Looking for the Lost City." Lorn snorted. "Thought it would be full of gold and alien tech. Looks like I got *that* wrong."

Malik sighed. "This damn Lost City legend is causing us no end of trouble."

"Let me guess," Lorn said. "Trumak?"

Malik's eyes narrowed. "You know him?"

"Knew he came this way. Knew he disappeared suddenly. That's why we decided to follow."

"Bad mistake," Malik said.

"Worse for Ekwansi," Lorn said. "Your robot killed him."

"It was supposed to if he demonstrated he was a threat. Which firing at the robot absolutely did. Friend of yours?"

"Guide. But I liked him."

"Too bad," Malik said. "You're just lucky you didn't draw your weapon, or you'd be in the same body bag." He studied Lorn for a long moment. "You look military," he said at last.

"Ex-military," Lorn said. "Dishonorable discharge. Got a little too greedy on the black market with some proscribed armament. Got out here ahead of the MPs. They don't much care as long as I don't go back to Bagnell."

Malik regarded him, pursing and unpursing his lips. After a moment, he said, "And will someone else be coming out here to see what happened to you?"

"Doubt it," Lorn said. "What *is* going to happen to me?"

"Still to be determined," Malik said. He scratched the back of his neck, then turned to the two giants. "Hold him," he said.

"What—" Lorn began, but before he could finish his question, one of the guards had spun him around and bent his right arm painfully behind him. The other grabbed his right arm and forced it straight. Unable to move, Lorn watched Malik calmly take a small black case from his belt. He opened it, revealing a syringe. The needle gleamed in the harsh light of the glowtube as he stepped forward. Without a word, he jammed the point into the crook of Lorn's arm and drew a blood sample. He jerked the filled syringe free and returned it to its case.

The guards spun Lorn around and shoved him away so hard he bounced off the wall with stunning impact and slid to the ground. Groaning, he righted himself as the door closed behind Malik and the other two. *What the hell?* he thought fuzzily. *What do they need a blood sample for?*

And why haven't they just killed me?

No answers presented themselves. And of course, just because they hadn't executed him yet didn't mean it wasn't still on the agenda. He hauled himself to his feet, using the wall for support, staggered over to the bed, and flung himself down on it again.

He fell asleep almost at once. Unlike during his previous unconsciousness, he dreamed. In his dream, he lay chained to the floor of a pit. Above him, robots moved. They began throwing corpses into the pit. They piled up around Lorn, threatening to crush him. The headless Ekwansi thudded down on his right, and then the pregnant woman he had shot in the Skywatcher enclave hit the ground to his left, and as their blood pooled beneath him, he came awake, gasping...

It was still dark. And it wasn't only the dream that had awakened him.

Someone was sitting on the end of his bed.

"Hello," said a soprano voice. "We need to talk."

Lorn blinked at the strangely small silhouette. "Who are you?"

"My name is Kiri Ishida. And you're Lorn Kymbal."

That sent a chill through him. "Who?"

The indistinctly seen woman sighed. "The blood Malik took was cross-referenced to the planetary ID records we extracted from the Peregrine 'Net. DNA doesn't lie. You're Lorn Kymbal."

"Then Malik knows...?"

"No," Kiri said. "Malik relied on me to check your results against the computer records. And I lied and said I couldn't ID you, that no record of your DNA existed."

Lorn sat up. "What?"

"Shut up and listen," Kiri said. "We don't have much time, and this is the only chance I'll get to talk to you." She glanced up at the tiny window. "You know what that egg-shaped thing out there is?"

"United Earth Starship *Falcon's Egg*." Her head swung back around to him. He still couldn't see her in detail, but he could see she was much smaller than him, slender, and had long hair drawn back into a ponytail. "Its name is written right on it," he pointed. "Not exactly a Sherlockian deduction. Trumak saw it, too."

"Trumak?"

"First guy to stumble on it," Lorn said. He paused. "Do you know what happened to him?"

"Nothing good," Kiri said shortly. "He tried to disable a guardbot with a rifle grenade. There wasn't enough left of him to identify."

Lorn winced. "Not a friendly place."

"That's one way to put it." She took a deep breath. "Okay, look. I know you're here because Javik told you about the transmissions he intercepted. So the first thing you need to know is that the only reason he was ever able to intercept those transmissions was that I interfered with them. I disabled some of the security protocols and made sure the 'anomalies' were flagged for his attention."

Lorn blinked. "You *knew* him?"

"No. But I figured out pretty early on that there was some kind of intelligence plugged directly into the 'Net. He left traces." He saw a quick flash of teeth from a smile. "'Anomalies.' He and I had that in common—we're both good at spotting anomalies." The smile disappeared. "But I had a technological advantage. I was able to figure out who he was, and what, while he never even knew I existed—or that I was the one feeding him information."

"You could have fed him a bit more of it," Lorn said bitterly. "He's dead."

"I know." Kiri shook her head. "Believe it or not, I was trying to protect him. I let him have as much as I thought was safe...but I screwed up. I'm the best compgeek we've got, but a couple of others aren't far behind me. That little turd Jokinen twigged to Javik's existence. Didn't twig to the fact I was the one feeding him information, fortunately, or we wouldn't be having this conversation, but that didn't help Javik." She took a deep breath and finished savagely, "I got him killed."

"I know how you feel," Lorn said, thinking of Ekwansi.

"Anyway. I intercepted Javik's message to you telling you to meet him. But I also saw the message from our agent that you'd been killed. I thought that was it. I thought I'd failed. Then suddenly, there you were, right on top of us. And now, *here* you are."

"Here I am." Lorn shook his head. Anger welled in him. He felt like a fish that had been played out, only to be reeled in again. "So what the hell do you want with me? And what the hell do you expect me to do?"

"I'll start at the beginning."

"Please do."

"No Earth starships have called here in some two local centuries, am I right?" Kiri said.

"Not unless you count *Mayflower II*."

"I'm not counting that."

"Then, no."

"Well," Kiri said, "let's start by me telling you why." She paused as if marshaling her thoughts. "The starships quit coming to Peregrine because of a rebellion: not *on* Earth, but *against* Earth. Peregrine was never trusted with starships, but other worlds were, and they led an uprising against Earth, against what they saw as a corrupt and dictatorial government, skimming the wealth of many worlds to enrich the plutocrats back home. And, of course, they were right, but the mere fact they were right did not guarantee success. Earth had very carefully withheld certain advanced technologies from the colonies, and as a result, despite being outnumbered, Earth pushed back the initial assault. The war has raged ever since, fading and flaring on multiple planets for decades.

"Peregrine has been spared because it has always been a backwater. But it will be spared no longer. The rebel forces have taken Earth itself, but the net they closed around it was not tight-meshed enough to keep loyalist forces from escaping.

"To retake Earth, the loyalists need new bases of operations. And that's where Peregrine comes in. That ship out there," she gestured at the tiny window, the movement just visible in the dark, "*Falcon's Egg*—it's what's called a seed ship. It's designed to settle down in some out-of-the-way place and start churning out an army."

"A robot army," Lorn said.

"Exactly. Like the guardbot that nabbed you. Other robots are digging for metals in the deposits we identified in this valley, raw materials for the microfactories underground. So far, they've produced only a few units. I think you met some of them at Javik's."

"Unfortunately, yes." Lorn pulled his feet up under him and sat cross-legged on the bed, ignoring the twinges of pain the movement still caused. "So you're building a robot army to take over Peregrine and establish it as a base from which you can strike back at the rebels. Is that right?"

"You've got it."

Lorn glanced up at the dark ceiling, thinking about what lay beyond it. "*Mayflower II* must have been a bit of a shock."

Kiri snorted. "You could say that. We had no idea it had survived, much less made it this far. But from our commander's perspective, it was serendipitous. No ship that size still exists anywhere else. She immediately saw the possibilities."

"I'm not sure I do," Lorn said cautiously, but in fact, he had a pretty good idea, and he didn't like it.

"Our initial clandestine surveillance—you have no technology in this system that can penetrate our cloaking systems; even now, this entire base, blazing with light, is invisible to your surveillance satellites—gave us a clear picture of recent events. Knowing that *Mayflower II* was largely abandoned but that those who remained aboard were no friends of the planetary government *and* were still loyal to Earth, Commander Almeida initiated contact with them. She found them very welcoming."

"I'll bet she did," Lorn said sourly.

"We now have a mixed human/robot team aboard *Mayflower II* working clandestinely to outfit it with a full stardrive and associated control systems," Kiri said. "Not to mention modern weapons. Commander Almeida has also, as you well know, made contact with discontented elements of the Peregrine government. They are under the impression we are somehow related to this 'Skywatcher' cult that has caused you so much trouble; none of them know the truth. They're what used to be called, on Earth, 'useful idiots.' When their usefulness is at an end, I suspect they will be very unhappy with the results."

"Why?" Lorn said.

Kiri's head turned sharply toward him. "Why what?"

"Why should they be unhappy with the results? It may seem to them—it may seem to a *lot* of people on this planet—that the benefits of all the new technology you are bringing, not to mention the resumption of star travel, are worth more than propping up the current regime."

"Is that how you feel?" Kiri said softly.

"I'm a member of the SSIN," Lorn said. "It's my duty to

prop up the current regime." Even as he said that he knew how it sounded.

Clearly, so did Kiri. "Not where your heart lies, though, is it?" She shook her head. "Perhaps people will feel that way at first. Commander Almeida may well be counting on it. But it's all a façade. Almeida has no interest in the people of this planet except for how they can help her strike back at the rebels. She will use them as slave labor, and when the rebels come calling—as they surely will—as cannon fodder or human shields. She is bringing war to this planet, and I doubt what comes out the other side of that war, if anything does, will be the world that any of you dream of."

Lorn said nothing. He felt the same longing he'd had as a boy, to go to the stars, to explore the worlds the people of Peregrine had been cut off from when the starships stopped coming. He'd been into space, but he'd barely been alive for most of his time there, and he'd been bound to the ground ever since. The woman at the foot of his bed had actually been to Earth—*Earth!* —and seen stranger and more terrible things there and on other worlds than he could imagine. But he *wanted* to be able to imagine it. More: he wanted to *experience* it.

Even if it meant leaving Peregrine behind forever. *Especially* if it meant leaving Peregrine, and everything he had done here...and had done to him...behind forever.

"If your cloaking systems are so good," he said at last, "why was I able to see your camp from the ridge?"

Kiri shrugged. "Because we weren't concerned with anyone seeing us from the ridge; the guardbots nab anyone who comes close, and no transmission can escape from kilometres around the ship. The cloak preventing satellites from seeing us is essentially a field of force projected overhead, a lens that bends light so that from above the forest seems unbroken."

"No transmission can escape?" Lorn said.

"Only the ones I *allowed* to escape, the ones Javik intercepted."

"Why did you do that?" Lorn asked. "Why are you sabotaging your own mission?"

"It's not my mission," Kiri said, with the tone of a mother explaining to a toddler why he needed to wash his hands before eating dinner. "I'm a rebel spy. I rather expected you to have figured that out by now."

And indeed, Lorn felt rather foolish. Why else would she be telling him all this? "Oh," he said.

"The rebels—we call ourselves ELF, by the way; it's an abbreviation for *Egalité, Liberté, Fraternité*—knew early on we could never seal off Earth's system tightly enough to prevent potential counterrevolutionaries from escaping. So we chose to infiltrate them long before the final assault." He caught a glimpse of teeth as she grinned. "And someone with my computer skills is always highly valued. I wrangled my away aboard this ship." The grin faded. "But now I find there is little I can do. I'd hoped Javik might send someone who could really put a stop to this abomination. Instead, I got you."

"Javik was not the person to contact if you wanted any kind of official response."

"Javik was the only person I *could* contact—the only one who could receive the signals I arranged to send. I always knew it was a forlorn hope, but I hoped I might at least delay things here on Peregrine while I moved on to the real plan."

"Which is?"

Another shrug. "Get back to Earth. Tell ELF what's going on here. Have a strike force sent out to deal with it."

"A strike force?" Lorn leaned forward. "You just told me that Commander Almaida wants to bring the war to Peregrine," he said accusingly. "You said that as if it was something to be avoided. Now you tell me it's what *you* want to do?"

"Big difference," Kiri said. "If I can get the message to Earth fast enough, the strike will be limited to where we are sitting right now. The robots are capable of only limited independent action, and even then, only if they're programmed to take it. To seize control of the planet, they must be under centralized control—from *Falcon's Egg*'s main computer. Destroy *Falcon's Egg*, and you cut off the head of the snake, leaving the body to flail uselessly. The rest of the planet will be largely unaffected except by local mopping-up action against whatever robots might be running around on their own and haven't simply frozen in place. And after that, Peregrine will *really* be opened up to the rest of the galaxy. Isn't that what you want?"

"Why are you telling me any of this at all?" Lorn said. "For that matter, *how* are you telling me? How did you get in here without triggering any alarms?"

"Mad computer skills, remember?" Kiri said. "For an hour, the systems are being fooled by a virtual feed indistinguishable from a real one, one that shows you sleeping soundly here and me working away at my station on the other side of the compound. As for why I'm telling you...well, I admit it's a bit of a whim, but here's the thing. I've got brains. I've even got a modicum of brawn—but," she spread her hands, indicating her small frame, "only a modicum. I may need more than that. You're military-trained, and the fact you're here means you already evaded two spiderbots and our monitoring agent—the one who reported you were dead just before he was eliminated."

"Leghev," Lorn said. He remembered Leghev's blood covering him after the spiderbot exploded. "His name was Leghev."

"I'm sorry," Kiri repeated. "Leghev." He could just see her eyes, looking at him intently. "So. I think I can use your help. Will you give it to me?"

"What if I refuse? What if I report you?"

"You really don't want to do that," Kiri said, and there was such flat certainty in her voice that he believed her.

But even discounting the implied threat, he didn't *want* to report her. The vision of Peregrine overrun by robots, forced to serve the Earth that had kept the technology from them two hundred years ago that would have enabled them to spread out among the stars, locked them on this one small planet, made him angry. "All right," he said. "I'll help you. What exactly do we have to do?"

"It's easy," Kiri said. "We're going to escape. We're going to steal a scoutship. Before we leave, we're going to cause as much damage as we can, to slow down Almaida's plans." She paused, and again he caught the flash of white teeth. "And then, Lorn Kymbal...we're going to Earth."

Chapter Six

KIRI SAID she needed a day to put her plan in place, which left Lorn nothing to do but stew in his cell. He fully expected a second interrogation, but whether due to Kiri's intervention or for some other reason, the day dragged past with no interruption—or interest—beyond the delivery of two small meals, slid through a small opening at the bottom of the door. Neither was immediately identifiable. The mid-morning meal had a kind of dark brown bread or cake with a nutty flavor, smeared with something that might have been butter but wasn't, and a bowl of what he guessed was a kind of porridge, although he found the pale purple color off-putting. Later in the afternoon, a second tray arrived, this one bearing a perfectly square slab of protein, though whether fish, fowl, pork or beef he couldn't have said, a blob of some kind of mashed root, and another blob of something green—pureed vegetable matter of some kind, though again he found it unrecognizable. Unless he missed his guess, he was eating some kind of reconstituted or synthesized food made on board the starship. He ate it dutifully but thought ruefully as he did so that he'd hoped to never encounter anything less appetizing than SSIN field rations...and he just had.

To drink, there was nothing but the water from the tap in the small bathroom; they'd provided him with a small plastic cup.

He spent most of the day wearing nothing but a towel, having showered on getting up and then done his best to wash his clothes in the small sink. By the time the second meal arrived, he was dressed again, smelling and feeling cleaner, although still a bit damp in spots, with the aching aftereffects of being stunned also much reduced. After the meal slid through the slot, the unseen delivery person outside said, "Pass through the morning tray, please." Lorn complied. An hour after the evening meal was delivered, a different voice asked for that tray to be returned.

And that was that. The sky outside the tiny window darkened and he lay down fully clothed on the narrow bed. Kiri hadn't said what time to expect her and had warned that if everything did not go exactly as she hoped, she might not show up until the following night. He figured he might as well get whatever sleep he could.

It turned out not to be much. Bloody nightmares woke him twice. The third time his eyes flew open, and he sat up at the sound of the door opening. It didn't close again. Kiri stood silhouetted against the faint blue glow of the corridor outside his cell. "Time to go."

He swung his legs over the side and reached for his boots. Ideally, he'd have already been wearing them, but he hadn't wanted to arouse any suspicions among whatever unseen watchers might be keeping an eye on him. He jerked them on, buckled them up, and stood. "Now what?"

"Barring the unexpected," Kiri said, "we should now have a leisurely stroll along a long, dull corridor to a lift which will take us up into the ship. A short walk through its interior will bring us to the courier vessel. It has already been programmed for an automated launch. A magnetic cannon will hurl us upward, the atmospheric engines will fire and lift us into orbit, and the Umstattd drive will have us on our way to Earth within an hour of launch."

"That easy?"

"That easy." Kiri's teeth flashed white in the dim light. "Barring," she repeated, "the unexpected. Here." She handed him a sheathed knife.

Lorn took it, glad to have some sort of weapon, though he would have preferred a gun. "What's that for?"

"The unexpected."

He attached the sheath to his belt. "What about the idea of creating some havoc to disrupt plans here?"

"I left them a little surprise in the computer," Kiri said. "The minute we launch, they're going to have their hands full. Now come on."

At first, her escape plan—bolstered, Lorn could only assume, by some computer wizardry on her part to keep their casual stroll through the empty corridors from being detected or seen—seemed just as straightforward as she'd described it. They walked down the corridor, dimly lit by blue nightlights. They descended a slightly brighter staircase for a considerable distance—four or five stories' worth, Lorn estimated—and emerged into another corridor running at right angles to the one they'd just strolled through. Unlike the prefabricated-hut-hallway up above, this one had been cut through solid rock. There were cross-corridors at various intervals, though no doors. "Top-level access to the mine," Kiri said as they left the stairway. "Lifts at the ends of the cross corridors. Not much else. Mostly robots down here, and they don't take breaks, so it's usually empty." She pointed at a small glassy dome at the center of one of the intersections. "Security cameras are showing a video loop. Easy enough down here where nothing hardly moves. But as we get closer to the ship..."

She stopped, peering ahead. "Ah," she said. "That's what I was afraid of."

"What?" Lorn had been trailing her; now he stepped up beside her and saw what she had seen. "Ah," he echoed.

Another seventy-five metres or so along the corridor, there was a pool of brighter light. Beyond it were the doors of a lift, surely their ultimate destination. But standing in that circle of illumination was a large man in a uniform like the ones Lorn's interrogators had worn, staring up at another of the little glass domes with his hands on his hips. "That camera," Kiri said in little more than a whisper, "is on a different system than the ones down here. It's controlled from the bridge. I couldn't access the bridge systems to loop it. So I just cut the power."

"You could do that from your station?"

"No," Kiri said. "But I could do it from about twenty metres farther along this corridor, where I snipped a cable."

"Oh."

"In a minute, he's going to start tracing that cable back this way," she said. "My being down here won't alarm him much. Your being down here will."

"This is one of those unexpected occurrences you hoped would be barred?"

"Actually, I rather anticipated this one," Kiri said. "That's why I cut the cable at an intersection. I just hoped it wouldn't happen." She took a deep breath. "Okay. There's no way he can see us while he's standing in that light. We ease up to the inter-section, you slip into the cross corridor, I lure him up to me, and you silence him. Can you do that?"

"Of course."

They moved forward slowly, trusting to the dimness to keep them hidden from the repairman's light-dazzled eyes. At the intersection, Lorn slipped into one of the side corridors.

The minute he was out of sight, Kiri shouted, "Hey! Sanders! Is this what you're looking for?"

"Who's there?" a man's voice called back.

"Kiri Ishida. We met at Gilbert's birthday party, remember?"

"Kiri? What the hell are you doing down here this time of night?" The voice came closer as he spoke. There was a strange tone to it. "Not that I'm complaining. I've been hoping to run into you."

"I'll bet." Kiri's voice was cool. "I'm just taking a shortcut. Had to reboot a router in the brig building. But look what I found." She pointed up. "Broken cable. Is that the malfunction that brought you down here?"

"That's the one. Damn diggerbot must have snagged it. The things barely fit through the corridors." He came into Lorn's view, but he wasn't looking up at the cable. "So, Kiri," he said. "You dumped me at Gil's party just when things were getting interesting. But I'm willing to give you a second chance."

"Sorry, Sanders. No second chances for you."

He took a step toward her. "Come on, Kiri—"

He never finished the sentence. Lorn leaped out of the corridor, covered Sanders's mouth and nose with his left hand, and with his right, drove the knife into the small of the man's back. He pulled Sanders back onto it to drive the blade as deep as possible, held him there for a couple of seconds, then jerked the knife free, tilted Sanders's head back, and slashed the blade across his throat. Blood poured out, and he stepped back, letting the body fall. Kiri, who had jumped back as he'd attacked, stared down at the dead man and the growing pool of blood around his body.

Lorn leaned down and wiped the blade clean on Sanders's clothes. His heart was pounding, and he felt slightly shaky. He didn't want to look at the blood. It reminded him of the woman. Of Ekwansi...

Blood has never bothered me before, he thought as he sheathed the knife again. *What the hell's wrong with me?*

"You've done this before," Kiri said, her voice tight. "That was very slick."

"Yeah, I've done it before," Lorn said, schooling his own voice to steadiness. He would *not* show weakness. "Shouldn't we be moving?"

"We should. Eventually, they'll try to radio him. When they don't get an answer, they'll send someone else." She leaned down and pulled a rectangular white card from Sanders's breast pocket, then turned away and headed on down the corridor.

Lorn's heart quieted as they reached the brightly lit lift. The knife wouldn't be much good against a robot, but against a human, especially one that wasn't trained in knife fighting, it could be a godsend. Just the appearance of a blade made most people hesitate, and if you acted fast in that instant, you had them.

And if you got them from behind, like he had Sanders, it was one of the quickest and quietest ways to kill someone. Something the SSIN well knew and had made sure he did, too. Like any military force, much of SSIN training was focused on overcoming the natural human aversion to killing another human. He'd practiced that "sentry-killing" move a thousand times before he'd used it for real a dozen more on various missions against Skywatchers. It was practically second nature.

He hadn't always been inured to violence. He remembered

when his father had shot the Skywatcher who had traced Art Stoddard to their house. He'd been horrified, though he'd tried to hide it. He'd had nightmares, then, too, but he'd hidden those, as well. He didn't want his father to think he was weak. He didn't want Art Stoddard to think he was just some dumb kid who wasn't good for anything. Besides, despite how horrible it had been to see a man die in his own yard, he'd been proud of his father for having the skill and bravery to use force to protect his family, and in the service of a greater cause. And scant weeks later, he'd done the same. His father had told him how proud he was of Lorn for opening the airlock on the *Mayflower II* and saving the small band of Crawlspacers from the Crew closing in on them. But he couldn't hide the shadow in his eyes as he said the words. Lorn hadn't understood it, then, though it had registered, but he understood it now, knew that he'd crossed some kind of Rubicon when he'd killed for the first time, and changed himself forever. Most people never killed anyone. He'd been fifteen when he'd killed the men on the *Mayflower II*. How many had he killed since?

He'd always believed he'd only killed people who had to be killed. He'd always believed he was just fighting for what was right, like his father, like Art Stoddard. He'd believed all the killing would lead to a better world. Maybe he still believed it: he'd killed Sanders so Kiri could escape and prevent the war from coming to Peregrine.

But not everyone he had killed had deserved killing. The pregnant woman...and who knew how many before that? Maybe he'd been lying to himself all the time, trying to convince himself he was a hero when really all he was was a killer, warped as a young man, like a young tree bent beneath a spring snow that never again grew straight.

Maybe what he really was was a monster.

He forced the thoughts from his mind. This wasn't the

time; this wasn't the place. *Survive now. Get Kiri off the planet. Then freak out all you want.*

"This may buy us some time," Kiri said. She swiped the card she had lifted from Sanders's body across the blank metal plate to the right of the lift. It left a smear of blood. "I was going to use my own, but now we're going to look like Sanders coming back up."

The doors opened, and they stepped into the plain white interior. The door closed again. Kiri swiped the card one more time across the interior plate. "Sixteen," she said into thin air.

"Sixteen," a disembodied woman's voice said. The lift accelerated upward.

For the first time, Lorn had leisure and light to take a really good look at his companion. As he'd guessed from her name, she appeared to be of Japanese ancestry. She was so small and slender that if he hadn't known better he might have taken her for a teenager, especially since her straight black hair was drawn back in a ponytail. "This takes us directly into the ship?" Lorn said.

Kiri nodded. "The ship is designed to be set down right on top of a promising mineral deposit and drill straight down. Last I heard, the mine is twelve levels deep."

"But the ore doesn't come into the ship." Lorn made that a statement, not a question; it clearly didn't.

Kiri shook her head. "The main mine head is right up against the valley slope. That's where the processing units are."

"I didn't see any smoke. Surely a smelter—"

"A smelter?" Kiri snorted. "We don't use anything that primitive. Nanobots rip through the ore and separate out anything of use...which is pretty much everything. No smoke. No waste. The processed material either goes straight to the robot microfactories or, if it's something that isn't immediately needed, into storage."

"Entering ship," the lift said. "Level one."

"What's on level sixteen?" Lorn said.

"Level two," said the lift.

"That's the boat deck." Kiri spoke over the lift's continuing rising count. "And that's where, if the unexpected has not been properly barred, we will encounter it."

Lorn drew the knife and waited for the doors to open.

Except they didn't open. The lift stopped but didn't let them out. "Corporal Timothy Sanders," the lift said, "you are not authorized to enter the Boat Deck. Please wait for the Deck Officer and present your authorization when requested to do so."

"Shit!" Kiri spat. "I thought Sanders was authorized. What, nothing breaks on this deck?" She tossed Sanders's bloody card aside and drew out a glassy square about ten centimetres on a side. "Well, back to my original plan." She pressed the square against the plate. "Override. Authorization Kiri 1080 Delta."

"Override authority recognized," the lift said.

Just like that, the doors swung open. Kiri pulled the glassy square—though, watching, Lorn saw that it bent more like plastic—from the plate. "That," she said, "just raised a huge red flag in the bridge. We've got maybe five minutes before this deck is full of armed Marines."

Lorn nodded. Kiri led him into the hallway, which curved to left and right, presumably following the hull of the ship. She darted right. He followed a few steps behind and was just out of sight of her when he heard her collide with someone else. "Who are you?" a woman's voice growled.

"Please, you've got to help me, it's Sanders, he attacked me!" Kiri said breathlessly. "He's after me—"

"Quiet." Silence for a moment. "I don't hear anything."

"He's shut up in the lift. I was doing some late-night maintenance, he heard I was here alone, he said he'd come up, but he couldn't get out, you can't let him out—"

She sounded genuinely terrified.

"He can't get out unless I let him out," the second woman said. "You come with me. We'll figure out what this is all—"

She came around the corner. Lorn was ready with the knife, but he didn't need it. Kiri spun, her foot slammed against the woman's temple from behind, and the woman went down as if shot. Kiri reached down and pulled the woman's sidearm from its holster, then snagged a keycard like the one she'd taken from Sanders.

"You've done that before, too," Lorn said, impressed.

"Once or twice." Kiri turned and hurried on along the curving corridor.

Maybe thirty metres farther, they came to what was clearly the inner door of an airlock. Kiri swiped the card. The door swung open—

—and in the same instant, an earsplitting rising shriek sounded. The door began to close again.

"In!" Kiri cried. Lorn crowded after her and barely dragged his foot in before the door closed. They were in a tight space, no bigger than a closet. Kiri swiped the card again, and the inner door swung open.

"Surprised that worked," Lorn said. "Considering the alarm."

"This door isn't controlled by the ship," Kiri said. "It's controlled by the courier boat."

A pounding sounded on the inner airlock door. "We know you're in there!" a voice shouted thinly, attenuated by the steel between. "Come out, or we're coming in!"

Kiri said nothing. The inner door had opened. She stepped through, Lorn on her heels. The door closed behind them. She turned and poked quickly at a touchscreen. Icons flashed yellow, then red.

"What'd you do?" Lorn said.

"Evacuated the space between the inner and outer doors," she said. "They'll still get through, but they're going to have to override a couple of more layers of safety features before the ship will let them open something onto vacuum, even on the ground." She turned. They were in another tight space, so Lorn had to suck in his gut and press his back against the wall behind him to let her manage the turn. He found himself extremely distracted by the nearness of her body.

Been in the field a little too long, haven't you? he told himself. *Down, boy.*

Kiri reached up for a bar over an opening that seemed to be nothing more than a smooth silvery metal tube. She swung her legs into it and vanished, sliding down. Lorn followed.

The slide was only a few metres long. Lorn emerged, stumbled to his feet, and found himself standing in what was clearly a control room, with two seats facing each other across a glowing insubstantial ball of what looked like thick gas, lights glowing within it—though how a ball of gas held a spherical shape, he had no idea. Busy flatscreen displays, meaningless to Lorn, covered most of the wall space, punctuated by three doors and a couple of closed white cabinets.

"Sit," Kiri said, pointing at one of the seats. "And strap in."

Lorn did as he was told.

She slid into the other chair and strapped in herself. Then she slapped the small glassy square she had used to override the lift doors onto the smooth black metal surface of the round table over which floated the glowing ball of gas.

"Authorized," a voice said—the same voice as the lift, which was a little disconcerting. "Kiri Ishida, you now have command of Earth Forces Courier Vessel *Ninshubur*. Welcome aboard."

"Emergency ground launch protocol," Kiri snapped.

"Initiating emergency ground launch protocol," the computer said. A dull thud shook the ship. Lorn guessed the Marines had gotten tired of waiting and had blown the airlock. "Sealing vessel."

The distant shouts he was just beginning to hear ended with finality as the opening through which they had slid into the control room snapped sealed.

"Magnetic launch system online," the computer said. "*Falcon's Egg* requesting confirmation."

"Confirmed," Kiri said. Her fingers flew over the little glassy square again. "Note that I have override authority over any commands from *Falcon's Egg*."

"Noted and confirmed," the vessel said. "Orders?"

"Launch," Kiri said.

"Launching," said *Ninshubur*.

Vicious acceleration jammed Lorn hard down into the chair, which suddenly seemed to have turned hard as a rock. He couldn't breathe. His vision closed down to a tunnel, a tunnel growing smaller and smaller—

The acceleration stopped. His body creaked up against the restraints as, for a moment, they went ballistic. Then more acceleration, not as violent as before, but it still felt like being sat on by a dragonbear...or at least how he imagined being sat on by a dragonbear would feel. This went on for minutes. Then...

"Orbit achieved," said the *Ninshubur*. "Orders?"

"Lay in a course for Earth."

"Course laid," the ship replied instantly.

"Take us there."

"Running preflight checks," the ship said. "All green. Umstattd drive spinning up. Drive active. Drive engaged."

Lorn felt a strange twisting sensation, as though every atom in his body had reversed spin, if that made any sense...and that was that.

"That's that?" he said out loud.

"That's that," Kiri said. "We're on our way to Earth."

And then she lifted the pistol she'd taken from the Deck Officer and aimed it squarely at his head.

Chapter Seven

LORN SAT VERY, *VERY* STILL. "KIRI," he said, "what's all this about?"

"This is about," Kiri said, "being locked in a small spaceship with a killer." She gestured at his belt. "Take off the knife and toss it over here."

He complied, but he felt a flash of anger as he flipped the sheathed knife onto the control table. "You were happy enough to have me kill for you down below."

"Actually," Kiri said. "I just told you to *silence* Sanders. *You* chose to kill him." She took the knife and tucked it into the seat beside her, the gun never wavering.

"If I hadn't killed him, he might have stopped us right there," Lorn said, keeping his voice calm, reasonable. "Even jumping him from behind, I couldn't be sure I'd put him down. He was a big guy. If we'd gotten into a struggle, anything could have happened. The only way to make sure our escape succeeded was to kill him, quickly and quietly. It's what I've been trained to do." It was technically true, of course, that he could have tried to throttle Stevens from behind until he lost consciousness or hit him on the temple with the hilt of his knife. The trouble was that knocking someone out with one blow wasn't nearly as easy with real people as it was with fictional people. It hadn't even occurred to him to try.

Should it have?

No, he thought. *I did what I had to do.*

But apparently, Kiri didn't see it. "You said you needed brawn, and you gave me a knife. What did you expect?"

"Don't try to blame me," Kiri said. "Sanders was a jerk, but he didn't deserve to die."

"Very few people deserve to die," Lorn said. *The pregnant woman...Ekwansi...* "But sometimes people have to die if a mission is to succeed." The words sounded hollow in his own ears, and even as he said them, he realized he might have just made an argument for her to pull the trigger and shove his body out the airlock. All the same, he pressed on. "The question you have to ask yourself is, is the mission worth it? I assumed you felt that preventing a robot-assisted takeover of Peregrine and its conversion into a military base from which to launch attacks on your rebel friends was worth at least one death. Was I wrong?"

Kiri held the gun on him for another long moment. "That's not what concerns me. Millions have died in this rebellion. And I've been directly responsible for my share. But I only kill when I have to. Do you?"

"I don't kill for fun if that's what you mean."

"Maybe. But is it fun when you kill?"

Lorn felt a flash of anger and shook his head. "Of course not. You never really get used to it." But even as he voiced that platitude, an icy part of his own brain called him a liar. *Hadn't* he gotten used to it? He'd killed a lot of people; so many he couldn't give an accurate tally. Until recently, it hadn't bothered him. He'd killed Sanders without thought, without even considering another option.

Maybe Kiri was right to pull a gun.

The barrel pointed unwaveringly at him a moment longer. Then Kiri thumbed on the weapon's safety and set it down on the table. "All right," she said. "I won't shoot you. At least not yet."

"Uh...thanks." Lorn glanced around the control room. "So, now what? This is all new to me. How long does it take to fly to Earth? What do we eat? Where do we sleep?" He smiled. "Where's the bathroom?"

"Let me give you the grand tour. It won't take long." She unstrapped, then picked up the pistol, not making a big deal of it, but Lorn got the message anyway. He was still on probation.

She got up from the acceleration couch, bouncing a little as she stood. Lorn had already noticed the low gravity; presumably kept at the minimum necessary to make getting around easy, without drawing too much power from the engines, since the focus of a courier ship must be on speed. "There are two sleeping spaces," Kiri said. She pointed the pistol toward the two doors situated ninety degrees around the circumference from the door through which they had entered. "A shared toilet/shower space." She pointed to the third door directly opposite the entrance. "We do everything else in here." She gestured around the control room. "The galley, if you want to call it that, is in that cabinet." She pointed to her right. "Entertainment player's in there," she pointed to the second cabinet. "Millions of books, vids, music, games. As for how long we'll be in here..." She indicated a flatscreen displaying a countdown in green characters on a black background. "Our ETA to the Earth orbit challenge point is twelve days, fourteen hours, and thirty-seven minutes, as you can see."

"Challenge point?"

"That's where we go into orbit and try to convince the fleet protecting the planet not to blow us out of space."

"Ah." Lorn cleared his throat. "You're not anticipating a problem convincing them, are you?"

"Not if Earth is still in ELF hands," Kiri said. "But I've had no contact with anyone in ELF ranks for well over three months. A lot can happen in three months."

"A lot can happen in twelve days, back on Peregrine," Lorn said. "And who knows how many days after that before anyone on Earth does anything about it. How quickly will Almaida's robot army come together?"

"I don't know," Kiri said. "There are very few of them so far, and the little computer surprise I left for them will slow them down, taking all the control systems offline—but there's too much redundancy for me to do any permanent damage. They'll have it sorted out within a few days. Once they're back on track, robots will be built as quickly as resources become available. They build each other, so they're like a bacterial colony: small at first, but expanding exponentially."

"Couldn't you have destroyed the computer completely?"

"Only by smuggling a bomb into the main computer room. But even that wouldn't accomplish anything as long as ELF doesn't know Peregrine has been invaded. Almaida would simply replace the computer and restore it from backups."

"So we could get back to Peregrine and find it's already firmly in the Earth loyalists' grip."

"We could," Kiri said.

"In which case, the planet becomes a battleground."

Kiri nodded.

"And there's unlikely to be much left when the battle is over."

"No," Kiri said. "Probably not." She met his gaze squarely then, with a flash of defiance. "And it wouldn't be the first. My homeworld will take years to rebuild from the battles fought there. But it *will* be rebuilt. It will be rebuilt better—and it will be *free*."

It was Lorn's turn to say nothing. *What is freedom worth?* he wondered. *Worth all the death and destruction? Worth what the SSIN did to that Skywatcher compound—what I did there— a hundred thousand times over? Worth the lives of everyone I've killed? Worth all the suffering?*

But the suffering was coming either way. How many would die when the robot horde—the *infection*, if you took Kiri's metaphor of a bacterial colony literally—spread out across the planet? The SSIN couldn't fight something like that. He'd barely managed to destroy a small unarmored spiderbot. Military robots, powered by technology decades in advance of anything on Peregrine, would be all but unstoppable.

He remembered an old saying: "You may not be interested in war, but war is interested in you." Like it or not, the decades-old war between authoritarian Earth and its at least nominally freedom-loving rebels had become interested in Peregrine and everyone who lived there. There was nothing he could do to stop it. The best he could hope for was that the rebels would act quickly enough to short-circuit Almaida's plans and minimize the damage to the planet...and that somehow, at the end of it all, Peregrine would end up a better place for his little sister to grow up on than it had been for him.

The wild card was the planetary government itself. There were clearly factions within it who intended to help Almaida, and the dead-enders on *Mayflower II*, even now being converted to a massive battleship, were as Earth-loyal as they came. The SSIN might actually side with Almaida rather than the rebels. In which case, civil war could descend on Peregrine for the second time in less than a decade.

He felt powerless. He *was* powerless. Nothing but a useless passenger, seen as a potential threat, now that he had helped Kiri gain access to this courier vessel.

But when they got to Earth...then maybe, just maybe, he *would* have some value because of his knowledge of the situation on Peregrine. And maybe, just maybe, he could barter that knowledge for some smidgen of power, some slight leverage of the course of events.

Maybe.

But for now...

He unbuckled. "Let's see what they've got in that galley. I'm starving."

———

TWELVE DAYS AND FOURTEEN HOURS. It didn't sound like much. At first, Lorn enjoyed it. It had been days since he hadn't been on the run, in peril, or fighting for his life. R&R should have been just what the doctor ordered.

Except he didn't know what the doctor would have ordered because he'd run away from his doctor.

The problems began that first "night," arbitrarily set to correspond to the Peregrine day/night cycle they'd just left. Falling asleep wasn't the problem. Staying asleep was.

The nightmares were waiting. The pregnant woman, eyes glazing, clutching the hole in her stomach, trying to stop her blood and the blood of her unborn child from pouring steaming into the night air. Ekwansi, one minute full of life, the next a headless corpse. Sanders, his hot blood spilling over Lorn's hands. And others, so many others. Skywatchers. Skywatcher sympathizers. Blood. Bone. Gore. The images brought him gasping awake. An hour or two later, he'd finally doze off again, only to face the ghosts of his dead once more.

Waking brought little relief. He had nothing to do. He tried to read, but he couldn't focus. He tried to listen to music, but it all sounded like mindless cacophony. He would have drunk himself into a stupor, but as far as he could tell, the courier ship carried no alcohol. And it felt wrong to be without a weapon. Vulnerable. If Kiri decided to take him out after all, he had nothing with which to fight back.

The second night he woke from another nightmare, heart pounding, sure Kiri was even then creeping toward him across the crew compartment, knife in hand, ready to slit his throat. He clenched his fists, waited, tense, ready to spring up the moment she opened the hatch. He could grab her, kill her, he was bigger and stronger...

It took him several minutes to quiet his racing pulse and realize how stupid he was being. If she wanted to kill him, she could shoot him at any moment. She had a gun. He had nothing. The fact she hadn't killed him proved she didn't want to.

Not yet, a part of him whispered. *But if you kill her first...*

He gasped. He sat up. He stared at his closed door in the dim illumination of the pale blue nightlight that gleamed above his bunk. *No*, he thought. And yet, the urge remained.

He lay back down.

Sometime in the next hour or so, he slept.

This time, he woke, screaming, to find a dark figure standing over him. He cowered away from it, still screaming, hands in front of his face, "No! No! No! No!"

"Lorn! *Lorn!*"

Arms, encircling him. A warm body next to his. He jerked and trembled like a frightened horse. Where was he? What was happening?

"Lorn! Sh. Shh...."

He quieted. Kiri. The courier ship. He knew where he was. He knew how he had gotten there. He clutched at Kiri like a drowning man clinging to a log. He felt himself shaking, heard himself weeping. It all seemed to be happening to someone else, while the real him looked on, separate, apart, with no control over any of it.

Is this what it feels like to be crazy? he thought.

He slept.

He woke to find himself alone in his bed, the door closed. Had he imagined it?

He got up, pulled on his pants, reached for the door.

It was locked.

He pounded on it. "Kiri? Kiri!"

Silence for a moment, then, "Lorn?"

"Why have you locked me in here?"

"One second." A paused, then the door slid open. Kiri, fully dressed, stepped back as it did so. She had the gun in her hand and looked at him warily.

That alone told him he hadn't imagined the events of the night. He stared at her. Then he backed up the three steps to his bed and sat down on it. "Shit. I lost it last night, didn't I?"

"Yeah." She still didn't move. "Question is, have you found it again?"

He took stock. He still felt...unsettled. Naked, and not just because he wasn't wearing a shirt. Exposed. Raw.

Vulnerable.

He didn't like it.

"Something's happened to you recently," Kiri said. It wasn't a question. "Something that broke the soldier-armor in which military training encases you. I'm guessing it was a mission that went wrong. Am I right?"

Lorn nodded.

"So tell me about it."

Lorn shook his head. "I don't want to talk about it," he muttered. He felt embarrassed now. Falling apart like that, in front of her...it was humiliating. His father would never have broken down like that. Or Shadow. Even Art Stoddard...

"You *will* talk about it," Kiri said, "or I'll keep you locked in that sleeping compartment for the rest of our journey...and hand you over to the military shrinks the minute we get to Earth. You want to be part of my mission, you want to help save your planet, maybe it's time you tell me what the hell's wrong with you."

Anger surged in him. He wanted to jump up, leap at her, knock her down, take the gun away from her...

But that urge shocked him just as much as his breakdown of the night before. And so he sat there, trembling...and then he began to talk.

He intended to give her a clipped, dispassionate account of the assault on the Skywatcher compound. But once he began, more and more words came pouring out of him. He told her about growing up in the Wild, about the day he and his Dad found Art Stoddard, the attack on their home, following Art, getting shot, going into space, blowing the airlock...the years of training, missions, mayhem...and, finally, the day he shot the woman: the day something broke inside him. He described her in detail, the blood, the glazing eyes, the awful knowledge that the gaping hole in her stomach had come from his bullet, that he had killed her when all she had been trying to do was escape the fire, save herself, save her baby...the words tumbled out of him faster and faster until, in the end, they were all gone, and he ended up sitting on the bed, head bowed, hugging himself, shaking.

A shadow fell on the floor plates in front of his bed, and he looked up to see Kiri standing there. She had holstered the gun. She sat beside him and once again put her arm around him, her hand warm on his bare shoulder. "You're not crazy," she said to him in a low voice. "You're becoming human."

He'd tensed as she touched him, but now he forced his muscles to relax. Her hand remained where it was, skin to skin. He took a deep breath. "I've always thought of myself as one of the good guys," he said, still looking down. "I grew up surrounded by heroes. My Dad. Art Stoddard. Shadow. Avara. They all risked everything for what they believed in. They saved the world. Millions of lives. I wanted to be like them. I wanted to save the world, too. But I haven't saved many lives. I've mostly just taken them. And at first, that seemed all right. The Skywatchers were a real threat. Terrorism...revolution...it all seemed possible. We had to prevent that. We had to stamp them out. But now...yeah, there were fighters in that compound. But they didn't attack us. They hadn't attacked anyone else. They were just living there, trying to stay hidden. Someone betrayed them. We got the orders to move in. They were only trying to defend themselves. Defend their spouses and children. And we...I..." His voice choked off. "I wanted to be a hero, and I turned into a monster," he whispered. "That night, I saw myself clearly for the first time."

"Your self-image shattered," Kiri said softly. "And now you have to build a new one."

"But how?" Lorn raised his head now and looked at her. "I can't take back what I've done."

Kiri released his shoulder, then clasped his hands in hers. "Lorn," she said. "You've already begun. You could have blown off Javik's warning. You could have decided not to get involved. But you didn't. You decided you had to act. You saw a potential threat to Peregrine...to your friends and family...and you acted on it. That's how you ended up here. That's how you ended up with me. You don't have to start from scratch. You don't have to change everything you've believed. You just have to take a step back from what you've become and turn in a slightly different direction." She leaned closer, her eyes locked on his, dark brown pools sparkling in what he had been told were Earth-spectrum lights. "Peregrine still needs you, Lorn. ELF—Egalité, Liberté, Fraternité—needs you. And I need you. If we're going to stop the Loyalists, we all need each other. You can still be a hero."

He felt his breath catch in his throat, though whether from her words or the fact he had suddenly been struck by her beauty, he couldn't have said. "I'll...try."

She squeezed his hands, then released them. He wished she hadn't. "Good," she said. She smiled at him, then. "Enough drama for the morning. Breakfast?"

He nodded, not trusting himself to speak.

They talked more as the day went by. She told him about her own upbringing on a planet that had been among the first to rebel against Earth. It had also had the misfortune to be located in a highly strategic spot and to boast both valuable resources and a strong manufacturing base: or at least it had until successive counterattacks had left much of it in ruin. By the time Kiri had been born, the tide was turning in the rebels' favor, but the planet, Sefuhabad, had long since ceased to be the "safe harbor" that its name had originally meant and instead was largely ruined and impoverished. Blame for that had fallen, in the eyes of the populace, squarely on Earth. That, combined with the fact that joining the rebels was one of the only ways to escape the unforgiving life and poisoned environment, meant that Sefuhabad, and many other worlds in similar straits, provided a steady stream of recruits to ELF—far more than the dwindling Loyalists systems could give Earth. Those numbers, in the end, had been what had overwhelmed her homeworld and finally allowed the rebels to "liberate" it—although from what Kiri said, Earth itself was now nearly ruined.

Kiri's younger brother had joined the rebellion after she

had and had died during the final assault on Earth. It was at that point in her account that her voice broke for the first time.

They were sitting on the floor of the crew compartment, backs to the galley, the light gravity making the hard floor plates more comfortable than they would have been anywhere else. It turned out he'd been wrong about there being no alcohol in the galley: she'd just had it locked away from him. She'd pulled out a bottle of red wine, "pure Earth cabernet sauvignon," she'd said, as if that would mean something to him; all he knew was that it was rich and smooth, and he liked it a lot. They were each on their second glass.

He looked up from his to see her looking deep into hers. "I'm proud of him," she said. "I am. He helped free Earth. He helped free us all." She took another swallow of wine, and he knew from the way her lip trembled after she lowered it that she would rather Loyalists still held Earth and her brother were still alive. He thought of what he would feel like if something happened to Melissa, his little sister. If she were shot down by a robot, or a soldier...someone like him...

It was his turn to take a deep drink of the heady wine.

"My father died shortly after I was born," she went on. "I never really knew him. My Mom died..." She pressed her lips together again. "Sorry," she muttered. "It's the wine."

"Uh-huh," Lorn said.

"Mom died while I was away on my first off-planet mission," she continued after a moment. "I was only nineteen. General Vermani broke the news to me personally."

"Vermani?" Lorn said.

"Atash Vermani," Kiri said. "Head of Field Intelligence for ELF, now. He was a little farther down the hierarchy then, but still my commanding officer. He knew my mother and father. When he told me...I broke down." She shook her head. "Worse than you did last night. He helped put me back together again.

He was widowed, had no children of his own. He took me under his wing, almost as a daughter. He didn't pull any strings for me, but he's the one who guided me into undercover work. He thought I might have a knack for it. Turns out he was right."

"Why undercover?" Lorn said. "Your brother joined the regular forces."

"I think," Kiri said, "I went into it because it meant that, for long periods of time, I could be someone else. At the time, that's what I wanted. And I guess he knew that."

That made him raise an eyebrow. "What's wrong with who you are?"

She snorted. "Look who's talking."

"That's not an answer."

Kiri lifted her glass again. "I don't want to talk about it."

"You didn't let me get away with that," Lorn said. "Why should I let you?"

She turned toward him, eyes flashing, but the momentary anger passed. She smiled a crooked smile. "Fair enough." She sighed and leaned back against the wall again. "I fell apart when my mother died because it was my fault. Or at least I thought it was." Her voice roughened. "She didn't just die. She was murdered by Loyalist terrorists. They'd identified the families of Rebels and gone after them. She was one of fourteen family members of ELF fighters killed that night. The only reason my brother didn't die *then* was that he was out with friends. Then he joined up partly to avenge her...and ended up just as dead." Her voice was shaking again now, and so was her hand. She raised it, stared at it. "See? This is why I don't like talking about it. This is why I prefer to be someone else. When I'm undercover, I fill myself with the cover story of whoever I'm playing. That way, I don't have to think about my *real* story."

Lorn stared at her; and then, to his own surprise, he found

himself chuckling. She turned toward him again with another flash of anger. "What's so funny?"

"Us," Lorn said. He slapped his own chest. "We're both barely holding it together, and yet we're the ones who have to save Peregrine." The chuckle died in his throat. "Although, now that I think about it, maybe that *isn't* really funny."

"Don't worry," Kiri said. She raised her glass again. Her hand no longer shook. "I'll hold it together." Then she turned to him and smiled. "And I'll help hold you together."

Something about the way she said it brought an immediate reaction from his body. *Down, boy,* he thought, very carefully not looking down at himself. *What are you, fifteen again?*

"I'll drink to that," he said, instead of all the other things he could have said, and touched his glass to hers.

———

THEY PASSED the remaining days to Earth far more comfortably and companionably than they had begun, though the hint of something more Lorn thought he had detected over their glasses of Earth wine did not materialize into anything physical. *It was just the wine,* he thought. *Nothing more.*

The nightmares didn't go away, exactly, but they were just dreams now, at least for the moment. He felt rested and more like himself than he had in weeks when, at last, the countdown on the flatscreen wound down to the last few minutes.

Lorn sat once more in the acceleration couch in which he had begun the journey, staring at the holodisplay. He'd spent hours during their journey learning the ship's systems, partly because he thought it might be useful, partly because keeping his brain engaged kept him looking forward rather than back, and looking forward, if Kiri were to be believed, was the way out of the emotional trough into which he had plunged.

Now Lorn gazed at the blue-and-white sphere of the Earth in the holodisplay and wondered at his lack of wonder. All his youth, he had longed to escape Peregrine, had wished that someday he could travel among the stars like his ancestors. Now he had done so, the first man from Peregrine to leave the system in two centuries, and it seemed to hold no thrill at all.

Because when I was a kid, I thought I could escape Peregrine's problems if I left it behind, he thought. *Instead, I find out that Peregrine's problems are everywhere.*

The display showed, as a red circle around the holographic Earth, the orbit the ship was automatically guiding them into so that they could, in Kiri's memorable phrase, convince the rebel fleet also in orbit not to blow them out of space.

"They're tracking us," Kiri said. A red light glowed in the display; she waved her hand, and it disappeared. "And they've locked weapons on us."

"Not very trusting."

"They've got no reason to be."

"Shouldn't you hail them?"

Kiri shook her head. "Don't speak until spoken to, that's the rule. Earth had some success in transmitting destructive computer viruses via routine ship-to-ship communications. Took out half a dozen ships and a few thousand of us that way alone. Our ship enters the challenge orbit as we're supposed to, they'll stand down from red alert, but only as far as yellow. And then *they'll* contact *us*."

The next few minutes passed in tense silence while the blue dot representing them in the holodisplay merged with the red circle of the challenge orbit. Even then, the silence stretched on until Lorn was convinced they would hear nothing before the missiles arrived and nothing thereafter for all eternity.

But then, with no warning at all, a female voice spoke,

apparently from thin air. "Courier Vessel *Ninshubur*, this is Earth Control. Be advised Earth is now under the control of the ELF Forces of Liberation. You may now transmit."

"They've got us locked into a firewalled receiver so we can't send any viruses," Kiri said, and then waved her hand over the control console, activating *Ninshubar*'s transmitter. "Earth Control, this is Lieutenant Commander Kiri Ishida of ELF Field Intelligence, accompanied by a passenger. Transmitting biometric information."

"Receiving," Earth Control said. "Stand by."

Kiri looked at Lorn and, to his surprise, gave him a wink.

"Kiri!" a new voice boomed, a male voice. "For God's sake, woman, what are you doing in a Loyalist courier ship?"

"As if you don't know, Atash."

The man laughed. "It's good to hear your voice, Kiri. And who is your passenger?"

"I'll explain when I see you, Atash."

"Intriguing." A pause. "You're cleared through the challenge orbit, Kiri. We're transmitting rendezvous coordinates for *Caleb*. I'll meet you in the docking bay. Atash Vermani out."

"See you soon, Atash. Kiri Ishida out." She gestured to stop transmission.

"Vermani?" Lorn said. "That's your general?"

She nodded.

"And *Caleb*?"

"Flagship of Field Intelligence."

"We're not landing?"

"No need."

The *Ninshubur* blue dot was already separating from the red circle, which faded away. It began a long pursuit of a green dot that had just appeared, presumably marking *Caleb*. "We're still a good hour from rendezvous," Kiri said. "Any other questions?"

"What happens next?"

"We report to Atash...General Vermani. He sent me to infiltrate *Falcon's Egg*. So he knows full well what it means that I'm back...though not the details."

"And once you've—we've—provided those details? What happens then?"

"Then," Kiri said, "*he* reports to the Provisional Command Council. And makes his recommendation. Which they may or may not follow through on."

"And meantime Almaida is still building robots."

"Atash is a good man," Kiri said. "He'll understand the urgency of quick action. And he holds quite a bit of influence with the PCC."

"But not *unlimited* influence."

"No," Kiri said. "No one does. Not now." She smiled a small smile. "That's kind of the point of the rebellion. No more dictatorial government."

Lorn shook his head but said nothing.

The completely automated docking with *Caleb* impressed Lorn more than he liked to admit. The Field Intelligence flagship was only a quarter the size of the massive *Mayflower II*, but it had a brutal look to it the ancient worldship lacked. For all *Mayflower II* had carried city-busting matter-antimatter missiles, it had been intended primarily as a peaceful colonization vessel. *Caleb*, on the other hand, bristled from bow to stern with antennae and weapons turrets. Nor did it rotate like *Mayflower II*: it had no need to since the Umstattd Drive technology that provided true starflight capability could also generate artificial gravity, just as it did on the courier vessel. That would also, he guessed, make it easier to aim and fire weapons.

Lorn had never seen or imagined anything like it, and as it swelled in the holodisplay, now displaying real-time video from the hull of the *Ninshubur*, he realized again just how primitive Peregrine was by current technological standards and how outclassed the SSIN would be in any conflict. The robot warriors building themselves in the jungles of Margaret's Land were at *this* level of technology, and that meant the best the SSIN could throw at them would be little better than flint-tipped spears.

Just when he thought they would smash themselves against that formidable black hull, an opening appeared in it, rimmed with blue light and brightly illuminated within by white, and they swept in and settled smoothly into a cradle clearly designed specifically for courier vessels like the *Ninshubur*. The holodisplay showed the giant hatch through which they had entered *Caleb*'s hull sliding shut again and then shut itself off, as did all the flatscreens. Suddenly, the *Ninshubur* was asleep.

The hatch behind Lorn's chair slid open, and chill air wafted into the control room, air that was dryer and also somehow smelled different than the air in the *Ninshubur*. "Time to go," Kiri said.

Lorn nodded and got out of his chair as Kiri moved past him. She clambered on hands and knees into the tunnel through which they had slid on their entrance to the ship. Lorn hesitated. Emerging into an unknown ship on hands and knees didn't give him many options if the welcome wasn't friendly. But he didn't have much choice: he crawled after her along the tunnel's smooth metallic length, through an open hatch, and into the figurative arms of an official greeting party.

There were six in all. Four were soldiers—three men and a woman—wearing unmarked black uniforms, body armor, and helmets with mirrored visors that rendered them anonymous and insect-like. Those four stood well back, two to either side, holding short, stubby, and deadly-looking weapons at the ready.

Of the other two, one was a big dark-skinned man whose own black uniform was draped with enough gold braid that Lorn instantly knew he must be the General, though the rank designations were completely opaque to him. The woman with the General, slight, fair-skinned and blonde, wore civilian clothes: a pantsuit of a cut odd to Lorn's eyes, the legs too flared, the jacket too snug. She had some kind of communications earbud plugged into her left ear and looked at him like he smelled bad.

General Vermani enveloped Kiri in a bear-hug. "I swear, young lady, I feared I'd seen the last of you. You are a sight for sore eyes."

"Thank you, Atash...sir." Kiri's voice sounded a little choked as she drew back. "General, this is Corporal Lorn Kymbal of the State Security Intelligence Network of Peregrine. Without his help, I could never have escaped. And he has valuable knowledge of the state of play on that planet."

General Vermani stepped forward and offered his hand. Lorn took it and winced as the general crushed his fingers. "Welcome, son," Vermani said. "And thank you for helping Kiri. She's one of my best operatives...and a good friend."

"I didn't do it for her," Lorn said, pulling his fingers back and wondering even as he said it why he felt the need to be so brutally honest. "I did it for myself...and for Peregrine. Can you stop this robot-assisted coup?"

Vermani's left eyebrow raised. "I like a man who's direct. But remember, I don't know anything about Peregrine at all. Kiri hasn't told me yet. Robot-assisted coup, eh?" He glanced at Kiri. "Sounds like a most...*interesting*...debriefing to come."

The blonde woman cleared her throat slightly. Vermani immediately turned toward her. "I'm forgetting my manners. Kiri, Lorn, this is Embla Bruun. Ms. Bruun is the Undersecretary of State in charge of Field Intelligence Oversight."

His tone was perfectly polite as he said it, but Lorn still

knew somehow that Vermani considered Bruun's presence there an imposition. *Civilian overseer. Military man*, Lorn thought, somewhat amused to find that some things, at least, were the same on Earth as on Peregrine.

He looked at Bruun speculatively. She was clearly the one whom they would have to convince of the urgency of doing something to stop the coup on Peregrine. Kiri, by the looks of things, would have little difficulty convincing Vermani. But he didn't think the fact she apparently had Vermani wrapped around her little finger via little-girl/father-figure magic would hold much sway with the chilly blonde.

Maybe I could try my masculine wiles on her, he thought, and snorted a little at the thought. *More likely make things worse.*

"You can stand down," the General told the four guards. They stiffened to attention, saluted, and moved off with military precision.

"What were *they* for?" Kiri asked, watching them disappear in both directions along the long white corridors.

"A sensible precaution," said Bruun, the first time she had spoken. Her voice was unusually low for a woman's and had an accent Lorn couldn't identify—not surprisingly. Presumably, every planet had its own accent. He wondered what he sounded like.

Probably an ignorant hick, he thought.

"Really?" Kiri said coolly.

Ah. She doesn't like Bruun either.

"The computer confirmed you were Kiri Ishida. But you said you were accompanied by a passenger. You could have been under some kind of duress and planning an attack on this vessel."

"In which case, I would surely have simply blown up the *Ninshubur* the minute we docked," Kiri said.

"Which is why you were docked in a heavily shielded and armored bay," Bruun said levelly. "You were also targeted by both beam and projectile weapons during the entire pursuit phase of the rendezvous. Had you deviated even slightly from the approved flight plan in either trajectory or velocity, we could not now be having this conversation."

Kiri's eyes narrowed. Vermani stepped smoothly into the breach. "Which we are," he said. "Just good security practice, Kiri. You would have done the same—provided you haven't forgotten everything I taught you."

Kiri's frozen look thawed into a small smile. "I haven't, General."

"Excellent." The General stepped to one side and gestured for Kiri and Lorn to precede him down the corridor to the right. "So, come. We'll talk in my wardroom. More comfortable. Once we have heard your story, we will find you quarters..." he glanced at Bruun, "...while we decide how to respond to it."

Bruun inclined her head slightly in agreement.

"Then this way, please."

Lorn stared around him as they walked. The corridor was singularly unadorned: white upon white, except for the doors at regular intervals, which were colored according to some scheme he couldn't quite figure out since they bore only letter/number codes by way of identification—SS104, WS221, that sort of thing. *Spaceship Systems?* he wondered. *Weapons Systems?*

Of course, the abbreviations could just as easily refer to Secret Spies and Water Specialists. Or a dozen other things.

After they'd passed the eighth door on the left, they turned down a short side corridor that ended in silver sliding doors. The doors opened into a lift, as boringly white as everything else. "How is the ship oriented?" Lorn said as the lift rose.

Vermani glanced at him as though a little surprised he was capable of speech. "Hmmm?"

"*Mayflower II* is a spinning ship," he said. "Up is always toward the center. But you have artificial gravity. You could make any way 'up.'"

Vermani looked almost shocked. "*Mayflower II?*" He looked at Kiri. "*What?*"

"All part of my report," she said, with what Lorn now knew her well enough to read as barely concealed amusement.

Vermani shook his head. "I can't wait to hear about *that,*" he muttered. He focused on Lorn again. "To answer your question...it is traditional to orient the gravity toward an arbitrary side of the ship...we call it the keel, from sailing ship days, although of course it is nothing of the sort."

"I see," Lorn said. "So 'up' takes us first to the center of the ship and then to the opposite side of the hull."

"Yes," Vermani said. "But we're heading to the bow. So as soon as we reach the center..." The lift slowed, rotated, and then began smoothly accelerating horizontally rather than vertically. "There. Now we are traveling along the ship's long axis."

The lift slowed again, rotated once more, and then opened. The hallway they stepped into was far less utilitarian than the first one Lorn had seen. The floor was carpeted, the walls paneled in wood or some synthetic version of it, and niches held bits of artistic bric-a-brac, here an abstract silver sculpture, there a watercolor landscape, there a glowing, rotating ball of light that sang unintelligible songs in the voice of a little girl.

Vermani noted Lorn's surprised look and shrugged. "The Office of Field Intelligence is not exactly steeped in military tradition," he said. "We don't do Spartan for Spartan's sake." He glanced at Bruun. "Much of my job consists of meeting with civilians. We like them to be comfortable."

Bruun almost smiled...though not quite. "Someone thought it would make it easier to walk all over us," she said. "They were wrong."

Lorn saw Vermani turn his head and, out of sight of Bruun, wink at Kiri.

The General led them along the corridor to a rather impressive set of wooden doors that swung rather than slid open at their approach. Beyond was a meeting room, also paneled in wood, carpeted in dark blue, with a circular twenty-person table centered on an embroidered image of the Earth. Lorn thought it seemed overly grand for the four of them, but he sat without comment in the chair indicated for him by the General.

"Record proceedings," Vermani said.

"Recording," said the same disembodied woman's voice that seemed to be used by all Earth computer systems.

Vermani turned to Kiri. "All right," he said. "Tell us what you know. High-level overview for now; we'll get into detailed debriefing later after I've had a chance to review the data files you've provided."

Kiri nodded and began speaking. Lorn listened silently. He didn't hear anything he hadn't already heard from his traveling companion: *Falcon's Egg* had established a mining and construction base in Margaret's Land, had already begun construction of a robot army with which to seize control of the planet, and had already made contact with disaffected elements in the planetary government—closeted Skywatchers, Lorn figured. She gave a brief and accurate account of the *Mayflower II*'s unexpected arrival seven years before and the events that had transpired from it—and how Almaida already had agents and robots aboard the ancient vessel, working to convert it to a fully functional-and-armed Umstattd-drive starship. *Although presumably without the artificial gravity,* Lorn thought, since it would play havoc with every existing structure in the rotating vessel if "down" were any direction other than out from the Core.

Vermani listened with obvious interest; Bruun listened without any expression at all.

"Good work, Kiri," the General said when she'd finished. "And your recommendations?"

"A strike force should be sent at once to Peregrine to halt the *Falcon's Egg* project before it has time to," she smiled a little, "hatch. If we can take out the manufactory and mine in Margaret's Land and stop the conversion of *Mayflower II*, we can minimize damage to the planet and risk to its population, both by preventing the planet's takeover by the Loyalists and precluding the necessity of a more vigorous ELF response in the future."

Vermani glanced at Bruun. "Timeline?"

"I believe I said 'at once,' sir," Kiri said, frowning a little.

Vermani said nothing. He kept his gaze on Bruun, who was looking down at the table, turning a datapen over and over in her hands. Finally, she looked up. "Impossible," she said. "As you know, General."

"I know nothing of the sort," Vermani said, over Kiri's sudden intake of breath. "Orders can be rewritten. We have enough units still in orbit around Earth to—"

"Those units cannot be released, General," Bruun said. "The Provisional Command Council has made that clear."

"We have no evidence—none—that Earth loyalists still possess sufficient ships to attack Earth directly," the General said. "As I have made clear to the PCC several times. But if we allow these robot seedships to gain a foothold on 'lost-colony' worlds like Peregrine—"

"The PCC takes those seedships as seriously as you do, General," Bruun said. "But our ships are already dealing with half a dozen of them. Clearly, *Falcon's Egg* is still in the early stages of its efforts. We have time."

"*You* have time," Lorn said. It was the first time he had spoken since they'd come into the meeting room, and the other three looked at him in obvious surprise, as though they'd forgotten he was there. "The people of Peregrine do not."

"I'm sorry," Bruun said stiffly, "but the people of Peregrine are not my primary concern."

"They're not?" Lorn said. "Already second-class citizens of this brave new Earth empire you're building, are they?"

"It's not an empire," Bruun said. "It's not anything yet. We're still making it. And whatever it is, Peregrine is not part of it." She shook her head. "Until you two showed up, Peregrine was just a name on the long list of Earth colonies no one has heard anything from for two centuries."

"So the people of Peregrine are of no concern to you at all."

"I didn't say—"

"They're of concern to me," Lorn said. He could feel anger building in him and fought to control it. He suspected throttling the woman would do his cause little good. "They're *my people*. And I'm here on their behalf."

"You have no formal authority to speak on behalf of the people of your planet," Bruun said. "*Corporal*."

"I'm a member of the planetary military and police force. I was instrumental in preventing the mutual destruction of *Mayflower II* and Peregrine seven years ago when I was just a boy. I have connections to powerful people within the current government." Lorn leaned forward. "Those are my credentials as ambassador, *Undersecretary* Bruun." He emphasized the minor title with as much relish as she'd applied to his rank. "Under the circumstances, don't you think they're enough? At least enough for you to present me to your precious Provisional

Command Council and let me make my case for helping my planet?"

Vermani raised placating hands. "Settle down, boy. You've made your point."

Lorn, feeling his heart pounding and knowing his face had flushed red, sat down again, though not very comfortably.

The General glanced at Bruun. "Well?" he said quietly.

Bruun carefully set the datapen down on the table. "The answer is the same."

Lorn jumped up again, slamming his hands on the table. "Dammit, at least let me talk to someone with more authority than—"

Kiri grabbed his arm. "Lorn, don't," she said urgently.

Reluctantly, he let her pull him down into his seat.

Vermani looked from the stone-faced Bruun to Lorn. "There's perhaps something you should know," he said. He looked at Bruun again. "With your permission?"

She nodded.

"Madame Bruun is here incognito," Vermani said. "Upon hearing of Kiri's arrival in the system, she came up immediately from Capetown—that's the provisional capital. Whenever she wishes to confer with me in person, she uses the Undersecretary persona. In reality—"

"In reality, *Corporal* Kymbal," Bruun said, "I am President of the PCC and, by unanimous consent of my fellow Council members, Commander-in-Chief of the Armed Forces. In short, there *is* no higher authority to which you can appeal. My decision is made, and my decision is final. No ships will be sent to Peregrine from the fleet currently protecting Earth. I assure you, however, that *Falcon's Egg* *will* be dealt with. I will dispatch a courier ship as soon as possible to the Second Expeditionary Fleet, currently mopping up operations on Farr's World. As soon as they can disengage from that system, they will make their way to Peregrine."

Lorn stared at Bruun. "How long will it take the courier to reach the Fleet?"

Bruun glanced at Vermani. "Fifteen days?"

He nodded, face now as expressionless as hers.

"And how long," Lorn continued, keeping his own voice coldly level, "before the Second Expeditionary Fleet will be able to disengage from Farr's World and journey to mine?"

Bruun shrugged. "There's no way to be certain, but at the outside...two months?"

"And the journey time from Farr's World to Peregrine?"

"Another three weeks."

Lorn took a deep breath. "So Peregrine is at least three months from relief." He looked at Kiri. "And how long until *Falcon's Egg* 'hatches'?"

"I told you, I'm not certain," she said unhappily.

"I understand that," Lorn said. "But less than three months."

She nodded.

"Then send me back," Lorn said. "Alone. I can warn my government—"

"Out of the question," Bruun said instantly. "*Falcon's Egg* would detect your arrival in the system and know that they've been found. They couldn't meet us ship to ship, but they'd have more than enough time to shift their attention to preparing automated orbital defenses that could cost us dearly during the assault."

"They must know *already* that you know where they are," Lorn said. "Kiri stole their courier vessel and sabotaged their control systems, for God's sake!"

Bruun glanced at Kiri. "I assume you took that into account. Am I wrong?"

Kiri didn't say anything.

Bruun's eyes narrowed. "I asked you a question, Lieutenant Commander."

"Kiri," Vermani said, a note of warning in his voice.

She took a deep breath. "I know my job, Madame President," she said, her voice cold. "Of course, I took that into account. I left a false story in my personal datafile indicating I had been exchanging illicit communications with a local man—Lorn—with whom I had fallen in love, and that we had planned for him to be taken prisoner so that I could then free him and flee with him to the frontier system of Stepson to start a new life as far away from the war and rebellion as possible. They will certainly have found my little fantasy once they reconstructed the data systems I scrambled. They will also find the apology I left for sabotaging the computer—I said it was just to discourage them from pursuing me." She glanced at Lorn. "We had to kill a tech during our escape, but that still fits with my story—obviously, he was just in the wrong place at the wrong time. They may still be suspicious, but not to the point of altering their overall plans."

Bruun turned to Lorn again. "There. So, no. You will not travel to Peregrine to warn anyone. You will remain our guest until the assault is over; then we will gladly return you to your homeworld."

Lorn sat very still for a moment. "It seems," he said, "that *that* is the best I can hope for."

"I'm afraid so, Corporal Kymbal," said President Bruun. She stood and said to Vermani, "I look forward to reading your more detailed debriefing of Lieutenant Commander Ishida, General." She glanced at Lorn. "Please keep our Peregrine guest comfortable and informed of any pertinent developments." She turned and swept out, the double doors opening and closing behind her.

Lorn looked at Vermani. The General looked away. "Kiri," he said, "I'll leave you to look after Lorn. You know where the guest quarters are. The Deck Officer is expecting you." He got up and then met Lorn's gaze again briefly. "I'm sorry, son," he said. "My hands are tied." Like Bruun before him, he went out through the wide-swinging doors.

Kiri put a tentative hand on Lorn's. "I'm sorry, Lorn, I hoped—"

He pulled his hand free, then placed it on top of hers instead. "Tell me, Kiri Ishida," he said. "Do you believe in paying your debts?"

Chapter Eight

SHE LISTENED to him with eyes growing wider by the second. When she tried to pull back her hand, he clamped down on her wrist. "You owe me, Kiri Ishida," he said. "You would never have made it off Peregrine without my help. You needed it to complete your mission. Now I need your help to complete mine."

"No one has given you a mission," she said. "I had orders—"

"So do I," Lorn said. "Standing orders. The oath I took to preserve and protect Peregrine against all enemies." He surprised himself by meaning it. For once, the enemies wouldn't be fellow Peregrine citizens. It made a nice change.

"It's not the same!" she said. "If I help you, I'll be breaking my oath—"

"If you don't help me, I'll try to do it on my own," Lorn said.

"You can't get access."

"Then I'll get a weapon and force access."

"They'll kill you."

"Then I'll die doing my duty. *Being a hero.* Taking that

different path you urged me to take." He released her wrist. She jerked it back and massaged it. "Well?"

She swallowed. "I admit," she said, "that I'm not happy with the President's decision."

"She's throwing away your precious mission," Lorn said. "Everything you went through and risked to get here with your warning, out the window. But you and I, working together, can still salvage it. And it won't even affect her decision."

"You heard what she said. *Falcon's Egg* will have time to launch orbital defenses—"

"Not if Peregrine acts first."

"Your government is compromised. You go to your leaders, and Almaida will know about it."

"I'm not planning to talk to the government. I'm planning to bypass it."

Kiri shook her head. "Even if you launch a strike, your forces can't beat the robots, and your ships can't destroy *Falcon's Egg*."

"No," Lorn said. "But tell me: would *Falcon's Egg* withstand a direct hit from a matter-antimatter missile?"

Her eyes narrowed. "No," she said. "But they're not aboard *Mayflower II* anymore."

"But they weren't destroyed. I know because I heard Art Stoddard talking about it when I was still a kid. They've been tucked away. But they're still in working condition." He spread his hands. "So we have a possible means of destroying *Falcon's Egg* and, as you put it, cutting off the head of the snake. But only if you help me get back to Peregrine."

Kiri looked down, chewing her lip. "You're asking me to throw away my career."

"I'm asking you to *complete your mission*," Lorn said. "I'm asking you to save countless lives. I'm asking you to do what you know is right." He kept his gaze on her face. "Are you the woman I think you are or have I misjudged you?" And then he let his tone soften, *because* he was looking at her face, at those remarkable eyes, and remembering them looking at him aboard *Ninshubur*, pulling him back from the dark place into which he'd fallen. "Kiri," he said. "*You* told me I could still be a hero. You told me I could still save my planet. You said we could do it together, holding on to each other, keeping each other from flying apart. I believed you. Did you believe yourself?"

She let out her breath in an explosive rush, as though she'd been holding it. Then she smiled, not much, but a little. "Yeah," she said. "Yeah, I did." She took a new breath, a deep one. "All right, then. The faster we act, the more chance we have of pulling it off. We've got to get back to *Ninshubur*. It's still keyed to my voice, and nobody here has authority to override that, since it isn't an ELF vessel. Unless they've disabled the ship completely, we've got a chance. If they have—"

"Then we think of something else," Lorn said. "Let's go."

Lorn half-expected to be stopped before they got anywhere near *Ninshubur*, but clearly Kiri—*Lieutenant Commander Ishida*, he reminded himself—pretty much had *carte blanche* when it came to moving around *Caleb*. The most they faced were the startled salutes of two young officers getting off the lift as they got on. Kiri returned the salutes smartly and watched them go. "They'll remember us getting on here," she said in a low voice.

"I don't think us stealing a courier ship is going to go unnoticed for long anyway," Lorn said dryly, and she laughed a little.

"No, I suppose not." She sighed. "You know, I never really cared about my supposed military rank. But I'm going to miss it once I'm court-martialed."

"You can replace your rank insignia with the medal Peregrine will give you," Lorn said. *Hell*, he thought, *they actually might, if we pull this off.*

Of course, it was equally likely he'd end up facing his own court-martial, and possibly firing squad, if the government changed hands again...but no need to say anything about that just now.

The long white corridor leading to the docked *Ninshubur* was bright and empty. In moments they stood at the now-closed hatch through which they had entered *Caleb*. Kiri took a deep breath. "The minute we open this," she said, "the bridge will know about it. It won't register as an alarm, though, because as far as *Ninshubur* and, therefore, *Caleb* are concerned, I'm authorized personnel. I'm hoping that buys us a few minutes because I'm going to have to do some fancy talking to *Ninshubur* to get it to do what we need to do after that—which absolutely *will* set off alarms."

"Will they fire on us once we're away?" Lorn said.

"Guess we'll find out." She faced the hatch. "*Ninshubur*," she said. "Access, please."

"Granted," the familiar female voice said at once. The hatch opened, and Kiri crawled back into the smooth-walled tube they'd already passed through twice before.

Lights came up in the all-too-familiar control room as they entered it. Lorn sniffed: now *Ninshubur* smelled funny. He'd gotten used to the ambient scent of *Caleb*. "I can't believe I came all the way to Earth, and I didn't even get to land," he said.

"We could still go back aboard and ask if you could take a tour," Kiri said. "As long as you avoided the fallout, the glowing craters, the slag fields, and the rather extensive plague areas, I understand there are still a few sights left worth seeing."

"I'll do it another time," Lorn said.

"Probably best." She slipped down into her acceleration couch, and Lorn did the same. Both buckled in. "Ready?"

"Ready," Lorn said.

Kiri nodded. "*Ninshubur*," she said. "Please confirm my authority to command."

"You currently have voice command capability for this vessel," the woman's voice replied.

"Very good." Kiri looked across the holodisplay at Lorn as she continued. "Secure all communications channels. No data —and no command codes—to be received by this vessel from any other source unless I authorize it."

"Communications channels secured," *Ninshubur* said.

"If they're awake on the bridge, someone just saw an alarm go off," Kiri said to Lorn; then, "*Ninshubur*," she continued, "initiate emergency launch protocol with evasive maneuvers. Expect attack."

"Understood," said *Ninshubur*. "Powering up." The banks of screens around them lit; so did the holodisplay, still showing the inside of the docking bay. "Blowing docking bay doors."

A brief flurry of mist obscured the holodisplay's view of the bay, clearing at once. The view shifted to show the doors that had sealed the bay a moment before tumbling away into space.

"How...?" Lorn said, startled.

"Courier ships have unusual capabilities," Kiri said. "Because sometimes couriers have to escape from...unfriendlies." She looked grim. "Never thought I'd consider my own branch of the forces 'unfriendlies.'"

"Launching," said *Ninshubur*, and just like that, they were out. The camera view vanished, replaced by a tracking diagram, *Ninshubur* once again represented by a green dot, *Caleb* by a blue.

"*Ninshubur*," Kiri said. "Activate passive monitoring of voice transmissions."

"Activating," the ship said, and instantly General Vermani's voice filled the cabin.

"...come in, dammit! Kiri, what the hell are you playing at?

Answer me!" A pause. "Answer me, Lieutenant Commander Ishida. That's an order!"

"Are you going to answer him?" Lorn said.

"And say what?" Kiri said. But she sighed and added, "*Ninshubur*. Active communication permitted. Voice only, security filter Alpha." She paused. "Hello, Atash."

"General Vermani," the general corrected, voice grim. "Lieutenant Commander Ishida, you will return that courier vessel to *Caleb* at once."

"And face court-martial for taking it without authorization—and blowing the doors off your docking bay in the process?" Kiri said. "No, thank you...General Vermani."

"But why did you take it in the first place? Where are you going?"

"You know that, General. Or you should."

A pause. "Peregrine." It was a statement, not a question. "Kiri, you are disobeying the President's direct orders that Peregrine not be warned. By taking this action, you are putting the lives of potentially thousands of your fellow ELF fighters at risk. I can't let you do that." His voice grew icily formal. "Lieutenant Commander Kiri Ishida, you will cut all power to your engines and await boarding and arrest."

"Or?" Kiri said. She was talking to Vermani, but her eyes were locked on the holodisplay. Lorn glanced into it and saw that the green dot of the *Ninshubur* was approaching a yellow line.

"Or I will fire upon your vessel and destroy it. Vermani out."

Lorn looked at Kiri. "Can he destroy us?"

"He can try." She chewed on her lip. "But he won't."

"How can you know?"

"He just won't." She glanced up at a flatscreen showing a countdown. "In four minutes and 15 seconds, we will be past the gravity-well limit for engaging the Umstattd Drive and on our way. He'll delay just long enough for us to escape."

"You're sure of that?"

"Absolutely," Kiri said, but she didn't sound absolutely sure of anything.

"Bruun will call him on it."

"He made the threat to fire. He's got plausible deniability." She cleared her throat and said, "*Ninshubur*, compute course for Peregrine."

"Computed," *Ninshubur* said.

"Engage Umstattd Drive automatically upon passing the gravity-well limit. Fine tolerance authorized."

"Understood," *Ninshubur* said. "Fine-tolerance engagement of the Umstattd Drive in three minutes twenty-two seconds."

A countdown appeared on one of the vidscreens. They watched it in mutual silence. As it reached the one-minute mark, General Vermani's voice filled the control cabin once more. "Lieutenant Commander Ishida, you have thirty seconds until I open fire. Will you stand down?"

"Atash," Kiri said. "It's me. You already know the answer."

"Lieutenant Commander Ishida," Vermani said, voice cold. "I ask you again: will you stand down?"

"I don't think I can do that, Atash."

"Then God have mercy on your soul. Vermani out."

"We have been targeted by the firing control systems of *Caleb*," Ninshubar said an instant later.

Kiri jerked upright. "What? Evasive maneuvers and targeting disruption! Now!"

"Beam weapon near miss," Ninshubar said. "Missiles en route." A pause. "Engaging Umstattd drive."

The scale of the holodisplay suddenly altered by a factor of ten as *Ninshubur* leaped out of the system far faster than light.

Kiri looked white, her hands gripping the arms of her chair. "He actually fired at us," she said, voice shaking. "Atash *fired* at us."

"He missed," Lorn said. "Maybe deliberately?"

She shook her head. "No," she said. "No way to do that. Once he committed to fire...the only reason we survived was *Ninshubar* is state-of-the-art." She stared at the holodisplay. "I never thought..."

"He delayed," Lorn said. "Delayed long enough to give us a chance. He could have fired sooner."

"I guess so," Kiri said, but she still sounded shaken. *He's like a father to her*, Lorn thought. *How would I feel if my father shot at me?*

"Will they send ships after us?" he said then, trying to break her out of her shock.

It seemed to work, a little; her eyes moved from the holodisplay to him, and a little color came back into her face. "It doesn't work like that," she said. "All Umstattd Drive ships travel at the same apparent velocity, regardless of size or power. They would chase us all the way to Peregrine and emerge into normal space with precisely the same time interval between us as when they launched their pursuit. After that, they could catch us, but they'd also *guarantee* that the Earth Loyalists would figure out what's going on. *Ninshubur* just might go undetected. A pursuit fleet certainly wouldn't. And once they were spotted, they'd be committed to attacking, which would be a direct violation of the President's orders."

Lorn took a deep breath. "So," he said. "We did it. We're heading back to Peregrine. And now we're on *my* mission." He got out of his chair and headed to the galley. "Food first. I'm starving. And then...plan."

"Oh, good," Kiri said. "I kind of hoped you had one."

"Not yet," Lorn said, as he opened the galley door. "Not

yet. But I will." He pulled down his favorite of the limited variety of pre-packaged rations—if you could *have* a favorite flavor of sawdust. "After all, we have twelve days."

"All the time in the world," Kiri said and came over to join him.

Sometime later, they were sitting on the floor of the control cabin, their backs against the wall, legs stretched out in front of them. Kiri hadn't hesitated at all on this leg of the trip to open up the courier ship's somewhat surprisingly sizeable store of liquor. This time, though, she'd poured whiskey, not wine. He sipped from the glass he held in his hand. Kiri had sunk into silence, staring at her own glass, clearly still stunned by the fact her commander had opened fire on her.

"Is there any chance," Lorn said finally, putting his glass down on the floor beside him, "that you *won't* be court-martialed for helping me?"

Kiri shook her head. "None," she said. "Court-martialed for sure. Based on what just happened...possibly shot." She tried a small smile. It didn't look very convincing. "You'd think rebel forces would be more forgiving of rebellion."

"In my experience," Lorn said, "they're often less so."

Kiri looked up at him, then. She studied him for a long moment. She drained her glass. Then she set it to one side. She reached out her hand and placed it on his thigh. "We've still got several days to go, Lorn Kymbal. We have both thrown away our careers and thrown in with each other. We've promised to help hold each other together. I think I know an excellent way to begin that process."

Lorn momentarily lost the ability to speak. He swallowed. "Um...are you suggesting what I..."

Kiri leaned over and kissed him, long and lingeringly, on the mouth, while the hand on his thigh moved to even more interesting territory. She pulled back her mouth, but not her hand, and he swallowed. "I...guess that answers that."

Kiri got to her feet. "You'd be surprised," she said, holding out her hand to him, "just how easy it is to fit two people into one of those little beds. As long as they're close together. Holding on."

Lorn let him pull her up. "It sounds like an interesting experiment," he said.

It was.

Chapter Nine

THE REST of the return journey to Peregrine passed much faster than the outward journey had, and far more pleasurably. Not that they spent *all* their time in one or the other of the tiny beds...or, during one incredibly awkward and unrepeated experiment, in one of the two control chairs. They also spent a lot of time talking, more time, Lorn realized, than he had ever spent talking to a single individual in his life. Yet despite the pleasure he was taking in circumstances as they had evolved, Lorn couldn't stop a seed of doubt from taking root in the back of his mind concerning Kiri's feelings for him.

It came partly from what he knew of her...and partly from what he knew of himself.

She liked to pretend to be other people, she'd told him. What if she was pretending now? Was she truly attracted to him as him, or was she just using him as a handy way to try to blot out the fact that her surrogate father had tried to kill her, choosing duty over personal loyalty?

But if he were truly honest, the bulk of his doubt lay not with her, but with himself. He did not see how she could love him with what she knew of him, after seeing him kill in cold blood, hearing him scream during his nightmares, learning of the atrocity he had committed in the Skywatcher compound.

He could see her now, sprawled naked and asleep, through the open door of her cabin from where he sat—clothed, though that was a recent development—in his usual seat in the cabin. He hadn't mentioned his doubts to her. How could he? What-ever they had between them, questioning it would surely destroy it...and selfishly, he wasn't going to risk that. Their rela-tionship might be based on insecurity and doubt and possibly deceit...but the pleasure they were taking in each other was undeniably real, and he didn't want it to end until it had to.

He tore his eyes from the extremely distracting view she offered and forced himself to focus his attention instead on the simulation he had booted up.

The courier vessel was designed to operate largely on autopilot, and there was certainly no way Lorn was going to learn to fly it manually. But the fact *Ninshubur* had blown the docking bay doors off of *Caleb* had revealed something else he hadn't thought about: the courier vessel had weapons. And those, he thought, he would be well-advised to learn to operate.

They were hardly as destructive as the matter-antimatter missiles *Mayflower II* had carried, but on the other hand, unless he misread the specifications, they were roughly ten times as powerful as even the most powerful beam weapons carried by Peregrine's small fleet of armed interplanetary craft—and even the Peregrine versions of such weapons could have sliced open *Mayflower II* like metal shears through soft tin.

As for what *Ninshubur*'s weapons could do...well, he intended to find that out right now.

Ninshubur's database had the specifications for *Mayflower II*, buried deep in what would have been, in a physical library, a shelf of musty old books in some forgotten corner of the stacks.

Now, using gesture rather than voice control so as to avoid waking Kiri...who rolled over as he thought of her, distracting him for several seconds more as he appreciated the new view... he had *Ninshubur* create a virtual version of *Mayflower II* and place it in orbit around a virtual version of Peregrine. Then he set up an attack run on it. *All right*, he thought to himself. *Let's start with something easy. The Forward Service and Propulsion module.* He turned his hand, directing the crosshairs of the targeting system to the massive sphere at the bow of the ship, behind the rust-red Forward Shield. He turned his hand over and lifted it. Full power.

The ship swelled in the holodisplay. He clenched his fist to fire the weapons.

The energy beams were invisible. Their effects were not. The Forward Service and Propulsion Module vanished in an eye-searing flash of light. The Forward Shield was hurled away, turning over and over, while behind the Module...

...behind it, the ship came apart. Gases from the explosion raced down the Core, splitting it open like a shelled pea. The habitats, each large enough to house five hundred people, each attached to the core by an adjustable stalk, came off like the peas from that pod being scraped out with a giant finger. Some spun off into space, jetting oxygen and water into the vacuum. Others slammed into their neighbours, the hulls rupturing. Secondary explosions ripped through them, flashes of light and then expanding spheres of hot gas rippling out from the ship.

Then the blast wave hit the Rear Service and Propulsion Module and the matter/antimatter reactor it housed. When the flash from *that* detonation had cleared, there was nothing left of *Mayflower II* at all except a glittering, expanding sphere of tiny metallic droplets and glowing gas.

Lorn realized his mouth was open. He closed it and swallowed.

"A bit of overkill, don't you think?" Kiri said. He looked up and saw her standing in the doorway to her cabin, a sheet draped around her and clasped loosely at her breast with one hand.

"I just wanted to see..." He shook his head. "It's hard to believe something as big as *Mayflower II* could be destroyed that easily."

"The *unmodified Mayflower II* could be," Kiri said. She came over and sat down in her own chair. "But if Almaida has time, *Mayflower II* will have the latest shields and other defensive systems." She leaned forward, letting the sheet drop away, distracting Lorn once more. "*Ninshubur*, run simulation again. Replace *Mayflower II* with *Caleb*. Simulate automatic defense response from *Caleb*."

"Ready," the ship said.

"Watch," Kiri said. She moved her hands. Once again, a ship swelled in the display, but this time it was the bristling cigar-shape of *Caleb*. Once again, the red crosshairs appeared on the ship. Once again, *Ninshubur* fired. Once again, there was a flash of light, but *Caleb*'s hull showed no effects. An instant later, however, there was an answering flash from the turrets near *Caleb*'s bow, and the image disappeared.

"*Ninshubur* destroyed," the courier vessel said. "Replay?"

"Unnecessary," Kiri said. She gathered the sheet around her shoulders again and sat back in the chair. "That's what will happen to us if we attack *Mayflower II*, and Almaida has had time to install its defenses. You want to be *very* sure before you launch that attack."

"I don't want to launch that attack at all," Lorn said. "The plan is to use *Mayflower II* to destroy *Falcon's Egg*, remember? And there are still hundreds of people on board *Mayflower II*."

"Then, why run the simulation?" Kiri asked.

Lorn sighed. "Because if we can't get on board *Mayflower*

II, and it's been outfitted with modern weapons, we may have to take it out instead, so it isn't a factor in the battles still to come." He chewed on his lower lip for a moment, then said, "*Ninshubur*, please display *Mayflower II* again."

The ship he had just seen so convincingly destroyed appeared once more.

"Assume installation of weapons and defensive systems equivalent to those of *Caleb*," he said. "Display change in external appearance."

"Done," said the computer.

"Damn," Lorn said. The ship looked unchanged.

"They don't have to be visible," Kiri said. "And it would be in Almaida's interest to keep them hidden."

"*Ninshubur*," Lorn said. "Would you be able to detect the installation of those systems?"

"Yes," *Ninshubur* said.

"Well, that's something."

"However," *Ninshubur* continued, "in order to do so, I would need to come within the operational envelope of those systems."

"Meaning," Kiri said, "that if *Mayflower II* is under Almaida's control, you might discover her modifications by becoming part of an expanding ball of hot gases."

"We don't dare get close enough to *Mayflower II* to find out, then," Lorn said.

"It would be a bad idea," Kiri said dryly.

"Well, it's not like we intended to dock *Ninshubur* with *Mayflower II* anyway," Lorn said. "No way to do *that* surreptitiously. We have to sneak aboard one of the regular supply shuttles. And that means..."

"Art Stoddard," Kiri said.

Lorn nodded. They'd discussed his rather vague plan several times. Art Stoddard had the connections to smuggle them aboard *Mayflower II* and knew where the matter/anti-matter missiles had been taken. It all came down to Art.

Lorn hoped he wouldn't prove a disappointment...again.

"First things first," he said. "We land."

"We can get by *your* planet's ancient defensive systems, no problem," Kiri said. "But we could still be seen. And the bigger concern is Almaida's sensors, not just on *Mayflower II*, but on orbital platforms. *Ninshubur* is stealthed, but no stealth is perfect. Where can we set down where we won't be seen?"

"I know a place," Lorn said. "We land, we hook up with Art, we figure the rest out from there."

"Then we're as prepared as we can be," Kiri said. "And we're still five days out." Kiri stood up. She left the sheet in the chair, and Lorn's heart suddenly shifted into high gear. She held out her hand. "Guess we'd better find a way to pass the time."

"I guess we'd better," Lorn said and let her pull him up. But even as they moved to her bunk, even as he let his body take over, in the back of his mind, that little seedling of doubt spread a new leaf.

———

THE FIVE DAYS passed pleasurably but slowly. At last, they reached Peregrine's star system. At the very fringes, in the local equivalent of the Oort Cloud, they switched from interstellar flight to interplanetary mode, and Kiri activated the courier ship's full suite of stealth measures. "*Ninshubur* has in her database a record of the sensor platforms Almaida had in place when we left," she said. "How many more she might have launched, where she placed them, and what their capabilities are, we can't know. It depends on how spooked she was by our abrupt departure. If she bought my cover story, we should be able to sneak into the system with little risk. If she twigged to the fact I was an ELF spy..."

"Then we're in for an unpleasant surprise," Lorn said.

"Yes," Kiri said. "She knows the stealth capabilities of this kind of courier ship and could tune her sensors to search for the stray energy that can't help but escape the shields. But if it's any consolation, while it might be an unpleasant surprise to be detected, it probably wouldn't be a fatal one. Not right away. Almaida would almost certainly attempt to capture *Ninshubur* rather than destroy her. She'd be much more interested in questioning me than killing me right away, and she's going to want the ship intact." She smiled a little. "I can't be sure she feels the same way about you, I'm afraid."

"Let's try not to find out." He waved his hand in the general direction of the holodisplay. "Well, let's get on with it."

"*Ninshubur*," Kiri said. "Maximum stealth approach to Peregrine, for landing at coordinates already supplied. Please flag all energy sources as we approach for my consideration. Begin."

"Beginning maximum stealth approach," *Ninshubur* said, and in the holodisplay, the green dot of their ship began the long, slow fall in-system toward the blue dot of Peregrine.

Two more days passed. Lorn and Kiri forestalled their previous personal pursuits for the duration, alternating watches in case *Ninshubur* flagged anything for their attention: which she did, beginning two hours into the approach. "Modified Mark 6 Long Range Ship Identification Platform bearing 317 by 24, range 570, 241 kilometres."

Both of them were still awake at that point, and Lorn glanced at Kiri. "Any concern?"

She snorted. "From a Mark 6? That thing's not just an antique, it's a museum piece."

Lorn felt vaguely insulted. "Hey, it's not our fault the starships quit coming and bringing us the latest tech. And our museum pieces at least managed to pick up the approach of *Mayflower II*."

"Which is so much of a museum piece it's practically a covered wagon," Kiri pointed out. "You'd be hard-pressed to miss *anything* that big decelerating from one-third lightspeed using matter/antimatter reaction drives. Hell, an amateur astronomer with a homemade copy of Galileo's refractor could have seen it coming."

Lorn started to argue but bit off his retort before it emerged. Kiri was absolutely right. He was only arguing out of a sense that he should stand up for his home planet. A better way to stand up for it, since he couldn't really argue the fact that it was a backwater, would be to keep it from being overrun by killer robots and then turned into a smoking ruin by interstellar warfare.

Well, he thought, *soon enough, we'll be on Peregrine. And then I'll be the one who knows the ropes.*

Although possibly just enough to get us both hung.

In the end, *Ninshubur* also detected several more-advanced sensor platforms, but the stealth held, and Kiri thought that the number and kind of sensors had not changed since they had fled in the courier ship almost a month before—a good indication, she thought, that Almaida had bought her cover story. "Or," she added, "she simply decided that she wasn't worried about anything as small as a returning courier ship, and she's set up her sensors to keep an eye out for a strike force instead."

"If she expects that, wouldn't she have more weapons platforms in orbit?" Lorn said.

"Maybe she does," Kiri replied. "We're not the only ones with stealth technology."

Lorn groaned. "My head hurts."

Kiri shrugged. "Nothing we can do about it. All we can do is press on with your plan."

They slipped into orbit around Peregrine without apparent detection by anyone, SSIN or Earth Loyalists. Lorn began to hope they'd made it free and clear.

But then, as they descended into the atmosphere on their final descent, just as the roar of air outside the hull began to be audible inside the cabin, *Ninshubur* spoke up. "Low-Orbit Reconnaissance Satellite 701C linked to *Falcon's Egg* automated systems has detected ionization trail. Data has been transmitted."

"Damn!" Kiri swore. "They know we're here."

"But do they know what we are?" Lorn said. "'Ionization trail'—couldn't we be a meteorite?"

The ship, beginning to vibrate as the atmosphere buffeted it, suddenly jerked sideways. "We'll be correcting our trajectory all the way down," Kiri said. "Meteorites don't do that. No, they'll know we're a ship. But not what kind of ship."

"Maybe they'll think we're local," Lorn said. "Peregrine has plenty of its own ships—even if they are 'museum pieces.'"

"Maybe," Kiri said, but she sounded far from convinced.

"Altitude 15,000 metres," *Ninshubur* said. "Landing coordinates identified and locked in. Request permission for autonomous adjustments before landing."

"Granted," Kiri said hastily. "Almost forgot that," she said to Lorn. "If the ship isn't given permission to make last-second adjustments, it could set down on a mountain peak or a house or in the middle of a volcano. This way, it will be sure to pick a spot that's clear and level."

"It won't have to adjust," Lorn said. "There's plenty of space. And no houses to land on. Not anymore." Kiri gave him a questioning look. "You'll see."

"Ten thousand metres," *Ninshubur* said. "Satellite tracking continues."

"Can't they tell just by looking at us we're *Ninshubur*?" Lorn said.

"The stealthing will obscure that," Kiri said. "It bends light around the ship. They won't be able to get a read on our shape or our size."

Lorn nodded.

"Five thousand metres," *Ninshubur* said.

They waited.

"Two thousand...one thousand...five hundred...landing struts extended...one hundred...braking..." A pause that seemed to last forever, then, "Landed. Engines off."

"Oof!" With the Umstattd Drive engines powered down, the artificial gravity field that had encompassed them since their original launch disappeared. Lorn sagged in his chair, suddenly feeling enormously heavy. He'd almost forgotten they'd been under one-third normal Earth gravity. He'd also sloshed to one side as the gravity changed. Clearly, they weren't entirely level.

"*Ninshubur*, exterior view," Kiri said.

The screens surrounding them lit up, providing a panoramic view of their surroundings. Snow. Mountains. Trees. They were in a clearing. "What are we on top of?" Kiri said suddenly. "*Ninshubur*, pan down."

The image on one of the screens shifted, revealing scattered beams and stones, dusted with snow but still visibly blackened: nothing big enough to stop *Ninshubur* from landing, clearly, but undoubtedly the cause of the slight list.

Kiri looked at Lorn. "I thought you said this would be clear."

"Clear enough," Lorn said. He nodded at the screen. "That's where this all started. That was Javik's cabin. You remember him. He's the man who was killed by one of Almaida's robots because you made sure he picked up your 'anomalies.'"

Kiri frowned. "If I hadn't done that, you wouldn't know what's going on and be in a position to—"

"I'm not blaming you," Lorn said. "But Javik was someone I've known my whole life. And my parents knew him before I was born. He was a casualty of war. He accepted that, and so do I. But I don't want him forgotten. I know I won't forget him." He met her eyes. "And now you won't, either."

Kiri's frown cleared. "I won't," she said in a low voice. "I promise."

"Let's get moving," Lorn said. "If we were detected coming down, something unpleasant could be joining us very soon."

"True enough," Kiri said. "Packs are ready."

They'd had plenty of time to prepare before landing, so the packs, loaded with basic survival equipment—of which the well-stocked *Ninshubur* had an impressive array, since, as Kiri explained, courier ships could be called upon to land in any and all environments—were indeed ready. Even better, from Lorn's point of view: he was once again armed, knife, sidearm, and something that looked like a small-caliber rifle. Actually, it fired an even more impressive array of ammunition than his old multi-rifle, from beams to hypersonic needles to relatively low-velocity but very dense slugs. He'd set his to default to the latter: they were more likely to need stopping power than precision if they ran into a large predator—or another of the small spiderbots that had killed Javik and tried to kill Lorn.

Access to the outside when the ship was on the ground was through a floor hatch, which, once opened, revealed a round and—Kiri assured him—heavily shielded access tunnel/airlock. They climbed down the ladder rungs about ten metres to an outer hatch that opened at their approach, then down an extruded ladder another three metres to the rubble-strewn ground, which still steamed from the snow that had melted during their landing. Four massive landing legs with broad four-fingered claw-like bases splayed out from the bottom of the sleek cigar-shape of the *Ninshubar*. Metal still pinged as it contracted in the cold—and cold it was; far colder than when Lorn had first hiked to Javik's cabin. Winter was setting in in earnest here in the mountains—and summer back in Margaret's Land, where it must be even hotter and more humid than before. Lorn shuddered at the thought and took a deep cleansing breath of the mountain air in which he'd been born and raised.

Kiri must have done the same because she immediately started coughing. "It's c...cold."

"You'll need the heaters in your warmsuit and boots," Lorn agreed. "Especially tonight, when it gets *really* cold."

Kiri stared at him. "What do you mean, 'really' cold?"

"This," Lorn blew out his breath in a cloud of steam, then grinned at her, "is what we call a beautiful winter day for a hike. It's only," he checked the small control display on the left sleeve of his white warmsuit, "minus 15 Celsius. Probably be minus 35 tonight. Maybe colder."

"Oh," Kiri said. "Good."

Lorn shrugged. "We've got the warmsuits. Kind of cheating if you ask me—I only ever had furs and long underwear when I was a kid—but I can probably get used to it."

Kiri shook her head. "Maybe I won't notice the cold so much if we get moving." She walked out from under the black overhang of *Ninshubur* and stared around. "Which way?"

Lorn followed her and moved to the edge of the clearing, pointing up to where shattered, blackened tree trunks were still visible, though partially shrouded in snow. "That way," he said.

Kiri raised an eyebrow. "Nasty predators you have around here if they can make trees explode."

"That one," Lorn said, "wasn't native to the planet." He glanced back at *Ninshubur* and blinked. Even this close, it was hard to see, more a disturbance in the air than a physical object. You could tell something wasn't quite right, but you couldn't put a name to it. Trees and rocks were visible through where he knew the ship had to be, but they looked strangely distorted, and when he focused, he realized one rock and the distinctive leaning tree beside it were repeated three times. "Wow," he said.

Kiri followed his gaze. "Won't stop it from being discovered if someone actually enters the clearing," she said. "It's much more effective from above, but still not perfect. If Almaida is suspicious a cloaked ship set down, she *will* find it eventually. Your own surveillance satellites won't, any more than they've spotted *Falcon's Egg*."

"For all we know, they have, and whoever in the government is working with Almaida is covering it up," Lorn said grimly.

Kiri shrugged. "As you say."

Lorn turned away from *Ninshubur*. "No one will hike into this clearing," he said. "Javik chose it to be hard to get to and far off any trails or roads. He also had a local reputation for shooting first and asking questions later. Nobody who lives within fifty miles would think of hiking to Javik's cabin without an invitation. And nobody will ever get an invitation again." He started up the slope toward the shattered trees on the ridge. "We've got hours of daylight yet," he said. "Let's use them."

Chapter Ten

DESPITE THE COLD and the exhausting drudgery of hiking through deep snow, Lorn enjoyed the rest of the day, in a way he hadn't enjoyed anything for a long time...even the days he'd just spent with Kiri. He'd had grown up in those mountains, and he felt at home there in a way he never really felt at home anywhere else. That was one reason he'd headed this direction when he'd taken his not-actually-authorized leave from the SSIN. Yes, he'd had the message from Javik, but even if he hadn't, he would have ended up out here. The cabin in which he used to live with his parents wasn't all that far away, though long-abandoned now, his parents having moved even further into the wilderness after Art Stoddard showed up and turned everything on Peregrine upside down.

He frowned as he thought that. His father had shown no inclination to rejoin SSIN, or even rejoin mainstream society, even after the Skywatchers were routed. "I'm retired, son," he'd told Lorn. "I just want a quiet life in the Wild. I've never wanted to be a hero." He hadn't even come to Lorn's graduation from the Academy—a bit of a sore point between them. He'd made it clear he wouldn't try to stop Lorn from joining the SSIN, but he'd also made it clear he didn't approve. And Mom had made no bones about her disapproval at all. Truth was, though he kept in touch with them pretty regularly, he hadn't been to see them in...how many months?

He couldn't remember.

The cabin he'd grown up in was abandoned, Javik's lay in ruins, Javik was dead. It all seemed a little too metaphorically applicable to his youthful aspirations and ideals, so he shoved the grim thoughts aside and concentrated on moving one leg after the other, breathing fresh air, looking ahead for the best route through the trees, keeping an eye on the weather. When he was a kid, just hiking through these woods had seemed a great adventure. But then Art Stoddard had shown up on their doorstep, and he'd followed him in search of greater adventures.

He'd never really found his way back.

A line from the 20th-century classic *The Hobbit*, a childhood favourite of his, ran through his head. *"We are a plain quiet people and have no use for adventures. Nasty disturbing uncomfortable things! Make you late for dinner! I can't think what anybody sees in them."*

You got that right, Mr. Baggins, he thought.

He sighed. Unfortunately, "adventures" seemed to be following him around. *Well,* he thought, *what's the alternative? Settle down with a nice girl and get a quiet office job in Bagnell?* He glanced behind him at Kiri, following in his footsteps, so she didn't have to work quite as hard toiling up the current snow-covered slope. She met his eyes, her face red with exertion. "What?"

"Nothing," he said. He turned his attention back to the trail. Somehow Kiri didn't strike him as the settling-down type. Even if she'd *want* to settle down with him. He still wasn't sure about that. *Well, we can work out the details of our relationship later*, he thought. *If we're still alive.*

And never mind killer robots. Lorn suddenly realized he'd been seeing something above the ridge they were climbing for some time without quite registering it. *The mountains can do a perfectly good job of killing us all on their own.* "There's bad weather coming," he said to Kiri.

"What?" she panted.

He stopped and pointed up the slope. "We're heading down into the valley on the other side of this ridge, and we'll be following it out into the more travelled areas of the mountains to where I left my groundcar. But it's going to snow on us before we get there. See those cirrus clouds?"

She looked up. "The high feathery ones?"

"That's them. They're streaming over the mountain ridge on the other side of the valley we're heading into. Around here, that means precipitation within a day to a day and a half. And we're still most of two days from my car."

"Great," Kiri said. "I love snow." She said it so flatly it took a minute for Lorn to realize she was being sarcastic.

"Good," he said. "Because you're going to get a lot of it." He readjusted his pack and resumed forging his way up the slope.

He'd hoped to make the floor of the next valley by that night, but nightfall found them just the other side of the ridge. He called a halt, and they set up camp: the equipment from the *Ninshubur* included a fold-to-next-to-nothing tent with built-in warming in the glistening silver walls. It was a snug fit for the two of them, but they were used to that from the narrow bunks of the courier vessel. Not that sex was on the agenda: although the camping equipment included perimeter sensors, they'd agreed to take watch and watch about.

The wind shifted during the night, coming from the south. The temperature, which Lorn monitored with the tent's built-in sensors, rose. That didn't make him happy. If he'd read those clouds right, sometime within the next day, the wind would swing around to the northwest, and the temperature would plunge again, sharply. And then the snow would come. Probably a great deal of it.

They wouldn't get lost, not with all the navigation equipment they carried, and they wouldn't freeze, thanks to the warmsuits, but they'd be slow and blind, and Lorn didn't like either of those. The only saving grace was that they should be on the valley floor by the time the storm hit, and that was far preferable to being up in the peaks.

One perimeter sensor went off, very early in the morning, but none of the others were triggered, which meant whatever it was had just brushed the edge of their monitored zone and hadn't come any closer to the tent. From the reading, it had been sizeable, whatever it was, and both of them spent a half-hour wide awake, waiting, before Kiri, whose watch it was, took over, and Lorn lay down to grab a couple of hours more sleep before they set out again.

At first light, they packed up and started off once more, now heading downslope, a far nastier proposition on slick rocks than climbing. Still, the boots that came with the warmsuits were remarkably grippy, and he only fell once, bruising his backside and his dignity but doing no permanent damage. His excuse was that he had been looking up again at the clouds streaming over the mountains: thicker now, and as he had guessed, the wind had shifted and strengthened, becoming an icy blast pouring down the valley from the northwest.

They reached the valley floor by noon and immediately set out along it to the south, walking in the woods alongside the frozen river that coursed along the valley, being careful not to get too close to the riverbank, where the snow hid ice-covered, rounded rocks that almost guaranteed a fall and possibly a broken bone or sprained ankle.

The temperature continued to drop, and the clouds continued to thicken, but the storm held off until they'd made camp: and then it hit, without warning, while they were huddled together in the tent, eating more of the rather tasteless rations *Ninshubur* had carried. The wind rose to a howl and shook the walls of the tent, and there was a scraping, fluttering sound against the silvery fabric. "Snow," Lorn said.

"How long will it last?" Kiri said.

"If we're lucky, it'll blow itself out overnight. If not...it's going to be a miserable hike tomorrow." He scooped out the last spoonful of gray gravy and crumpled up the rectangular ration box: it was made of a thin, light metal that reduced to almost nothing. He stored the tiny silver ball in the garbage pouch of his pack. "We should still keep watch. The snow could confuse the perimeter alarms."

She nodded. "I'll go first. You broke trail. Get some sleep."

He nodded, then stretched out and closed his eyes. "Wake me in four hours."

But he woke far sooner than that.

The first hint of trouble was the chirping of a perimeter alarm. Followed by a second. Then a third. *Not a false-positive from the snow, then,* Lorn thought, sitting up even as his eyes snapped open. Something big was coming toward them through the night. He grabbed his rifle and snapped "Out!" at Kiri.

She didn't argue: she seized her own rifle, and the two of them plunged into the night. They'd kept on their warmsuits and boots, of course, and together they barreled through the swirling snow away from the tent, in the opposite direction from the triggered alarms. After twenty or thirty metres Lorn stopped, turned, and threw himself down, motioning to Kiri to do likewise. She aimed her rifle back in the direction they had come without him telling her to. They could still hear the perimeter alarms' high-pitched chirps, but they couldn't see the tent: no light escaped through the opaque fabric.

The warmsuit came with high-tech goggles that included night-vision capability, among other things. Lorn reached up and flicked them into place, but they showed nothing, defeated by the thick snow. "Stay low," he whispered to Kiri. "I'll—"

But something about the quality of the silence to his left told him that Kiri was gone. He jerked his head to the side, where he'd expected to see her, and through the goggles caught a glimpse of movement as she squirmed away from him on her belly. *Dammit, what's she playing at?* he thought. He glared after her a moment, then turned his head back toward the tent.

Nothing moved there, or in the forest beyond. Lorn turned his head, scanning to the left, but the snow continued to play havoc with the goggles. He briefly glimpsed Kiri, crouched twenty feet away, then her green glow vanished again.

He scanned to the right. Still nothing.

The chirping of the perimeter alarms had changed. Now there was just a single chirp at the same pitch. Which meant something inside the circumference of the alarms but not closing with the tent. Which meant...

Circling it!

He rolled over onto his back and just had time to glimpse a faintly glowing figure among the trees before their attacker's weapon flashed and cracked. His shoulder blazed with pain. He gasped and tried to raise his weapon, but Kiri was faster: her rifle thundered, and the dimly glowing figure dropped where it stood.

"You all right?" Kiri called.

"No," Lorn said. "He hit me." He twisted his head to the left. Bright green smeared his left shoulder: blood. But he couldn't see a hole. It hadn't been a bullet, it hadn't been a laser, and it sure as hell hadn't been an explosive round. His shoulder even worked, after a fashion, though the pain made him gasp. He could flex his arm and wriggle his fingers. He got awkwardly to his feet, grunting, and trudged over the man's body, the snow around it spattered with bright green in his night-vision, the color already fading as the blood cooled.

The man wore a facemask and his night-vision goggles, standard SSIN issue. Much bulkier than the ones he wore, but effective.

Kiri reached him an instant later. "You're bleeding! Where did he hit you?"

"Shoulder," Lorn said. "Not a bullet."

"Hold still." She came over, took off her night-vision goggles, and pulled a tiny flashlight from her pocket. She flashed it on the wound. "Buckshot, I think," she said. "Shotgun, and he just winged you with it, looks like."

"Shotgun?" Lorn looked down at the man. His weapon was a multirifle, like Lorn's former weapon. Lorn's did not have a shotgun setting, but he knew they existed. "Why would he use a shotgun?"

"Probably made a mistake," Kiri said. "Lucky for you."

"Yeah," Lorn said. "Why did you crawl away? Not that I'm complaining..."

"Because the perimeter alarms showed only one signal," she said. "Which meant only one attacker. Which meant if we split up, we had a better chance of surprising whatever was coming."

Lorn blinked. "Good thinking," he said. *And I should have thought of it first and told her to do it before we left the tent*, he thought. *But my first instinct was to keep her close to protect her. As if she needed my protection.*

"Let's get you patched up," she said.

"I'm all right," Lorn said. "For a minute." He was studying the body. "Those goggles are SSIN issue, but he's not wearing SSIN winter gear."

Kiri knelt to search the body. "No ID." She straightened, holding the man's rifle. "But I don't get it. If he wanted to kill us, why not just blow up the tent with us in it? This thing fires grenades, too, doesn't it?"

Lorn nodded. The movement brought an involuntary gasp of pain from him.

"All right, that's it," Kiri said. "Back to the tent." She hefted the rifle. "I'm keeping this. Never know when another weapon will come in handy."

"We've got to get out of here," Lorn said. "He might not be alone."

"Soon as I tend to your shoulder," Kiri said. "You passing out on the trail won't help." They left their attacker to the elements and local scavengers and returned to the tent. With Kiri's help, Lorn peeled the warmsuit down to his waist and took off the T-shirt he wore underneath it. She probed the wound. "Weirder and weirder. Whatever he hit you with seems to have melted away. There's no shot in the wound." She gave him a sharp look. "You're not feeling sick or woozy, are you? It could be a drug of some kind—"

"Aside from having a bunch of little holes in my shoulder, I feel fine," Lorn said.

Kiri examined the man's rifle, but there were no shells left in the shotgun ammo drum.

"It could have been birdshot," Lorn said. "Lot of hunters use a biodegradable kind, so they don't have to worry about getting the shot out when they clean the bird."

"You're saying that guy was just a hunter who took a dislike to us?" Kiri said.

"No, I think he meant to kill us and set the rifle wrong,"

Lorn said. "If he's been out here living off the land waiting for orders, he'd be using his weapon for hunting. He could have been some kind of sleeper agent waiting for orders. Quiet backwater, he's not really expecting to be called on, suddenly he gets word to track us down. He gets nervous, forgets to switch to his military ammo. Could happen."

"Good an explanation as any, I guess," Kiri said. She hadn't stopped working: Lorn had kept talking partly to take his mind off the fire in his shoulder as she cleaned it, but once that was done, she applied something else that reduced the pain considerably, then bandaged the wound. He tried rotating it. It hurt, but not as badly as before. "Don't do that!" Kiri said. "I've applied a FastHeal dressing, but it can't work its magic if you keep reopening the holes."

"Not moving my shoulder isn't exactly going to be easy while we're hiking through the mountains in a snowstorm," Lorn said. "Perhaps you'd like to carry me?"

She stuck her tongue out at him.

Working by the uncertain vision of the night goggles, they struck the tent, stored it in Lorn's pack, gathered up the all-important perimeter sensors and stored them in Kiri's, and set off through the storm, moving slowly because of the dangers of the terrain, following their built-in navigational displays, which would have been more useful if they'd contained a detailed map of their surroundings instead of just a few landmarks from the *Falcon's Egg*'s limited database.

Still, they managed to put a few kilometres between themselves and the camp by the time the light began to grow and the snow to lessen, kilometres well shrouded in fresh heavy snow that Kiri thought would defeat even robot trackers.

Eventually, exhaustion forced them to halt. Snow still fell, but only lightly. In the early morning light, they found a new campsite, set out the perimeter alarms, and climbed back into the tent they had vacated so abruptly a few hours before. Lorn had every intention of staying awake and on watch, but Kiri ordered him to bed and gave him something to dull the renewed pain in his shoulder that also sent him right to sleep. He jerked awake an indeterminate amount of time later as the tent flap opened and cold air flooded around his face.

He sat up to see Kiri's rear end disappearing into the great outdoors. He followed her. She glanced at him. "Shoulder?"

He flexed it. "Much, much better," he said, somewhat surprised. "Must be that...what did you call it?"

"'FastHeal,'" Kiri said. "Speeds cellular regeneration. It's not magic, but on small wounds like those punctures, it's the next best thing. Your being asleep and immobile gave it a chance to work."

"Something from *Ninshubar*'s stores?"

She nodded.

The snow had stopped, and though thin clouds still covered the sky, the sun shone through them as a dim white disk. All around, the shapes of trees and rocks were blurred by thick shrouds of fresh snow.

After a quick meal, they packed up and set off again through the forest. After about three hours of hard slogging on their part, the valley curved to the west, and the amount of snow on the ground lessened. "Weather patterns shift here," Lorn said to Kiri as they began to move a little faster. "The mountain range bends, and that makes a difference."

She nodded but didn't waste breath on a response.

That night their camp was undisturbed. About two hours into their hike the next day, in brilliant sunshine, Lorn stopped and pointed right, to the west. "See that notch in the valley wall?"

Kiri nodded.

"It'll take us about three hours to climb up and through it...

and we'll find my ground vehicle tucked away on the other side."

"If it's still there," Kiri said. "You've been gone more than a month."

"It'll still be there," Lorn said. "I hid it well to begin with, and after all this snow, you'd have to trip over it to spot it by accident."

"Won't your SSIN have tracked it down?"

"I deactivated its tracking system before I left Bagnell," he said. "And my own ID tag is buried in a public campground fifty kilometres to the west. They may have found *it* by now if they bothered to come after me, but they won't have found my vehicle." He grinned. "Come on. Only a few more hours of walking."

Kiri groaned. "I'm never walking anywhere again."

They made the notch a little faster than Lorn had anticipated, and sure enough, his ground vehicle was where he had left it, though it looked like nothing but another snow-covered rock when they first approached. Lorn strode up to it confidently, brushed away snow to reveal bright white metal, then took off his right glove and touched his bare hand to the vehicle's side.

The snow blew off in a sudden flurry, uncovering the groundcar: a hulking, squared-off backcountry model with six large blue tires and silvery one-way windows. "It looks military," Kiri said. "Except for the colour."

"It *is* military," Lorn said. "Well, ex-military. Special deal for SSIN members. It's not armed—but it *is* armored." He touched the vehicle again, placing his hand against a black square on the side. The door slid aside, revealing four black-leather seats and a spacious storage area. "Throw your pack in the back, and let's get out of here."

"You can drive it through this snow?" Kiri said, tossing her pack into the storage space and then clambering into the far seat.

Lorn threw his pack in after her, then climbed into the control seat. "It drives itself," he said. "And it can drive through almost anything." He touched a control, and the door slid shut, sealing them inside the interior, cold but already warming up. "Hi, Suzy," Lorn said.

"Hello, Lorn," said a female voice.

"Suzy?" Kiri said, giving him a look.

"My mom called all our vehicles Suzy," Lorn said defensively. "It's a perfectly good name."

"Uh-huh."

Lorn ignored her. "Suzy, connect to 'Net."

"Connected," the car said.

"Won't that give away your position?" Kiri said.

Lorn shook his head. "Suzy is programmed to always hide her true identity and location when online." He turned back to the console. "Suzy, do I have any messages?"

"You have twenty-four messages," Suzy said. "Sixteen are marked urgent."

"Suzy, how many of those 'urgent' messages are from Lieutenant Molitor?"

"Fifteen."

"Your commander?" Kiri guessed.

"Yeah," Lorn said. He wondered what Molitor had to say. *He thinks I'm a headcase. Probably started with well-faked concern and ended with threats. Well, screw him.* "Suzy, Delete all messages from Lieutenant Molitor unread," he said. "Do *not* send read receipts."

"Are you sure you want to do that, Lorn?" Suzy asked, as she was required to do.

"Yes, Suzy, I'm sure."

"Messages deleted."

Kiri looked at him with one eyebrow raised. Lorn shrugged, a little uncomfortably. "No need to listen. I'm resigning anyway." He turned back to the console. "Suzy, who is the remaining urgent message from?"

"Arthur Stoddard," Suzy said.

Lorn felt a surge of relief. "Suzy, please display."

A screen lit up on the control panel. There was no image, just text. Lorn leaned forward to read it out loud. "Got your letter. Sounds like you are having an interesting vacation. Let us know when you get back, and we'll get together where we met last time. Art." The message was time-stamped; Lorn flicked his eyes to the date and time display on the control board. It had come in four days ago. "Suzy, were any other messages from Art Stoddard received after that one?" Lorn asked Suzy.

"No, Lorn," Suzy said.

"That's it?" Kiri said.

"That's enough," Lorn said. "He got my message. He's waiting to hear from me. He hasn't gotten worried enough to take any more action on his own. We've still got time."

"Where is it he wants to meet?"

"Mirror Lake. They've got a cabin there. And it's close— only about a three-hour drive. We can be there by nightfall. They can fly in in less time. Suzy," Lorn said.

"Yes, Lorn?"

"Message to Art Stoddard."

"Ready."

"Begin message. Hi, Art. I'm back! Had a great time. Can't wait to tell you all about it. Let's get together this evening. Lorn. End message. Send."

"Message sent, Lorn."

The vehicle suddenly vibrated as the engines started up. Then they were rolling, backing up, turning, and bumping along through the snow.

"You've put a lot of faith in this Art Stoddard," Kiri said. "I hope it's justified."

"So do I," Lorn said.

Chapter Eleven

AFTER AN HOUR of jouncing over rutted tracks through snow that would have stopped any lesser vehicle, they reached a relatively smooth, ploughed road that led higher up into the mountains to the north. Now the speed increased, the trees flashing past on both sides. Suzy took switchbacks at a speed Lorn was used to, but which made Kiri gasp and grab the arms of her chair. "The computer is a very good judge of road conditions and safe cornering speeds," he told her, amused, after the fifth time.

"No offense," Kiri said, "but the computer in this thing is roughly equivalent to an abacus by my standards."

Lorn "tsked" and patted Suzy's dashboard. "Don't listen to her, darling," he said. "You're doing wonderfully."

"Darling?" Kiri said. "The closest thing to feminine companionship you've had up until now has been your car?"

"Jealous?" he said.

He hoped for a comeback that would better illuminate her feelings for him, but all he got was a snort. He spent the next twenty minutes trying to decipher that but came up blank. For all they'd been through, Kiri Ishida was still a mystery to him.

Yeah, well, she's a woman, he thought. *Aren't they supposed to be mysterious to clueless men?* Just because it was a cliché didn't mean it wasn't true.

Twilight descended. They'd passed no other vehicles. "I'm surprised this road is even ploughed," Kiri said.

"We're in the Rhewlif Wilderness Park," Lorn said. "The 'safe' part of the Wild for tourists to visit. So the automated ploughs keep it clear. But there's no skiing up at Mirror Lake, and so almost no one goes there this time of year. It should be deserted, except for us."

Full darkness, and still they drove on. Finally, Suzy slowed and turned left along a much narrower and unploughed track that wound through the trees until it dead-ended in a clearing. Light glowed through the windows of a snug log cabin, firewood stacked neatly outside, smoke rising from a fieldstone chimney. "They're here," Lorn said. "Suzy, park and secure once we're out."

"Park and secure," Suzy repeated. "Yes, Lorn."

He and Kiri clambered out and pulled their packs and rifles from the storage space. As they trudged toward the cabin, Suzy's engine died, her lights went out, and Lorn heard a faint hiss and then a "thunk" as the doors sealed and locked.

Lorn kept the rifle ready. He didn't think there was any way anyone could have figured out where they were meeting Art, even if they'd read the messages they'd exchanged. But he'd been surprised a few too many times recently to take anything for granted.

But nothing jumped out at, shot at, or exploded near them, and as they stepped up onto the porch, the door opened, silhouetting a man against warm yellow light from the cabin's interior. "Lorn! Good to see you." The man's head turned, and even with the light behind him, Lorn saw his eyebrow rise. "And I see you brought a friend."

"Good to see you, too, Art," Lorn said. "Art, this is Lieutenant Commander Kiri Ishida of," he cleared his throat and pronounced carefully and awkwardly, "*Egalité, Liberté, Fraternité*. Kiri, this is Art Stoddard." His mouth quirked. "Sometimes known as the Conqueror of Space and Time."

"Not by choice," Art said. He gave Kiri a curious look. "Lieutenant Commander? *Egalité, Liberté, Fraternité*? This promises to be a *very* interesting conversation." He moved to one side. "Well, come in, both of you."

Lorn waited for Kiri to step inside, then followed. Art closed the door behind them. Lorn looked around the interior of the cabin. It was just as he remembered: a large main room furnished with worn-but-solid overstuffed armchairs and a blanket-covered couch facing a massive fireplace in which logs crackled cozily, a wooden dining table with four chairs ranged around it off to one side, and on the other side, behind a bar with a couple of stools, a kitchen with incongruously modern appliances. On the same side as the dining table, a hall led, Lorn knew from previous visits, to two bedrooms and a bathroom.

There was no one else in the main room. He glanced at Art. "Where's Avara?"

"Couldn't get away inconspicuously. Tomorrow night is the Baggies, and she's the emcee."

Kiri, who had dumped her pack and rifle by the couch and was warming her hands by the fire, glanced over her shoulder. "Baggies?"

"The annual awards of the Bagnell Academy of the Theatrical Arts," Lorn said. "I can see how that would take priority over the upcoming Earth Loyalist takeover of the planet."

"If Avara Morali—of all people—suddenly bailed on something as high-profile as the Baggies, don't you think that would raise a *few* red flags among the people you don't want to know you know about them?" Art said, a hint of steel in his voice.

Lorn bit off his retort. He didn't want to argue with Art...again. They seemed to argue far too often these days, whenever they got together. And this was too important to get sidetracked by past differences. "Fair enough."

"Let's get something to eat and drink," Art said. "And then you can tell me what's what." He turned toward the kitchen, but Lorn stopped him with a hand on his arm.

"Is your security active?" Lorn said.

"Of course," Art said.

"*All* of it?"

"All of it."

Lorn released Art's arm. Art rubbed it. "Little jumpy, aren't you?"

"With good reason, Mr. Stoddard," Kiri said from the fire. "We were detected on landing. And someone tried to kill Lorn in our camp two nights ago."

Art glanced her way. "And where is this 'someone' now?"

"Feeding animals."

Art looked at Lorn again. "This gets more intriguing by the moment. All right. Food, drink, talk...plans." He went into the kitchen.

Twenty minutes later, they were all seated at the dining room table. The food, though prepackaged and autocooked, was so much better than the rations from *Ninshubur* on which they'd been subsisting that despite the urgency imposed by events, Lorn could think of little else for a few minutes. And the dark brown beer Art had poured him—Nightcatcher Ale, one of his favorites—was heaven in a glass.

But eventually, hunger and thirst assuaged and glass

refilled, seated in one of the chairs by the fire with Kiri in another and Art on the couch, he told Art everything that had happened since he had received the invitation from Javik to his cabin. "So what Javik uncovered—and I sent to you—was only the tip of the iceberg," he concluded some half an hour after he had begun. "Peregrine, like it or not, is about to be a new front in a war that's been going on since the starships stopped coming...unless we can stop Commander Almaida and her robot army from taking over the world."

Art's mouth twitched. "Although I understand the situation is dire, it's almost worth it to hear someone say something like that with a straight face."

Lorn stared at him, puzzled.

Art sighed. "Never mind. I forget sometimes I'm pretty much the only person left alive who has ever watched pre-starflight science fiction movies." He lifted his beer glass and took a thoughtful sip. "So. How do we go about that? From what you say, the SSIN will be outgunned by these robots."

"Outgunned by the robots, and probably infiltrated from within by traitors," Lorn said. "It will be the Skwyatchers all over again."

"And I don't have any pull with robots," Art said. "They're not likely to stand down just because I tell them to."

"No," Lorn said.

"Then what do you propose?" Art said. "I could put in a call to the Prime Minister, but she's not exactly hanging on my every word these days, and for all we know, she's been coopted. Avara could do what she did once before and broadcast a message to the whole population telling them they're about to be overrun by robots built by a starship from Earth that landed surreptitiously in Margaret's Land...and nobody would believe her. She's seen as an entertainer these days, not a revolutionary." Lorn was surprised at the hint of bitterness in Art's voice and at the echo of some of his own uncharitable thoughts toward Avara. For the first time, it occurred to him that the man he had once worshipped as a hero might have his own regrets about the way things had devolved for him since his glory days, that he hadn't *chosen* to become the glorified bureaucrat he had become.

"We need to destroy *Falcon's Egg* from orbit," Kiri said.

"Can the weaponry this Commander Almaida of yours has been installing do that?" Art said.

"I don't think so," Kiri said. "I think it's unlikely she's bothering with orbital strike weapons. She wants *Mayflower II* to take on attacking ELF ships. She's got no reason to bombard the planet. She wants the infrastructure intact."

"Then how...?"

"Our plan," Lorn said, "is to use the weaponry *Mayflower II* arrived with."

Art lifted an eyebrow. "The matter/antimatter missiles? The warheads were removed before *Mayflower II* entered orbit."

"Removed, but not destroyed. And you know where they are."

"Ah." Art looked down at his beer again. "Getting them won't be easy."

"But possible?"

Art nodded. "I think so. With the right help." He cocked his head to one side and looked at Kiri. "I don't understand why you don't just use this courier ship you came in. It must have weapons."

"Nothing that will take out the *Falcon's Egg*," Kiri said.

"But those matter/antimatter missiles are ancient. Surely her defenses—"

"One of those missiles would be useless launched against her in space," Kiri agreed. "But from orbit? Given the right launch vector, *Falcon's Egg* will never even see it coming, or at least not in time to stop it."

"And how do you propose to get aboard *Mayflower II* with the missile? Will you use your courier vessel for that?"

Kiri shook his head. "Won't work. The stealthing is good, but you can't dock without being seen. We'd be met by a very unfriendly welcoming party.

"I'm counting on you to help us sneak aboard, as well," Lorn said quietly.

"You're asking a lot," Art said. But his tone was almost absent-minded; he was clearly already thinking about how to accomplish it. "I can't do it myself," he said after a moment. "But there's—"

The windows suddenly flashed white, washing out colours, turning all of them, for an instant, into pale white ghosts with staring eyes and black, open mouths. As quickly as it had come, the light vanished. "What—" Lorn said, then grabbed the arms of his chair as the ground shook. And then came the sound; an enormous thunderclap of sound followed by rumbling echoes that died away slowly.

Art was already out of his chair. In one corner of the main room was a nondescript wooden desk; he waved his hand over it as he reached it, and a holodisplay lit up, along with a virtual keyboard projected on the wooden surface. He typed, and waved his hand, and typed again. "Something just blew up in the mountains," he said. "Maybe two hundred kilometres east of here. The government is calling it an asteroid strike. But I know those coordinates." He turned to look at Lorn and Kiri. "Javik's cabin," he said.

"*Ninshubur*," Lorn said. "Almaida found it."

"And destroyed it from orbit," Art said, quietly. "So much for the theory Almaida doesn't need bombardment capability aboard *Mayflower II*. That was a kinetic strike, by the looks of it."

"The government has to know where that attack really came from," Lorn said.

"Almaida doesn't care," Kiri said. "If she was willing to attack that openly, it can only mean one thing: she's ready to move. The robots are coming. They may already be here."

"Right," Art said. "Then we have to move fast. First: do you still need the matter/antimatter warhead? Or can you somehow take control of the new weapons Almaida has installed on *Mayflower II*?"

Lorn looked at Kiri. "We still need the warhead," she said. "From what I was able to find out about the *Mayflower II*'s capabilities from the old records in *Ninshubar*'s databases, it should be possible to launch a missile from one of the missile bays independently, without bridge authorization, and it should be relatively easy to access one of those bays without drawing attention since the missiles have no warheads and are therefore harmless junk as far as Almaida is concerned. Trying to take control of the kinetic strike weapons would require accessing the bridge, and Almaida will have that fully secured. But it's not just a matter of getting the warhead. We need to know how to arm it and how to program the missile. The records I had access to didn't have those little details."

Art nodded. "Very well. So you need a matter/antimatter warhead. You need to get to *Mayflower II* without being detected. You need to reinstall the warhead in one of the *Mayflower II*'s missiles. You need to be able to program and launch it without being detected or stopped. Does that cover it?"

Kiri nodded.

"Then I've got a call to make. To an old friend."

Lorn stared at him. "Shadow?"

"Shadow."

"But why?" Lorn felt a surge of anger. "She shot you. She's a rabble-rouser in the Annex."

"Spoken like a true SSIN loyalist," Art said sharply, and Lorn clenched his jaw, angry not just at the rebuke but because he knew it was justified: he was parroting what he'd heard other SSIN officers say.

But, dammit, it was true! Shadow was a rabble-rouser. And she *had* shot Art.

"Shadow," Kiri said. "She's the daughter of the *Mayflower II's* captain?"

"Lorn told you about her?" Art said.

Kiri nodded. "Her real name is Cynthia Nikos, right?"

"Right," Lorn said. "But nobody calls her that."

"And if you do, you should duck," Art said.

Kiri laughed. "Let's see how well I listened to my briefing." She turned to Art. "As I understand it, Shadow, though the daughter of the captain of *Mayflower II*, was also one of the leaders of an on-ship revolutionary group called the Crawlspacers. She kidnapped you because you were a propagandist—"

"Information Dissemination Specialist," Art protested.

"—aboard the ship, and they wanted a message broadcast revealing the truth about *Mayflower II* approaching the end of its journey, which the Crew was keeping secret. You got arrested, then were kidnapped from the ship by a SSIN officer named Avara Morali—"

"Now, my wife!" Art put in.

Lorn glared at him. "Are you going to let her tell it or not?"

Art put up his hands. "Sorry! Just trying to add human interest."

"Go on," Lorn said to Kiri. "So far, so good."

"Of course," she said. "I'm a professional." She gave him a quick grin. She turned back to Art. "You were then kidnapped *again*, by the Skywatchers, whose leader had decided you would make a fine fulfillment of prophecy in the form of their promised messiah, the Conqueror of Time and Space. They'd already infiltrated much of the government and the SSIN—it's apparently a popular pastime on this planet—and used your arrival to launch a coup. But en route to a nice remote prison, your plane crashed—"

"—with a little help from yours truly," Art said.

"—and Lorn and his father rescued you. By that time, things were getting tense: *Mayflower II* was known to be armed with matter/antimatter missiles, and it was looking increasingly like either the ship or the planet—or both—would open fire. Avara was running a clandestine planetary counter-propaganda network, and Lorn's parents—and the late, lamented Javik—helped arrange for you to meet her, the plan being to tell the truth to the people of Peregrine and to the people of *Mayflower II* at the same time in the hope they could prevail upon their respective leaders to stand down. But things got complicated."

"Starting with a young man who ran away from home and managed to attach himself to me," Art said, glancing at Lorn.

"The coup began. Avara managed to get the three of you into space on a ship heading to *Mayflower II*. The plan was for you to get aboard and prevent the ship from attacking while at the same time Avara broadcast the truth on the planet, in the hope of preventing *it* from attacking. But things got even *more* complicated."

"Starting with the young man getting himself lasered in the back," Art said.

"You and Lorn made it aboard *Mayflower II*. Despite the best efforts of the Crew, the Crawlspacers stormed the bridge and seized control of the ship."

"With a little help from that wounded young man who

managed to take out an entire platoon of Crew and came within a hair of signing his own death warrant," Art added quietly.

Kiri glanced at Lorn, then turned back to Art. "Trouble was, Shadow was still prepared to fire missiles at the planet if Peregrine showed any sign of attacking...and sure enough, a fleet launched from Peregrine, a Skywatcher fleet. You used the fact you'd been proclaimed Conqueror of Time and Space to sow dissension in that fleet, however, and the attack fell apart... but not quite in time to keep Shadow from deciding to go ahead and launch her missiles. You tried to stop her, and Shadow shot you."

"And ever since," Lorn gave Art a sour look, "they've been the best of friends, though I can't really understand why."

"You don't have to," Art said. "Just believe me when I say that I trust Shadow completely."

"Even though she shot you?" Kiri said.

"Even though," Art said. "*Because*, in a way."

"So you trust her," Lorn said. "So what? I don't see what use she'll be now." He turned to Kiri again. "Once *Mayflower II* was in orbit around Peregrine instead of Merlin—"

"Merlin?"

"Ringed gas giant in the outer system."

She nodded. "Oh, that one."

"Once *Mayflower II* was orbiting Peregrine, all the passengers and Crew who chose it were ferried down to the surface and housed in a transition camp. It was supposed to be temporary, but it's been seven years, and there are still thousands of them living there."

"The transition from ship to surface is harder than you perhaps imagine," Art said.

"It's called the Earth Refugee Rehabilitation and Assimilation Transition Annex—ERRATA."

Kiri snorted. "Governments everywhere are the same. They all love acronyms."

"Unfortunately, that particular acronym," Art said, "makes it sound like the people in the Annex are errors that need to be corrected. I suspect that was deliberate."

"So there's unrest," Kiri said.

"There's unrest," Lorn said. "And Shadow is at the center of it. Even though she doesn't live in the Annex herself."

"She has good reason for that, too," Art said. "All right, Lorn, you obviously told Kiri the tale from your perspective. I understand—especially since you've spent the last four years ensconced in the SSIN—why you distrust Shadow, but there are things you don't know." Art glanced at his watch. "Which I don't have time to tell you right now. But I suspect you'll find out in the course of the conversation I'm about to instigate. I arranged for it before I came out here. I knew whatever you had to say, Shadow would have to be involved."

"What?" Lorn said. "Why?"

"I told you," Art said. "You'll find out." He returned to the still-active holodisplay in the corner of the room and waved his hand through the control field.

Instantly, the display lit with Shadow's olive-skinned face, her black hair cut shorter than a regulation SSIN man's cut, her eyes a deep, deep brown. "Art," she said without preamble. "What's this all about?"

"Good to see you, too, Shadow," Art said mildly. He glanced at Lorn and Kiri. "There's someone else here." He nodded, and Lorn reluctantly stepped into view of the camera.

Shadow's eyes narrowed. "Lorn Kymbal," she said. "Where's your uniform?"

"I've resigned," Lorn said. "The SSIN just doesn't know about it yet."

Shadow snorted. Lorn glanced at Kiri, who also stepped

forward. This time Shadow frowned. "Who is *she*? Can she be trusted?"

"Can *I* be trusted?" Lorn snapped.

"I don't know," Shadow said evenly.

"I've got my doubts about you, too!"

"Stop it, you two," Art said. "Let's take it as given we can *all* be trusted. Otherwise, this is going nowhere. Lorn, introduce your friend. And then tell Shadow what you told me."

Reluctantly, Lorn did as he was told. Shadow listened intently. *At least* she *didn't interrupt*, he thought as he finished.

Art stepped forward again. "In case you doubt him, something just destroyed the ship Lorn and Kiri arrived in...something from orbit."

"*Mayflower II*?" Shadow's eyes narrowed again. "Father."

"He's still up there?" Kiri said to Lorn.

He nodded.

"He would *absolutely* throw in with these Earth loyalists if they contacted him," Shadow said. "And help hide the work being done on the ship to modernize its weaponry."

"We have to get up there," Art said. "Or, rather, these two do. The only way to stop this robot army is to destroy its central command. And apparently, the only weapons we have that might do the trick are the matter/antimatter warheads *Mayflower II* originally carried."

"And you want me to give you one."

Art nodded.

"You have the warheads?" Lorn said, startled. "I thought they were under government control."

"They are," Shadow said. "All except two. They went...missing."

"Something you arranged?"

"Who else?"

Lorn felt a surge of anger. "To what end? Planning to stage your own coup?"

"No," Shadow said. "Planning to smuggle one aboard *Mayflower II* and detonate it if my father found a way to cause trouble. Which, it seems, he has."

Lorn's eyes widened. "You'd blow up *Mayflower II?*"

"In a heartbeat," Shadow said. "And every dead-ender Crew and Passenger on board." She made a sour face. "After giving them a chance to leave," she said. "I suppose."

"As we've discussed more than once," Art said softly, "my parents are up there, too, Shadow. And I don't hate them the way you seem to hate your father."

"Your problem," Shadows said, "has always been that you're soft." She shook her head, irritably. "But you're right, we've argued this out already. I said I'll give them a chance. I'll give them a chance." She looked back at Lorn and Kiri. "But you don't want *Mayflower II* destroyed. You want to use one of its missiles to destroy this *Falcon's Egg.*"

Lorn nodded.

"All right," Shadow said. "I'll give you one warhead. But only one. In case I still need one."

"It won't do us any good unless we have someone with us who knows how to install it, arm it, and program and launch the missile," Kiri said.

"I can arrange for that, too," Shadow said.

"And get us into space?"

Shadow glanced at something out of camera range. "There's a regular shuttle launch in six hours. We'll smuggle you on board. And the warhead."

"How can you do that?" Lorn demanded. "The SSIN—"

"The SSIN assigned to those shuttles are loyal to me," Shadow said. "They'll only see what I tell them to see." Lorn blinked, and she gave him a tight grin. "Shocked you, have I?"

Lorn said nothing, but he *was* shocked: not that there were SSIN with divided loyalties—he'd seen plenty of that, starting with the Skywatcher revolt—but that there were those whose loyalties divided *this* way. Being loyal to Shadow meant they disagreed with the way the government had been treating the erstwhile *Mayflower II* citizens in the Annex. Being loyal to Shadow meant they wanted the kind of Peregrine they'd all been promised when the Skywatcher threat had been dealt with. SSIN who felt that way... gave him an unaccustomed feeling: hope for the future.

"When and where do they have to be?" Art said.

"Annex Field Three, three a.m. local," Shadow said. "They can't just walk in. There's a warehouse—77 Riba Road. I'll meet you there. We'll hide you and the warhead in a cargo container."

Art nodded. "They'll be there." He lowered his voice. "Shadow. You know I'm doing the best I can, and we are making progress. Avara's had several guests who support more liberal approaches to the Annex. I've been quietly working on Councilors. Another few months, they'll introduce legislation that..."

"I've heard this all before, Art," Shadow said. "And nothing has ever come of it. Conditions aren't getting better in the Annex, they're getting worse. The police are getting more brutal and more corrupt. We've got drug rings and prostitution rings and crumbling infrastructure. The Annex is a powder keg. A lot of people there are ready to take more...direct action."

"But you don't have to light the fuse on that keg," Art said. "Not yet."

"Not yet," Shadow said. "But I won't wait forever. Shadow out."

The holodisplay went dark.

"I like her," said Kiri.

Chapter Twelve

THE PLAN WAS for Lorn and Kiri to take Suzy into Bagnell while Art flew back in the aircar parked out on the ice of Mirror Lake. None of them had anything to pack, so there was no need to delay. They stepped out of the cabin door. Art turned to lock it. In that moment of silence, as Art placed his palm against the biometer panel, Lorn heard a faint sound in the forest on the other side of Suzy—a sound he'd heard once before: the skittering sound of metallic legs sliding through snow.

"Get down!" he yelled as he leaped off the porch. He landed in the snow and went flat on his stomach, bringing his rifle to bear on the forest on the other side of Suzy, sighting between the vehicle's wheels. He caught the faintest glimpse of movement. It was enough. He squeezed the trigger.

The barrel belched flame, hurling heavy slugs underneath Suzy and into whatever was in the trees beyond her...and whatever-it-was, whether a spiderbot like the one that had killed Javik or something bigger, exploded, with enough force to shatter Suzy's windows and tip the massive groundcar onto its side. Bits of metal pattered into the snow all around Lorn, hissing as they cooled.

He started to get up, then threw himself down again as a *second* spider-like robot swarmed over the top of the car, nightmarishly big—as big as the one that had killed Ekwansi in Margaret's Land. If it exploded like the first one had, but without the car to take the brunt of the blast—

Something flashed in the corner of his right eye, and he flicked a look that way to see Kiri with her own rifle in hand. He looked back at the spiderbot. It had simply frozen in place on top of Suzy's corpse, two legs raised. In the dim light from the cabin windows, he could see a thick black barrel protruding from the center of its globular body—and, just above that, a neat round hole whose edges still glowed red.

"Why didn't it explode?" Lorn said.

"I knew where to hit it," Kiri said. "Also...slugs? Really?"

Lorn shrugged. "I'm a brute-force kind of guy."

Art looked a bit shaken. "One of Almaida's?"

"It's certainly nothing of ours," Lorn said. "But how did it follow us?"

"Tracker of some kind," Kiri said. She shook her head. "Dammit, I should have guessed. That's what that attack in the forest was for. He shot you with a nanotracker. Those things *followed* us here."

Lorn twisted his head to the left to look down at his shoulder. "Nanotracker?"

"Most of the shot in that shell was just to confuse things," she said. "Dissolved harmlessly in the body. But somewhere in the load was a nanotracker...and it's sending out a constant signal to anything close enough to pick it up."

"Can't we get it out?" he said in alarm.

Kiri shook her head again. "Not here. The thing is small enough to travel harmlessly through your bloodstream. It could be hiding anywhere in your body. You need specialized equipment to locate it and remove it. *Ninshubur* could have done it, but *Ninshubur*..."

"Is gone," Lorn said. He looked down at himself. "So I'm going to have robot killers chasing me for as long as I'm on the planet."

"The signal is pretty short-range," Kiri said. "The nanotracker doesn't have much power, obviously. So they can't use it to track you down from the other side of the planet. And Almaida can't find you from orbit. But whenever you *do* get within range of any robots...they'll know you're there, for sure."

"That's going to complicate things," Lorn muttered.

Kiri walked over to the dead robot and poked at its round black body with her rifle. "This is one of the new ground scouts," she said. "They were just gearing up the microfactories to produce them when we absconded with *Ninshubur*. They're the first true military bots."

"Didn't seem so tough," Lorn said.

"They're designed for speed. Hardly armored," Kiri said. "Even so, if you'd fired ordinary bullets at it instead of heavy slugs, they'd have just bounced off."

"But you took the second one out with a laser."

"That wouldn't have worked against an armored unit, either. Wouldn't have worked against *this* one, except I knew exactly where to hit it. Good thing, too." She pointed at the barrel. "Scout or not, this thing has roughly the same firepower as a whole squad armed with what I'm carrying."

"The guy in the forest could have killed Lorn," Art said slowly. "They wanted him alive so they could follow him to whomever he was planning to contact. And now they know. Me." He took a deep breath. "And if they were listening in..."

"Shadow," Lorn said.

"We've got to move," Art said. "And quickly. Nothing is

supposed to be able to get a signal through my security field here, but who knows how effective it is against these things? They tracked Lorn through it, after all. Somebody in Bagnell may already know that I've been contacted and that I've been in contact with Shadow.

"That groundcar of yours isn't going anywhere. We'll all have to take the flyer. But ground control will know it's coming, and someone could be waiting for us in Bagnell." He thought for a moment. "Okay, here's what we do. We go in low, below normal radar coverage, and land before we can't hide our presence anymore...I know a place. We all get off. The aircar flies on on its own. If anyone is waiting, they'll find it empty.

"I can have ground transport waiting at this landing field I'm thinking of. It can't take you to the Annex, but it can get you close enough to walk in."

"What about public transit?" Kiri said.

"Not while I'm AWOL from SSIN," Lorn said. "I'd be spotted by the automated security the minute I was within range of the cameras."

"On foot is the safest way," Art said. "Another reason we've got to get going. All this is going to eat up a lot of time, and I don't think your appointment with Shadow is one you can afford to miss." He went back to the door of the cabin. "Wait out here. I need two minutes inside."

They waited. Lorn walked over to the frozen military robot and studied out. "Ten times the firepower of our rifles, huh?"

Kiri nodded. "And it's just a scout, remember. The mainline infantry robots have ten times the firepower of *that*. And then there are the big ones, the ones they call 'sappers'..."

Lorn shuddered. "I get the picture."

Art reappeared. "This way," he said. "Hurry. " He led them around to the far side of the cabin and along a long boardwalk to what, in summer, was clearly a boat pier. The boats were out of the water for the winter, though, and in their place sat a squat metallic-green aircar, with the stylized bird-of-prey head that marked official government everything on Peregrine embossed on the side in gold.

"Nice flyer," Lorn said appreciatively.

"Perks of selling out," Art said shortly. He strode out onto the frozen-in dock, leaned down slightly, and placed his hand on another biometer panel in the aircar's flank. The gullwing door swung up, and soft white light came on inside. "Good thing there was only a four-passenger available, or we'd have a very snug flight." He climbed in, and Lorn and Kiri followed.

The seats were plush pale-gold leather, the carpet a darker shade of gold, and the interior paneled in dark-brown wood with a satin sheen. The door closed behind them. "Welcome aboard," said a female voice.

"That's the same voice as Suzy," Kiri said.

"More than half the computers on the planet seem to use that voice," Lorn said. "I've often wondered who she was."

"Probably someone long dead," Art said. "Or completely synthetic. Hello, *Kingfisher*."

"Hello, Art."

"*Kingfisher*, fly us to Northgate Rural. Ground-hugging mode, maximum altitude 100 metres."

"I'm sorry, Art, but that is in violation of my safety protocol."

"Safety protocol violation authorized, *Kingfisher*. Code AA9."

"Code accepted. Ground-hugging mode, maximum altitude 100 metres, to Northgate Rural. What cockpit display options would you like?"

"Rear view only for five minutes, *Kingfisher*. Then keep everything dark. But throw up a map on the main control display showing our progress and any other vehicles in our vicinity. Let's say...twenty-five kilometer perimeter."

"Yes, Art. Display activated."

The curving, smoothly polished black dashboard that wrapped around the front of the cockpit suddenly lit up with two images. On the left was a view out the rear of the aircar, showing the snug cabin, smoke still rising from its chimney. On the right was one of the standard navigational maps the government provided all vehicles. This one showed mountains to their north and east and hills to the west and south.

"Taking off."

There was the faintest of rumbles as the flyer presumably taxied out onto the ice, then a moment of acceleration—and then they were flying, though the only change in the cabin from when they had been parked on the lakeshore was a distant rushing noise, wind over the hull and wings.

The cabin dwindled in the view behind them without falling very far below, as the aircar reached its frighteningly low cruising altitude. And then, suddenly, the viewscreen blanked out in a flare of orange light, which faded to show a flaming ruin where the cabin had been.

"One of the things I did with those last couple of minutes inside," Art said. "Self-destruct mechanism." He sighed. "We loved that cabin. But I suppose we can always rebuild. You know, if the planet survives."

"A self-destruct mechanism is not exactly a standard option on home security systems," Lorn said.

"Shadow helped me set it up." He patted the control panel. "Helped me modify *Kingfisher* here so I could override those safety protocols, too."

The rear display went black. Lorn turned his attention to the map and, for a few seconds, watched it slowly scrolling, noting landmarks he was familiar with from the ground. But it was very comfortable in the leather seat, and Kiri had leaned against him, a solid, pleasant presence, and within five minutes after they were airborne, his eyes, which were becoming progressively harder to keep open, slid closed again...and this time, he didn't bother opening them.

He woke to a jolt and sat up suddenly as Kiri did the same beside him. He wiped a little drool from the corner of his mouth, then leaned forward. "We've landed?"

Art nodded. "*Kingfisher?*"

"Yes, Art?"

"As soon as we've vacated the cabin and moved to a safe distance, continue your flight to Bagnell, Municipal Port B. Upon landing, taxi to terminal, but remain locked and sealed, all security systems engaged."

"Understood, Art."

Art turned to Lorn and Kiri. "This is where we get out."

Lorn gathered his weapon and pack, and he and Kiri followed Art down the stairs into a light drizzle. The night air smelled of manure. There were cows nearby. A lot of them.

Kiri gagged. "What's that smell?"

"Agriculture," Lorn said. He looked around. They were at one end of a single tiny airstrip. The "terminal," a small, low building with a single light burning over a closed blue door, was clearly unoccupied at this time of the night. But a vehicle idled on the other side of it, low and sleek and black.

"There's our ride," Art said. "Come on."

As they left *Kingfisher* behind, the aircar pulled up its steps, closed its hatch, turned, and rolled down the airstrip. In seconds it was aloft, the blue glow of its takeoff jets disappearing a moment later into the low cloud cover as it climbed to a more normal altitude for its automated approach to Bagnell proper.

Art led them to the car. A window rolled down at their

approach, revealing a dim-lit interior. A woman sat in one of the front seats. A small girl slept in the back, clutching a stuffed cat. "Hello, Lorn," the woman said.

"Avara," Lorn said. He nodded to Kiri. "This is Kiri."

"Hi," Avara said.

"Hi," Kiri said.

"Get in," Art said. "Try not to wake Melissa."

Art went around to the other side and got into the front seat next to Avara, while Kiri and Lorn clambered into the back, one on either side of the raised seat into which Melissa was buckled. The interior was roomy enough to hold them and their packs and weapons without difficulty. "We're going on a family vacation," Art said as the windows rolled up and the car began to move. "And before you ask, yes, Shadow helped me modify this car, too. It won't show up on anybody's tracking system."

"I thought you had to host the Baggies," Lorn said to Avara. It came out more harshly than he intended.

Or maybe not.

"I think potentially saving the life of my daughter is perhaps slightly more important," Avara said.

"Glad to hear it."

"Stop it," Art said, with a touch of real anger in his voice. "You two can hash out your differences later." He twisted around to face Lorn more directly. "The car will take us to the edge of the city, just outside the start of the city's traffic control grid. You'll have to walk from there. You should still make your rendezvous, but it's going to be tight. Don't dawdle."

"Where will you go?" Lorn said.

"I told you," Art said. "Family vacation. He smiled. "A couple of old friends of mine live up in the mountains, off the grid. They'll take us in. They helped me out once before."

"Oh."

"I'll give them your love."

"Thanks." *I'm not entirely sure they'll take it,* Lorn thought.

They fell silent for the rest of the ride, only half an hour. As the car stopped, Art activated its navigation screen. "Display current location," he said.

A map of Bagnell lit up with a blue triangle glowing right outside the city limits.

"Indicate 77 Riba Road."

A red circle appeared. Lorn leaned forward. The Annex was at the southern end of Bagnell. They were on the city's eastern edge. "We'll stick to the city fringes. It's all industrial stuff over here. With luck, we won't see a living soul."

"With even more luck, you won't see a killer robot," Art said. He glanced at his watch. "Times a-wasting. You're going to have to move pretty fast." He looked back at both of them. "Good luck. I wish I could do more to help."

"So do I, Lorn," Avara said softly. "Believe it or not."

Lorn looked at her. A few weeks ago, he wouldn't have been able to believe her. From hero of the revolution to talk-show host? He'd been unable to feel anything for her but scorn. But suddenly, he felt ashamed. Who was he to blame people for falling off the pedestal on which he had set them? No one had fallen farther or harder than he had. He swallowed. "Avara...I'm sorry. I haven't been fair to you. I've...things haven't worked out the way I imagined seven years ago."

"For me, either," she said. "Art and I...were in the right place at the right time back then. Now we're not. I'm glad you are."

"You've both already done a lot," Lorn said and was almost surprised to realize he meant it. "Thank you."

"Yes, thank you," said Kiri. "If we manage to stop Peregrine from becoming a battleground, it will be largely due to you."

Art smiled briefly. "We've had previous experience."

Melissa lifted her head suddenly. "Daddy?"

"Here, sweetheart," Art said. "It's all right. We're going on vacation up to the mountains. Sorry we had to start so early!"

The little girl blinked sleepily at Lorn and Kiri. "Hi, Uncle Lorn."

"Hi, Melissa," Lorn said. "Say hi to Kiri, too."

The bright blue eyes shifted to Kiri. "Hi," Melissa said uncertainly. "Are you coming on vacation with us, too?"

Kiri smiled at her. "No, Melissa," she said. "We're getting out here. But it was very nice to meet you."

"You..." Melissa yawned. "...too."

Lorn reached out and tousled her hair. "See you later, alligator."

"After a while...crocodile." Melissa giggled at the old rhyme her father had taught her. "Bye, Uncle Lorn."

"Bye." Lorn turned and scooted out of the car, Kiri behind him.

"Good luck," Art Stoddard said. Avara flashed a brief smile. Then the door swung closed, and the car rolled off into the night, vanishing into the drizzling darkness.

Kiri tapped him on the shoulder. He turned toward her, and she surprised him by leaning in and kissing him, a long, passionate kiss. When she pulled back, he licked his lips and swallowed and then said, "What was that for?"

"For luck," Kiri said. "'Uncle Lorn.'" She grinned at him, then turned and looked toward the glow of the city lights, visible beyond the treed slope that rose to the west. "That way, I presume?"

"That way," Lorn agreed. He slipped his rifle off his shoulder, and together they set off into the night.

Chapter Thirteen

HOODS UP, heads down, rifles hidden under their coats, they entered Bagnell a few minutes later, following a deserted street that ran north and south past buildings that were little more than anonymous gray boxes. The trudge around the city's eastern fringe was unexciting, which was the way Lorn liked it. They saw a handful of ground vehicles but only two pedestrians, both from a distance and both uninterested in anything more than reaching shelter as soon as possible. The drizzle had become a steady downpour, but their coats were waterproof, so that didn't bother them. Both of them kept a wary eye on their surroundings in case Almaida's robots had already infiltrated Bagnell, and picked up Lorn's embedded nanotracker, but they saw nothing...not that that proved anything much in the streaming rain.

They only passed near one residential area, and it consisted of stacks of dreary apartments that had been heavily damaged during the Skywatcher rebellion and never rebuilt. Lorn kept his rifle ready as they skirted the ruins, knowing that the buildings almost certainly hid squatters, but again, the weather kept whatever unsavory residents might have been lurking there under cover and out of sight.

They reached 77 Riba Road at ten minutes to three. The warehouse was as dark as any of the others they had passed. Lorn *very* cautiously approached the gate in the chain link fence surrounding the building. It looked closed, but when he tugged at it, it slid open slightly. "Guess we're expected," he said, and pulled it a little bit wider, just enough for the two of them to slip through. He pulled the gate shut again, and then they splashed across the puddled, crumbling pavement to the building itself, two stories tall and sheathed in metal siding covered with peeling black paint. There was a kind of lean-to attached to the front of the warehouse with glass windows all around and a single door in it, obviously an office of some kind, but it was dark and the door locked.

They followed the wall to the left. Around the first corner they found only more wall, unrelieved by window or door. But around the next corner, on the backside of the warehouse, invisible from the street, they discovered a large transport vehicle parked in front of an open loading dock. Dim light glowed inside the warehouse, and shadowy figures moved there.

Lorn shouldered his rifle and instead drew his sidearm, Kiri following suit. Then they crept along the wall, Lorn in front. Metal steps led from the ground to the loading dock. A man came out of the warehouse carrying a white plastic crate in his arms, disappeared into the transport, then re-emerged a moment later without the crate. He vanished back into the warehouse, and Lorn led Kiri up the steps. He pressed his backpack against the warehouse wall and took a quick look around the corner.

"Five men, two women," he whispered to Kiri. "And a bunch of crates, including two very big blue ones."

"Shadow?" she whispered back.

"I didn't see her—"

"That's because I'm hard to see," said a voice behind them, and Lorn jerked so hard he banged his head against the warehouse's metal siding. Rubbing his scalp, he turned to look down the steps. Shadow stood there, rifle in one hand, dressed in black from head to foot. "Hello, Lorn. Hello, Kiri."

"Hi." Lorn holstered his sidearm. "Guess this is the right place."

"Good deduction," Shadow said. She climbed the stairs and walked into the light. Lorn and Kiri followed her, and heads turned in their direction. "They're here," Shadow said without preamble. "Jedda, open the crate."

The dark-skinned woman she'd addressed nodded and turned to one of the large blue crates. She placed her hand on a biometer panel and the middle part of the crate swung up and open like the hatch on the *Kingfisher*, revealing smaller wooden crates through whose slates showed green and white. "Cabbages, lettuces, broccoli and brussels sprouts to supplement the diets of the Passengers and Crew who have remained aboard *Mayflower II*," Shadow explained as she walked forward, motioning Kiri and Lorn to follow. "But we've removed just enough of its official cargo to make room for us."

"Us?" Lorn said, stopping and staring at her.

Shadow looked back at him, face unreadable. "Yes, us," she said. She indicated Jedda. "She's the missile expert you need to make this work. Until seven years ago she was Crew, and responsible for their maintenance. She helped me squirrel two away in the first place."

"Fine," Lorn said. "But why are *you* coming? That was never part of the plan."

"It was always part of the plan," Shadow said. "I just didn't tell you until now. And if you'd use your brain for half a minute, you'd understand why. If you're going to try to move around *Mayflower II* without being detected, you need someone who's an expert at it. Who better than the former leader of the Crawlspacers?" She shook her head. "Enough talk.We need to get in and get up."

"What's in those packs of yours?" Jedda said to Lorn and Kiri. She was older than Lorn had estimated at first sight, early 40s at least. "Anything you need in space?"

"Just camping equipment," Lorn said. "Extra ammo is on our belts. They can stay behind."

"Good," Jedda said. "Because I've got new ones for you."

"Warhead components?" Lorn said.

She nodded. "They're smaller than you might think."

"So one of us," Kiri said, looking alarmed, "will be *wearing* a city-busting matter/antimatter charge?"

"Don't worry, I'll carry that part myself," Jedda said. She laughed. "Not that I guess it matters, if it goes off. Which it won't!" she added hastily as Kiri's face grew even more alarmed.

"What are you waiting for?" Shadow snapped. "Dump your packs."

Lorn dug through his one last time, retrieving a spare knife he could make room for on his belt. Then he handed it over to one of the men, who took it without a word. Kiri disposed of hers, as well. Once that was done, Jedda led them into the cargo container. Following her, Shadow, Lorn and Kiri squeezed through a narrow opening between stacks of crates and into a small, green-smelling space at one end of the container. The floor had been covered with multiple layers of padded quilts of the kind used to protect fragile goods during transit. Once they were in, the people remaining in the warehouse stacked in more crates, walling them up. Then the hatch closed, cutting off all light and sound from outside.

"I suggest we sit down," Shadow's voice said, disembodied

by darkness. "It'll be bumpy as we're loaded into the transport and driven to the shuttle field. Once we're aboard the shuttle, we can lie down through the launch." A dim blue light suddenly lit up the enclosed space from a small flashlight clipped to Shadow's shoulder.

"What kind of acceleration forces are we talking about?" Kiri said uneasily, poking at the lumpy padding on the floor.

"Not too bad," Shadow said. "Three standard Gs. Unpleasant, but not dangerous if we're lying down."

"How long until we dock aboard *Mayflower II*?" Lorn asked.

"At least four hours," Shadow said. "So make yourself as comfortable as you can."

Lorn eased himself down onto the padded floor. Kiri slid down beside him. Shadow and Jedda sat down across from them. Their feet mingled in the middle.

Lorn felt Kiri's hand on his, and took it. *Maybe there is something there after all*, he thought. *Too bad we probably won't live long enough to figure out what it is.*

Engine noises from outside were followed by a grinding noise, a sudden sense of being lifted, bumps and sways, and then a jolt that banged Lorn's head against Kiri's. "Ow," Lorn said, rubbing the spot.

"Cuddling probably isn't safe," Shadow said dryly, and Lorn moved a little to the side. Kiri withdrew her hand. He missed it.

But he was glad they'd heeded Shadow's warning as the journey continued. The head-banging jolt was only the first of many. Lorn guessed they'd been loaded onto the ground transport, which felt like it was driving cross-country without regard for little things like paved roads. "Not really," Shadow said in response to his question, when a relatively smooth stretch allowed them to talk. "These *are* the paved roads. It's just that road repair near the Annex is not exactly a priority of the Peregrine government. Potholes are about the only thing being manufactured in this part of Bagnell."

Lorn didn't reply, mainly because the smooth stretch had ended and he was worried about losing teeth or the tip of his tongue if he didn't keep his mouth shut.

Eventually they jerked to a stop. "Spaceport gate," Shadow said.

"Will they inspect the cargo?"

"I'd be surprised," Shadow said. "They never have. Why would they? If someone smuggled a bomb aboard *Mayflower II* the planetary government would probably be secretly relieved."

The crate wasn't opened. In a few minutes they were rolling again. This time the ride was smooth, but short. Then there was another massive jolt, the sense of being lifted, more jolts and bumps, and finally they were still.

"We're on the shuttle," Shadow said.

"Figured," Lorn said. He rubbed the back of his neck, sore from all the jolting around.

"How long until launch?" Kiri said.

"Only a few minutes. We should lie down."

The space was so small that once they were stretched out they were all touching, Shadow sandwiched between Lorn and Kiri on his right, Jedda stretched out on his left. Each of them had a weapon that had to be accommodated, too: Shadow helpfully reminded everyone to make sure they were safetied.

They didn't have long to wait. The launch, when it came, was sudden and brutal, the acceleration pushing them down into padding which suddenly seemed little better than bare floor, though what it would *really* have felt like on the bare floor Lorn preferred not to think about. He concentrated on trying to breathe with a leviathan sitting on his chest.

Fortunately, the acceleration was relatively short-lived.

Then, of course, came the weightlessness. After some rather undignified flailing around they anchored themselves by holding onto the crates, and shouldered their respective weapons. "I hope no one is subject to space sickness," Shadow said.

"I really didn't need that image in my mind," Lorn muttered, and Kiri laughed.

"The shuttles dock at the bow," Shadow said. "There's a floating dock whose rotation can be cancelled. Once the shuttle is inside, it's spun up again. It's not very far from there to the missile compartments, but there's no direct route, and certainly nothing that won't be watched. We're going to ride with our vegetable friends down into Passenger country and then make our way back."

"Using your Crawlspaces?" Lorn said.

Shadow nodded. "I've never revealed them all," she said. "And truth is, no one even asked. Guess the deadenders figured there was no need to worry about them with all of us trouble-makers down on the surface. We shouldn't have any difficulty making our way to the missile bays surreptitiously."

"Even while lugging a warhead?" Lorn said. "How big are these packs we'll be carrying? And for that matter, where are they?"

"They're not much bigger than the ones you were wearing when you arrived," Jedda said. "They're tucked away in the cargo at the other end of this module. Once we're in the missile bay I'll reassemble the weapon. Three-hour job. Systems tests and programming will take another hour. Four hours after we get to the missile bay, we'll be ready to hit *Falcon's Egg*."

"Long time to remain undiscovered," Kiri muttered.

"It's a big ship," Shadow said. "And mostly empty."

"It *was*," Kiri corrected. "We don't know how many people Commander Almaida has put on board. Or how many robots."

"We'll deal with problems as they arise," Shadow snapped. "What other choice do we have?"

Kiri fell silent.

"None," Lorn answered for all of them. "Absolutely none."

After that they didn't say much. Their silent, weightless flight went on for two and a half hours, long enough Lorn began to entertain unpleasant worries about whether or not the automated shuttle had failed—they did, from time to time, age and the general disrepair of things on Peregrine taking their toll—and they were drifting helplessly in space.

At least we wouldn't starve for a while, he thought. Not with all these cabbages and broccoli. He shuddered. Better to open the airlock then have to live on broccoli!

But finally the module shuddered, and they all drifted to one side. "Rockets firing," Shadow said. "We're docking."

More slight adjustments, then another jolt. Five minutes passed with nothing happening. Then they all drifted slowly down to the padded floor, and stayed there.

"We've docked," Shadow said. "The bay has been spun up. They'll shift the cargo module into one of the big Core transports to move us aft, then they'll raise us hullward to full gravity in one of the habs. Not much longer now. We'll have to be ready to overpower the workers—there's probably only going to be a couple of them. Check your weapons."

Lorn nodded and pulled out his sidearm, Kiri doing the same. He unshouldered his rifle. He checked the action and ammo and battery, then slung it over his back again.

A half hour passed. More bumps and jolts, and then a growing sense of weight until they were once more sitting on the padded floor as heavily as they had on Peregrine. Shadow extinguished her flashlight and they sat in darkness and silence. More banging. A loud clank.

Dim light poured around them, seeping through the slats of

the crates of vegetables. Lorn thumbed the safety off on his weapon.

And then the crates were suddenly torn away in a flurry of cabbage leaves, blinding light pinned them in place, and from the multi-legged robot that seemed to fill the cargo module boomed an amplified voice: "Disarm or die!"

Lorn glanced down at the tiny red dot shining on his chest, and very carefully placed his sidearm on the thinly padded floor.

Chapter Fourteen

FIVE MINUTES LATER, Shadow, Jedda, Lorn, and Kiri knelt, hands behind their heads, on the cold deck plates of the cargo bay. The robot that had ordered them out stood watch over them. Spider-legged, identical, so far as Lorn could tell, to the one that had killed Ekwansi in Margaret's Land, it hadn't spoken again once it had told them to kneel where they were with their hands behind their heads.

A second robot, unarmed as far as they could tell, had already removed one of the four backpacks carrying the matter/antimatter warhead components from the module. It didn't examine it; it simply carried it over to a large wheeled transport and stowed it. There wasn't a human in sight, although surely some human *somewhere* now knew they had been discovered. A security force must already be on the way.

"This is all new," Jedda murmured as the cargobot scuttled back into the module. "*Mayflower II* has hundreds of maintenance bots, and some were programmed as security bots, but nothing this sophisticated."

"They're from *Falcon's Egg*," Kiri said. "Commander Almaida has been busy up here."

"But why no human supervisors?"

"Shortage of manpower," Kiri said. "Almaida has been retrofitting *Mayflower II* and building a base in the jungle. Robots are doing most of the work. Actual humans have to be few and far between."

The cargobot emerged from the module with the second backpack and carried it to the transport. As Lorn watched it head back to the module for the third backpack, a sudden thought struck him. All the Earth technology he'd seen relied heavily on voice control. Like *Ninshubur*. Which had accepted Kiri's authority without question...

"Kiri," he said slowly. "If these are from *Falcon's Egg*...how likely do you think it is that they've gotten around to disabling your command privileges? What with everything else that's been going on?"

Kiri shot a startled look at him. "I should have thought of that," she breathed. "It's worth a try."

Shadow looked from her to Lorn, eyes narrowed. "What is?"

Rather than respond to her, Kiri turned and looked at the robot behind them. "Safety protocol 777B," she said clearly. "Authorization Kiri Ishida. Voiceprint verify."

And just like that, the security robot lowered its weapons and froze...as did the cargobot, stopped in the act of placing the third backpack on the transport.

Shadow scrambled to her feet. "How long?"

"Minutes," Kiri said. "And maybe not very many of them."

"Right. Lorn, grab the weapons. Jedda, get the last component out of the module. Kiri, you and I will get the packs from the transport and the one that robot's still got its claws on. Go."

Lorn reached the cargo module ahead of Jedda and swore

when he entered his hiding place and saw all their long weapons in pieces on the floor: the cargobot, in accordance with some security programming, had simply destroyed them. But their sidearms, harder to break, had been set aside intact, no doubt for later disposal. He grabbed them. Jedda was digging through cabbages. "Damn bot knocked everything over pulling out the last pack," she said. "I'll have it in a minute..."

"Here," Lorn said, handing her her pistol. She took it, holstered it, and resumed rummaging around in the fallen vegetables.

He ran out to find that Shadow and Kiri had their own problem: they couldn't free the third backpack from the cargobot's manipulators or even open it. He handed them their sidearms. Shadow holstered hers, then pulled out her knife. "I'll cut the component out," she said. "We'll have to carry it some other—"

But the second her blade touched the pack, the robot woke up. Which meant—

"Take cover!" Kiri cried. She shoved Shadow down behind the transport. Lorn flung himself down behind Kiri.

Jedda emerged from the module, holding the fourth backpack triumphantly. "Got—" she began, then light flashed, her chest smoked, and she thudded lifeless to the deckplates, the fourth backpack still held in her hands. "Jedda!" Shadow screamed, the pain in her voice surprising Lorn. *Maybe she isn't made of ice after all.*

The cargobot dashed away, but other skittering noises drew nearer. "You take left, I'll take right," Lorn snapped. Sidearm in his hand, he rolled over and faced the end of the transport.

A second later, the bot burst into view. He didn't wait to see its body: the thing was so fast he figured if he saw the weapons barrels, he was already dead. Instead, he fired a burst of four explosive slugs at the first glimpse of a leg. He was way inside the "too close for comfort" radius for that particular choice of ammo, and shrapnel whizzed over his head and rattled off the transport, but nothing hit him. The slugs blew off one of the bot's legs and damaged another, so that it clattered to the metal floor and slid awkwardly across it with the momentum of its own rush, unable to bring weapons to bear.

"Other side of the transport!" Lorn shouted, and the three of them scrambled up and around it while the crippled bot began trying to force its body back around to aim at them.

"Missile's useless now, without Jedda," Shadow panted. "We've got to get out of here." She pointed across the deck-plates. "See that ventilation screen?" She drew her own sidearm and fired. The screen exploded, revealing a dark opening beyond. "Crawlspace. I know where we are. From in there, I can get us anywhere."

The transport suddenly hummed at their backs.

"And our cover is about to leave," Shadow said. "So...follow me!" She scrambled to her feet and, half-crouched, ran for the opening.

"You next," Lorn said.

"Lorn—"

"Go!" Lorn said. "You're more important than I am to stopping what's going on. Don't argue, just run!"

Kiri gulped, gave him a quick kiss, and then bolted after Shadow.

At the same instant, the transport began to move. Lorn rolled to his left, following it, and then, prone, just as it moved out of the way, fired the remaining four explosive slugs in his clip at the security bot, which had managed to bring its weapons to bear in their general direction. Apparently, it was too crippled to aim them low, though, because the beams slashed over Lorn's head, visible in the smoke hanging in the air, as his slugs tore into the bot. Its remaining legs were blown off, and its spherical body flung backward. Lorn didn't wait to see where it landed, instead rolling over, scrambling up, and running as hard as he could toward the opening in the far wall, into which Kiri and Shadow had disappeared. He'd slid feet first into it just as an enormous explosion filled the cargo bay. The blast threw him hard against Kiri and both of them to the deckplates. Ears ringing, he lay panting for a moment until a small voice underneath him said. "Can't...quite...breathe..."

"Sorry," Lorn said and rolled off of her.

"Next time, it's my turn to be on top," she said as she sat up, and he laughed shakily.

"Why did the bot blow up?" Shadow said.

"Seems to be standard programming," Lorn said. "They keep doing it."

Kiri nodded. "If a bot is disabled and there are no friendly forces in the vicinity, it blows itself up in a last-ditch effort to take its attacker with it."

"Nasty," Shadow said.

"Almaida's idea," Kiri said.

"The more I learn about her, the less I like her," Lorn muttered.

"How did you freeze it in the first place?" Shadow demanded. She sounded almost suspicious. "And why didn't it stay that way?"

"Lorn asked me if they would have disabled my command privileges."

"And they haven't," Lorn said, feeling a little smug.

Kiri shot him a glance. "Well...actually, yes, they have."

He blinked. "What?"

"There's no way Almaida would have left my computer privileges intact on *Falcon's Egg* after I stole *Ninshubur* and left that nasty bug in the system," Kiri said.

"Then how...?" he said, confused.

"I gambled that what she didn't think or bother to do was purge my command privileges from the *cloned* computer core they must have shipped up here to oversee the robots."

Shadow frowned. "Cloned computer core?"

"If they're programmed for it, robots are capable of some independent action when cut off from central commands," Kiri explained. "Like the ones that kept trying to kill us on Peregrine. But when coordinated action is required—as in building the base in Margaret's Land or reconfiguring this ship—they're closely controlled by a central computer. That's why taking out *Falcon's Egg* will put a stop to any effective takeover of the planet by robot soldiers.

"*These* robots can't be under the control of the *Falcon's Egg* computer because of speed-of-light lag and the risk of signal interruptions due to weather or a relay satellite failure. In those circumstances, standard procedure is to clone the command computer. This work has been going on for a long time, which means the computer would have been cloned from the *Falcon's Egg* computer *before* I abruptly resigned from the Loyalist forces. Which was why my commands still worked." She gave Lorn an apologetic smile. "But I wouldn't have thought of it if you hadn't asked your question."

"Well, that's something," he said.

"But why didn't it last?" Shadow said. Lorn thought he could hear the unspoken question, *Why didn't it last long enough save Jedda?*

"There's always a human monitor somewhere," Kiri said. "Who immediately guessed what had happened. My privileges have been cut off now for sure, so that was a one-time trick. And they know exactly who one of us is, anyway." She gave Shadow a pointed look. "And now don't you think we'd better get crawling through these crawlspaces of yours before some actual humans come to see if there's anything left of us?"

Shadow grunted. "Fair enough." She turned to her right and began to crawl. "This way."

Lorn holstered his weapon and gestured at Kiri. "After you. I'll bring up the rear." He grinned. "That way, I can watch your butt wriggle."

She laughed.

"Less talk. More crawling," Shadow said from ahead of them, her voice tight, and Lorn shut up, suddenly realizing how callous he must sound, joking just minutes after Jedda's violent death. He'd only known her for a few hours. Shadow had known her for years.

They crawled through the ventilation duct for what seemed like forever, then descended down a shaft via a metal ladder, only missing a *few* rungs, so that Lorn only *almost* fell fifty feet to a messy death. They jumped down into a new corridor, this one tall enough to stand upright in. To their left, it ended in a blank wall after about five metres. To their right, it stretched about ten to a rusty metal door. Shadow led them to the door, took a laser cutter from her belt—she seemed to be carrying an entire workshop's worth of tools in addition to ammunition, Lorn noted for the first time—and used it to slice through the simple padlock securing the door. "What kind of starship is this?" Kiri said, staring at the door. "Rust? Padlocks? Random corridors?"

"It's a very *old* starship," Shadow said. "Built by desperate people in a hurry. When they needed to, they simply cobbled components together the best they could. And the result is a whole hidden network of access shafts and corridors and beneath-deck spaces and forgotten chambers—even forgotten transports. Growing up, I spent years mapping them. And then I put that knowledge to use as leader of the Crawlspacers."

Lorn said nothing. He knew she hadn't been the only leader of the Crawlspacers—there had been a Ship's Councilor involved, too—but he didn't see any reason to correct her. She'd certainly been the operational leader of the group of mostly teens who had helped Art Stoddard gain access to the bridge and ultimately save both ship and planet—albeit shooting him in the process.

"But if these networks are in the ship's database—"

"They're not," Shadow said. "The ship's official schematics are much...tidier." She'd pushed open the door whose lock she'd just cut through. "There's an old workers' lounge down here. We can hole up there and figure out what to do next."

She plunged into the darkness beyond the door, Kiri behind her. Lorn started to follow but froze. From behind and above them, he heard the sound of metal moving on metal. He swore, then closed the door, bolted it, and hurried after the others. "I think there's a robot back in the ventilation duct," he said as he caught up with Kiri and Shadow.

"Well, we didn't exactly hide our tracks," Shadow said. "But there's no reason it should find us down here. That duct goes on for hundreds of metres. It'll search that first. And there are multiple shafts up and down we could have taken."

"Yeah," Lorn said, "but only one that a guy carrying a nanotracker went down."

Shadow stopped so abruptly, Kiri ran into her. She turned, her eyes shadowed by the light on her shoulder. "Nanotracker?" she snarled. "Someone might have mentioned this."

"Didn't expect it to come into play," Kiri said. "And we've been kind of busy." She looked at Lorn, chewing her lip. "I doubt the bots can really track through the ship, Lorn. Not with all this metal surrounding you."

"How sure are you about that?" he said. "Because you don't look very sure."

Kiri was silent for a moment. "Um...pretty sure?" Then she shook her head. "Actually, I have no idea," she admitted.

"So much for holing up in here," Shadow growled. "Okay. We have to get out of this hab. And we have to get the nanotracker out of you if we can."

"*Can* you on this rustbucket?" Kiri said.

"Yeah," Shadow said. "I think so. If we can get you to a docbot—an automated emergency medical station—it should recognize the thing as a foreign body, and depending on where it is, it might be able to remove it."

"Might?" Lorn didn't much like the sound of that.

"Can't be sure," Shadow said irritably. "But it's our best hope. There's a docbot not far from the shuttle docking port. *If* we can get there. Come on."

She hurried on along the narrow corridor. At the end, another door opened into the "lounge," a rather grand name for what was just a room about five metres wide and ten long, with a few hard folding chairs, a table, and two doors, one closed that presumably opened into another corridor at the room's far end, the other open, revealing a chemical toilet. The lid was closed, and considering how long the thing had been there, Lorn thought that was probably best. Lockers lined one wall. Shadow listened for a moment, then turned, leaving the door open. "All right," she said. "I don't hear anything, so maybe we have a minute to plan."

"Plan what?" Lorn said. Until that moment, he'd been mostly focused on surviving. Now it sank in how screwed they really were. "Our plan died with Jedda."

"I've got a backup," Shadow said.

Kiri's eyes narrowed. "Which you haven't bothered to tell us?"

"Didn't know if it would be needed. Hadn't, I wouldn't have needed to mention it. Since things didn't work out, though, aren't you glad I have it?"

"Depends," Lorn said. "What is it?"

"We need to stop this ship from being used as a battleship against Peregrine and your rebel forces, right?" Shadow said. "And we need to take out *Falcon's Egg,* so the robot army falls apart. Right?"

"Right..." Kiri said.

"So here's how we do it," Shadow said. She smiled or at least showed her teeth. "We don't have any weapons we can access, except one." She banged her palm against the bulkhead. "*Mayflower II* herself. We kill two birds with one stone. We de-orbit *Mayflower II*...and drop it right on *Falcon's Egg* and Commander Almaida's head."

Lorn stared at her. "You can't be serious."

"I'm serious," Shadow said. "Aren't you?"

"There are still hundreds of people aboard," Kiri said. "You'll kill them all."

"Including your father," Lorn said. "And Art Stoddard's parents."

"I'll give them a chance to get off," Shadow said. "Once I have command. Ever since *Mayflower II* reached orbit, there have been enough shuttles docked aboard to get everyone to the planet in an emergency. They'll have to move fast. They won't be able to take anything with them. But they can escape if they want to. If they choose to stay on board, that's their problem." Her voice might have been frozen steel, without a hint of warmth or softness. "How many *innocent* people will die if Almaida and her robot army try to seize control of Peregrine and turn it into a beachhead for the re-invasion of Earth? How many when your ELF forces arrive to try to take it back?"

"You can't control the descent of something this size that precisely," Kiri said. "You could miss *Falcon's Egg* entirely."

"Then I'd still take out *Mayflower II*, and when the rebels finally get here, there won't be anything in orbit that can face them as they take on the robots," Shadow countered.

"How is this even possible?" Kiri demanded. "You have access to the control room?"

"I got in there once. I can do it again," Shadow said.

Lorn felt a flash of anger. "For God's sake, quit being so arrogant," he snapped. "You may hate your father. It doesn't mean he's an idiot. He *will* have fixed that little security problem since your attack."

"Why should he?" Shadow said. "All the malcontents went to the surface. Nobody here but the die-hard Crew and Council types. He certainly wasn't expecting *me* to come back."

"Then what about the Loyalist forces?" Lorn said. "If they're in control, they'll have secured the bridge to *their* standards, not your father's."

"Lorn's right," Kiri said. "That's why I discounted the possibility of using *Mayflower II*'s kinetic strike weapons against *Falcon's Egg*."

Shadow waved a hand. "It's a hidden, physical opening into the bridge that doesn't show up on any of the ship's schematics," she said. "My father didn't know about it. Why should they? They can put up all the high-tech defenses they want, and I can still get in there."

Kiri glanced at Lorn. "If we could get in there...I might be able to use orbital bombardment against *Falcon's Egg* after all." She looked back at Shadow. "And you wouldn't have to crash the ship."

Shadow looked disappointed. "I suppose." She, too, turned her gaze to Lorn. "Even if it's a long shot—you got a better idea? Think fast. The robots are already heading into Bagnell."

Lorn imagined the giant starship hitting the atmosphere... starting to burn...vast chunks, entire habs capable of supporting hundreds of people, ripping off as it fell...hitting the center of Margaret's Land with the force of an asteroid. Would *anyone* on the continent survive? And if she missed, hit the ocean, or if even chunks of the ship hit the ocean...the potential for death and destruction was immense.

But once it was done, that would be the end of it. Kiri said the destruction of the *Falcon's Egg's* core computer would render any robots still on the offensive leaderless. Isolated and uncoordinated, they could be defeated one by one. By the time Kiri's compatriots from Earth finally deigned to enter the system, the fighting would be over, once and for all. Hundreds or thousands dead, untold destruction, yes...but in the end, peace, and a better world.

A better definition of a just war he couldn't think of. And wasn't this war just?

Trouble was, he'd caused his share of death of destruction in his years in the SSIN using the same rationale, and despite what he'd been promised, there'd been no sign of peace and a better world coming out of it.

Maybe this time will be different, he thought. *And there's a chance, at least, that Kiri can use the new weapons and* Mayflower II *stays in orbit.*

"If we can't use the kinetic weapons and have to crash the ship...we go down with it," he pointed out.

Shadow laughed. "Only if you're feeling suicidal. I'm planning on using an escape pod myself."

Lorn blinked. "There are *escape pods?*"

"That doesn't make any sense," Kiri said. "You can't just fling yourself out into interstellar space in low-powered pods from a ship travelling at a third the speed of light. What would be the point? It would be a death sentence."

"They weren't for Passengers," Shadow said. "Or even for Crew. They were installed for the construction workers' safety during the ship's assembly in orbit. Not readily accessible to passengers, so they'd be no use for evacuating the ship even now. But I know how to get to them."

"Are they steerable?" Lorn said.

"In a limited way," Shadow said. "They're designed to get you safely down to the surface. You've got a window of opportunity after launch to set landing coordinates. But you've got no control after that. Trust me. The pods are there. And they might even work if the maintenance bots have been doing their jobs." She looked from him to Kiri and back again. "Well?"

"I say we try it," Kiri at once. "It may be our only chance to stop *Falcon's Egg*."

More death. More destruction. But what choice is there? "All right," Lorn said. "So what do we do next?"

"We—" Shadow began but got no further. Bright light flared at the far end of the hall that led to the workers' lounge. The door Lorn had bolted banged open, and a multi-legged silver robot swarmed through like a demented spider.

Only the fact the door bounced off the wall and momentarily blocked the robot's sensors saved them. It gave time for Lorn to draw and fire an explosive slug down the corridor even as he flung himself (he hoped) out of the bot's line of fire. Kiri's laser slashed at the bot's sensors as she hurled herself prone beside him. Neither of their shots had any effect. But Shadow fired, not at the bot, but at a thick red pipe that ran along the corridor. It burst and filled the corridor with steam, blinding the bot's sensors. It overshot, bullets stitching across the back wall of the lounge as Shadow lunged forward in a crouch and slammed the lounge door closed. She bolted it.

Lorn hauled himself to his feet and helped Kiri to hers. "The other door didn't hold it. This one won't, either." A spot of red was already showing as the bot began cutting its way through the metal, and an acrid smell filled the air.

"It'll slow it down. Maybe long enough. This way." Shadow

jerked open the door at the far end of the lounge. Another corridor stretched away, lit by dim blue lights at irregular intervals. She motioned for Lorn and Kiri to go ahead of her, then leaped through and closed that door behind them, too. "This corridor should lead to a pod station," she said, as she led the way along it at a jog. "There was a secondary transport system for construction workers. Some of the stations are still in use. Others were shut down when the ship launched."

"*Should* lead?" Lorn said.

"Most of them do, when you find one of these old workers' lounges. But some of them are blocked off completely."

"So we could be heading into a dead end."

"Emphasis on the *dead*," Kiri said.

A few more metres, and they found out. The corridor didn't dead-end...but it didn't end in a pod station either. Not unless pod stations were usually marked by empty hatch openings revealing only blackness.

Shadow stuck her head through the opening. "It's a pod tunnel, but it's not in use. And there was never a platform here. This must be a maintenance hatch."

Lorn looked behind them. "That thing will be through the first door by now and working on the second."

"So, now what?" Kiri said.

Shadow turned around. "We climb," she said.

"Climb what?"

"Ladders. When the pods aren't working, you still need some way to move around the shaft."

Lorn groaned.

"That bot has legs," Kiri pointed out. "It can climb ladders, too. And once it's in the pod tunnel with us..."

Shadow grunted. "Got an idea for that. About five hundred feet coreward, we're going to come to where the tunnel bends into the 'stalk' that connects the hab to the Core. And right about there, we're going to find another bot...but not one of Almaida's. One of *Mayflower II*'s."

"Maintenance bot?" Kiri said.

Shadow nodded. "And a control station for it. It can be programmed on the spot—no need to trouble the central computer with something like cleaning rust."

"So we program it to clean out the tube..." Lorn said thoughtfully.

"But is it armed?"

"Cutters," Shadow said. "Which should be enough since as another robot, it won't register—until it's too late—as a threat to that thing on our tails. Which will be *literally* on our tails if we don't move them..."

Lorn sighed. "Lead on. Again."

Shadow turned and reached carefully out into the darkness, stepping out of sight to the right. "On the ladder," her voice came back after a moment. "Climbing."

"You next," Lorn said.

"Too dark to see my ass in there," Kiri said.

"So I'll imagine it. Go!"

Kiri gave him a quick kiss, then scrambled out into the dark.

Chapter Fifteen

WHEN IT WAS Lorn's turn, he found it easy enough to grab the rungs in the tube wall. In here, there were no friendly blue lights; only the lights they carried, attached to their right shoulders. Ahead of him, Shadow and Kiri seemed to be moving through a vast, formless darkness. He had no sense of the size of the tube except that it was large, and extended, it seemed, forever both below and ahead of them, though that made no sense. They were close to the outside of the hab already, so the tube had to end, or loop, or however the things worked, not far below them.

Of course, "not far" could still be far enough to kill him if he slipped off the ladder, so he quit worrying about where they were or where they were going and concentrated instead on where he placed his hands and feet.

The worst of it was that he couldn't hold a weapon while he climbed. His sidearm remained in its holster. He was uneasily aware of the opening beneath them. That killer robot could burst out through it at any moment and come swarming up the ladder after them. It wouldn't have to draw a weapon. It could see in the dark. It could pick them off the ladder like ripe fruit from a tree if they didn't get to the top of the hab before it emerged.

Five hundred feet. It didn't sound like much. He could run it in well under a minute, even in full military gear.

So why did climbing it seem to take forever?

Even though they weighed less with every rung they climbed coreward, their mass remained unchanged, alleviating the strain only slightly. His legs and arms ached when at last he clambered off the ladder into a chamber containing, as Shadow had promised, a maintenance robot, and a small control panel on a pedestal, presumably used to program the thing. Just as Lorn pulled his foot out of the shaft they had been climbing, a spot on the metal ceiling overhead flashed white and then slowly faded back to red. Lorn stared at it, breathing hard. *Way too close*, he thought. "It's on the way. Get programming!"

"No time," Shadow panted. "We were too slow." She slapped her hand on the control panel, and the metal brackets holding the maintenance robot in place snapped open. "Help me!" she shouted as she hurried around to the far side of the robot.

Lorn suddenly realized what she intended to do and scrambled after her. Kiri rounded the other end of the robot. "Push!" Shadow shouted, and the three of them shoved as hard as they could.

The maintenance robot, just a metal ovoid the size of a very large dog—or maybe a very small pony—when its legs weren't extended, dropped from the brackets and crashed to the deck plating. Lorn, Kiri, and Shadow scrambled around to the other side of the brackets and pushed it again. It rolled to the lip of the shaft they had been climbing—and dropped.

From the sound of it, the killer robot chasing them had almost reached the chamber. There was an enormous metallic crash, a long silence...and then another crash far below, one that went on a bit longer as bits of metal ricocheted off the walls and finally clattered into silence.

"I do love me some hot robot-on-robot action," Shadow said. Lorn, surprised, laughed out loud. She flashed him a grin. "All right. From here, we can get into the transport system proper... and maybe we can see about getting that nanotracker out of you once and for all." Her grin faded. "Before we try to get to the control room."

Lorn looked down into the dark shaft they had vacated. He could see nothing, but nothing shot his head off, either, so presumably, the killerbot was as *hors de combat* as it had sounded. "Lead on," he said and then grimaced. It seemed to him he'd been saying that a lot recently. When had he become a follower instead of a leader?

Since we moved into Shadow's territory.

Shadow crossed the chamber and opened a new hatch with a touch. "Nothing secured in here. No need for it since you can't even get *in* here without clearance." She grinned again. "Unless you're a Crawlspacer. Which I guess you both qualify as now. Congratulations!"

"Thanks," Kiri said. "It's a dream come true."

The hatch opened onto a short corridor that led to another hatch that opened into a well-lit chamber that Lorn *did* recognize: he'd ridden the ship's internal transportation system the last time he'd been on board. They'd found an active pod station at last. "Won't this be monitored?" he said.

"Doubt it," Shadow said. "There's almost no one on board. The pods run constantly, and they're almost always empty. Who would bother? Also," she unholstered her sidearm, "the camera in the next pod that comes along is going to suffer an unexplained failure. Which is hardly unusual on this rustbucket."

The pod arrived, the door on the other side of the chamber sliding open at the same instant as the door to the pod. Shadow held up a hand, took a deep breath, then ducked inside the pod, and fired in the same instant. There was a flash, and then she motioned them aboard.

As the pod accelerated, Lorn looked up at the neat round hole through the silvery dome that presumably held a no-longer-functioning security camera. "Good shot," he said.

"I've had a lot of practice," Shadow said dryly.

Kiri laughed.

Lorn and Kiri sat together on one bench of the pod as they zipped through the shafts. "Down" kept changing location—not much, but enough to push them this way and that. Their weight changed, too, increasing as they first accelerated, lessening after that, and vanishing altogether, along with *any* sense of "down," as they reached the Core. "Not long now," Shadow said. "Once we've got you decontaminated, we can make our way to the bridge. Then—"

The lights went out.

"Pod travel terminated unexpectedly," said a pleasant female voice. "Please wait for assistance."

"Shit!" Shadow said. The light on her shoulder flicked on again. She scrambled to the door. "We've got to get out of here."

"Someone figured out what we were doing?" Lorn guessed.

"Somebody on this ship has gotten competent," Shadow growled. "Never would have expected it." A panel by the door was marked EMERGENCY DOOR OPERATION. She opened it, revealing a handle and a hole in which to insert it. She stuck the handle in the hole and began to crank. The door slowly opened. It was as dark outside the pod as inside it. "They couldn't be sure we were in this pod—it won't be the only one with a dead camera—but they've figured out it's a possibility. So they've shut down the whole system. I'll bet there are bots headed this way right now." She shot him a look over her shoulder. "And you're still carrying a nanotracker."

"Can we still get to this 'docbot' you mentioned?" Kiri said.

"Not a chance," Shadow said. "And that's not the worst of it. We can't get to the bridge, either."

"Why not?" Lorn demanded.

"There's simply no way to get there without taking a pod. Even when we took the ship last time, we used the pod system."

"Then we're screwed," Lorn said. "There's no way to destroy *Falcon's Egg.*"

"No," Shadow said. "But we can still take *Mayflower II* out of the picture." She frowned. "I'll need something I don't have...but I know where to get it. Come on." She pulled herself out into the darkness before Lorn could ask, *What?* Kiri followed.

Lorn floated up to the hatch, a halo of metal lit by the flashlight on his shoulder, surrounding blackness, Shadow and Kiri having already moved out of his line of sight.

And suddenly, his heart raced, and he froze, seeing another hatch, the one he had blown open to save Art Stoddard and Shadow and the Crawlspacers with them. He saw it receding from him as his spacesuited body drifted helplessly away. He saw the bodies tumbling out after him, propelled by the escaping air. His first kills. But not his last. Not his—

"Lorn! Are you all right?"

The image vanished. The hatch opening was no longer a black hole. Instead, it framed a face: Kiri's face. A face he'd come to love. A face looking at him with naked concern. His racing heart slowed. He gasped air. "Coming. Coming!" He pulled himself out through the hatch. Kiri gave him one more worried look, but there was no time to talk. Shadow was waving at them impatiently to hurry up. He hoped she hadn't seen his moment of weakness. He couldn't afford to be weak. Not now.

The shifting illumination of their flashlights showed Lorn for the first time how the pod system worked. He'd pictured the pod as a kind of pea in a peashooter and had vaguely imagined some kind of jet propulsion, but in fact, it ran on a monorail, a thin silver line that vanished into the gloom fore and aft of the pod itself, which was shaped like a drug capsule, a short cylinder rounded at both ends. There had been no rail in the inactive pod shaft up which they'd climbed from the workers' lounge.

Shadow pulled herself up to the side of the pod away from the monorail, and in the pool of light from her torch, Lorn saw a ladder, like the one they'd climbed in the other pod shaft. "Stay away from the rail," Shadow warned. "If the power comes back on, that thing will fry you. Theoretically, you can hang on to the ladder, and a moving pod will shoot past harmlessly. But that's assuming the windblast doesn't rip you free and put you into the rail—or into the path of the next pod."

"So where do we go?" Lorn said.

"I have no idea exactly where we are in the network," Shadow said, "but every so often, there are access hatches. Inside the Core proper, you should find maneuvering units. They're simple to operate. Use those to head toward the stern. As soon as that damn nanotracker is detected, the bots will forget about everything else and come after you."

"Why?" Kiri said.

"The matter/antimatter reactor is in the Aft Propulsion Module," Shadow said. "They don't want anybody screwing with *that*. And there are emergency controls down there that would let you do exactly that. You won't be able to access them, but they can't be sure, so you'll draw their attention. Hopefully, long enough for me to get what I need."

"Which is?" Lorn said.

"A key," Shadow said. "Now get going."

"Into the Core, pursued by robots?" Kiri said. "Sounds like a suicide mission."

"Not necessarily," Shadow said. "Dangerous as hell, sure, but if it looks like you've gone as far as you can, look for one of the escape pods I told you about. Their access points are marked with red flashing lights."

Lorn nodded, then held out his hand. "Good luck."

Shadow took it, shook it firmly. "And to you." She withdrew her hand. "Now, get moving. The bots are on their way." She turned and began pulling herself along the ladder in the direction they'd been travelling.

Lorn led Kiri in the other direction. After about five minutes, they came to the promised access hatch, which opened to a touch of the control panel. Light, blinding after the dimness of the pod tube, poured through it as it slid open, and Lorn put up a hand to shield his eyes.

"Impressive," Kiri said, looking past him.

Lorn had seen *Mayflower II* from the outside, but somehow the vista before him brought home the sheer size of the starship in a way seeing it from space hadn't. Maybe it was because the Core was an enclosed space: an enormous open cylinder, illuminated by light strips spaced equidistantly around the interior, running to their left and right as far as they could see. Massive pipes and conduits ran along the walls between the lights, structures that would have been large buildings even in Bagnell stood up here and there, and the low throbbing hum of machinery in action filled the air.

Movement flickered up and down the walls of the Core. Kiri drew her sidearm. "Bots," she said, as a fat multi-legged robot clicked and clattered by, somehow gripping the wall despite the almost complete lack of centrifugal force this close to the ship's center. The machine ignored them. Twenty-five feet aft, it stopped, and a manipulator flicked out and twisted something.

"Maintenance bots," Lorn said. "They don't seem interested in us."

"For now," Kiri said grimly. "Let's get moving."

"I don't see these maneuvering units Shadow promised," Lorn said.

Kiri pointed past the maintenance bot, still fiddling with whatever had drawn its attention. A puff of steam suddenly surrounded it. "That structure over there looks promising," she said. "What are those things hanging inside it?"

Lorn followed her gesture. The structure, about the size of a gardener's shed, was just an open framework with no roof. Half a dozen bulky white objects hung from the metal pillars of the frame. "Could be..."

They pulled their way over to the "shed," past the maintenance bot, which still ignored them. In fact, it had quit moving altogether, even though steam continued to jet all around it. Lorn gave it an uneasy glance.

The bulky objects in the shed proved to indeed be the promised maneuvering units. Lorn had used something similar in training, although not nearly as big and clumsy as these. Still, the controls were intuitive enough: two joysticks, one on each of the rigid arms in which their forearms rested, the one on the left controlling puffs of gas in the Z axis, the one on the right in the X and Y axes. A control panel in the left-hand arm showed how much gas remained. That was all there was to it.

Lorn strapped Kiri into one unit. She'd just finished strapping him into another when the maintenance robot suddenly sprang to life outside the hut—and raced toward them, manipulators reaching. "Up!" Lorn yelled. He slammed the left-hand joystick forward, and the unit launched him straight up through the open roof of the shed, Kiri right behind him.

The maintenance robot soared after him with its own gas thrusters. But they were drawing away from it. "Aft!" Lorn cried. He pulled the left-hand joystick back briefly to slow his ascent, using the right to start moving sternward along the Core. Kiri matched his maneuver perfectly; she'd clearly had experience in these kinds of units before as well.

Unfortunately, the maintenance bot had no trouble matching the maneuver either.

The right-hand joystick twisted to fire puffs that could spin the unit in place without affecting its forward trajectory. He took advantage of that to face back at the pursuing bot. It was still slipping away behind them—but now he could see other bots lifting off from the walls of the Core to join the pursuit. Some of them looked considerably bigger than the one closest to them...and potentially faster.

Then Kiri said, "Turn around, Lorn."

He spun to face forward again.

Like the air around a disturbed bluestinger nest, the Core ahead of them swarmed with black dots, maintenance bots launching themselves into the air.

"Do we look for an escape pod?" Kiri said.

"You mean like that one?" Lorn said grimly, pointing past a half-dozen approaching bots at a flashing red light.

"I see your point," Kiri said. She drew her sidearm and flicked on the laser sight. "Well, then," she said. "I could do with a little shooting practice."

Lorn glanced behind them. The bots back there weren't making much progress; the biggest threat was definitely ahead of them. He drew his own sidearm. "I think you're right."

The nearest bot, a fat black upright cylinder with a single claw-like manipulator, was only a hundred yards away and closing fast. Lorn painted it with the laser and fired a single explosive slug. The maintenance bots weren't nearly as tough as *Falcon's Egg*'s military bots: the blast ripped the cylinder apart, and black globs of liquid sprayed out, turning into glistening globules covered with flickering blue flame...and heading straight toward them.

Lorn would have liked to have sworn, but he was too busy dodging. They made it through the burning globs and immediately faced four more bots, these more like the one that had first come after them. "Beam!" Kiri said, and Lorn switched his sidearm over to the laser. The invisible beams stitched bright, sizzling lines of molten metal across the shells of the bots: they simply froze and drifted past as dead hulks.

"Better choice," Lorn agreed.

"Yeah," Kiri said. "But the power won't last long. Here comes another one!"

Their journey aft took on a nightmarish quality. In some ways, it felt like the shooting simulations Lorn had fought through endlessly during training—but this was no simulation. Another of the fat black-cylinder bots exploded at the touch of Kiri's laser, and this time Lorn wasn't able to dodge all of the flaming contents. A burning black glob struck his backpack—and clung. He couldn't reach it. The white covering began to char. If it burned through to the gas tanks...

But Kiri was right there, belt knife in hand. She scraped the blazing gunk free and flicked it away.

"Thanks," Lorn said, and then just managed to get off the shot that turned the big bot barreling straight toward them into tumbling junk. He kicked Kiri out of the way, the action sending him spinning in the other direction. For a moment, they were both out of control, rapidly drifting away from each other, and in that moment, the big bot he had just shot exploded.

The blast shoved Lorn down hard, too hard for his jets to counteract. He barely managed to twist around so that he hit the bulkhead backpack first and felt it crunch beneath him as his breath whooshed out. He bounced up, the maneuvering unit useless, still unable to get his breath, gaping like a landed fish.

The blast had caught Kiri too, but she'd been farther from the wall and had managed to regain control. She darted back toward him. Halfway her backpack simply came apart as though sliced by a knife, and she, too, hit the wall hard. He heard her breath, too, whoosh out of her as she bounced back toward him. She collided with him, and helplessly tangled and unable to control their flight, they drifted back into the middle of the Core...

...and directly into the path of a bot completely different from the maintenance bots they'd been fighting, a bot Lorn recognized at once:

It was a killerbot from *Falcon's Egg*.

Chapter Sixteen

HAD IT FIRED, they would have died there and then. But instead, it simply hung in the Core, and an amplified voice said, "Hold where you are!"

"Can't!" Lorn shouted as he continued to drift up and away from the bot. "Can't maneuver!"

Something silvery exploded from the side of the bot and lashed out at him. He stared down at the shining cord wrapped around his ankle. He'd been lassoed.

So had Kiri. He followed the line of another cord and saw the end of it wrapped around her arm. Both of them were pulled inexorably toward the killerbot. "Marines are on their way," the voice from the bot said. "You will be brought to Hab One for interrogation. Do not struggle, or it will be worse for—"

Something flashed, and the bot suddenly went silent. The cord slithered away from around Lorn's leg, but his momentum carried him onward. He bumped up against the bot and just managed to grab one of its frozen crab-like legs. Using that as a lever, he hauled himself up to see down the Core behind the bot's bulk—

—to discover Shadow, wearing a maneuvering unit of her own, drifting steadily nearer and holstering her sidearm.

"You're a sight for sore eyes," Lorn said. "Did you get this 'key' you mentioned?"

Shadow nodded. "Tucked away right where I left it." She reached the defunct killerbot and booted it out of her way, countering the reaction with her jets so it drifted off toward the Core wall and she stayed put. "So now we're all headed to the Propulsion Module. I can't control the ship from there, but I can neutralize it...permanently."

The maintenance bots had frozen with the advent of the killerbot, temporarily shut down to avoid interfering with it, he guessed. But for how long?

"You all right?" Kiri said to Lorn as her momentum brought her up to the three of them. Shadow snagged her and, with a puff of gas, brought her to halt.

"Think so," Lorn said. "But this thing is shot." He unbuckled his maneuvering unit and pushed it away from him, forcing Shadow to puff more gas to keep them on station. She was forced to do it again a second later as Kiri followed suit.

"Can we find more?" Kiri said.

"We can do better than that," Shadow said. "Hang on." She puffed more gas, and they began to angle down toward a long low structure, open at the top like the one from which they had taken the maneuvering units. *Well, I supposed it doesn't rain much in here*, Lorn thought.

This structure was considerably larger than the first, though, and rather than holding several individual maneuvering units, it held a single large vehicle. "Cargo sled," Shadow said. "Faster than the individual maneuvering units and *way* faster than any maintenance bot."

"What about killerbots?" Lorn asked.

"That I don't know. So let's get a move on. Climb on."

With Shadow at the controls and Lorn and Kiri clinging to stanchions, the cargo sled rose through the top of the storage building and accelerated aft along the Core. They passed more maintenance robots, all still frozen in place.

The Core changed little as they flew: they saw the same small structures, the same massive equipment housings, the same lights, repeating over and over in wide bands of structures that looked exactly the same. Lorn assumed they marked the strata of the giant ship, the "stalks" that led from the stem of the core to the "seed-pods" of the habitats.

The stern bulkhead swelled ahead of them, a vast wall against which they would be mere insects. Lorn had begun to hope they might reach it unmolested when the frozen robots suddenly returned to violent life, a dozen launching themselves from the Core walls between them and the bulkhead. Glancing back, Lorn saw dozens more. "Clear a path!" Shadow shouted.

The shooting gallery had reopened. Keeping one arm wrapped tightly around his stanchion, Lorn fired and fired again, trying to make each shot count, as the power meter on the sidearm slipped inexorably to zero. When the laser failed, he switched to explosive slugs, but he had only a couple of shots left. Beside him, Kiri's weapon also died. Two bots ahead of them remained live. "There and there!" Lorn cried to Shadow, pointing them out.

"Never mind the little ones," she said grimly. "*That's* the one we need to worry about."

Lorn stared ahead and realized with a chill that what he had thought was a strangely shaped building was, in fact, a bot. Not only that, it was a type he had seen before: seven years ago he had glimpsed it as Art Stoddard pushed off into the interior of *Mayflower II* and left him, injured, alone in the giant airlock that housed the thing—the airlock he had blown minutes later to take out the Crew pursuing Stoddard and the Crawlspacers.

It had no weapons. It didn't look like it would need them. Manipulator arms reached out, drills whirring, blades spinning, claws opening and closing. "Hang on," Shadow said. "And be ready to jump." And then, rather than attempting to dodge the oncoming behemoth, she accelerated.

Lorn and Kiri said "Shit!" in stereo. And then flung themselves off the sled, following Shadow, just before the impact.

The bot's maneuvering jets hissed like angry snakes, but inertia and momentum defeated them. The bot hadn't altered course an iota before the sled slammed into it. Sled and bot crumpled into a mass of tangled and twisted metal.

And then the fuel in both machines exploded.

Something sharp sliced across Lorn's calf, bright-red drops of blood welling out in its wake. He contorted himself to avoid a larger piece moving fast enough to take his head off, then rolled into a ball to avoid another, even larger. Then he was through the debris field but still moving at an alarming rate of speed straight toward the bulkhead. He shot a look around.

Kiri was drifting away from him in a different bulkhead-ending trajectory, face contorted in pain, clutching her left arm, which also trailed tiny red globules. He twisted his head up. Shadow was "above" him. She had something in her hands that he didn't recognize, a slim black rectangle that she held in one hand while the fingers of her other moved across it.

The bulkhead loomed. He estimated he was still travelling at a good forty kilometres an hour. He might survive the impact, but not without broken bones. And there was nothing he could do about it. He tensed...

And then gasped as a silvery net suddenly writhed into view across the bulkhead. An instant later, he hit it, his breath whooshing out as the net gave, then stiffened, cushioning his impact and draining away his momentum. He had the presence of mind to grab and hold the silvery cords even as he struggled to draw air into his lungs and to twist and look behind him.

The wreckage of bot and sled continued forward. Beyond it, a few maintenance bots still jetted their way.

He looked closer.

Make that a *lot* of maintenance bots.

He managed to get a smidgen of oxygen into his lungs and used it to start pulling himself hand over hand along the netting, toward where Shadow clung like a spider at the centre of the web. She wasn't moving. Much farther away, Kiri came scuttling across the net as well, although, with one arm hanging limp, much more slowly than Lorn. He reached Shadow first.

She was unconscious, but her eyes fluttered as he touched her. "Shadow," he said. She muttered something. "Shadow!" He slapped her cheek lightly.

She opened her eyes and blinked blearily at him. "Ow. Harder hit than I expected," she said, her voice a little slurred—but then she looked over his shoulder at the onrushing bots, and her eyes widened. "No time to nap, though." She pulled out her sidearm. "Still some laser juice left," she said, and turned and burned a man-sized slice through the net. "Go help Kiri," she told Lorn. "I'll get us into the Propulsion Module." She handed him her sidearm. "You need it more than me."

Lorn glanced at the weapon. The power meter was yellow. He'd be lucky to get a half-dozen shots off.

Shadow was already slithering through the opening in the net. The bulkhead was another fifteen metres away: she launched herself to it. Lorn didn't watch to see what she did next. Instead, he scrambled toward Kiri, whose white face was also fifteen metres away as she struggled one-armed across the net.

Behind her, the first of the oncoming bots thumped into the net...and began scuttling after her like a metallic spider.

The "spider" stopped dead as Lorn's laser sliced through its skin, but two more thudded into the net close to it and began closing the gap.

Lorn fired twice more. One of the bots stopped and erupted in smoke. The other began moving in small circles, like a dog chasing its tail. But there were a dozen more closing fast. Lorn sheathed the almost-exhausted weapon and pulled himself across the net. "Grab my ankle!" he shouted at Kiri. She nodded, her white face shining beneath a sheen of sweat. The tear in her sleeve was blood-soaked, but she was no longer trailing scarlet globules. She took his ankle, and he turned and scurried back toward the opening in the net, pulling her along like a balloon.

They reached the opening. He shoved her through, not too hard, directly at Shadow, who had her legs hooked around one of the ladder-like rungs on the bulkhead clearly intended for that very purpose, busy with the strange flat rectangle he had seen earlier. "Shadow!" he shouted. "Incoming!" Shadow's head twisted around, and she let the rectangle hang in the air at the end of a cord around her wrist while she turned to catch Kiri, grunting with the impact. Kiri took hold of a ladder rung with her good arm, and Shadow snatched the rectangle back and returned all her focus to it.

Lorn turned himself around just in time to see a double-sized maintenance bot racing toward him down the Core, heading directly for the gap in the net. He gasped, thumbed the pistol to explosive shells, and fired three—all that were left—in quick succession. The recoil drove him through the cut in the net and away from the bot, which burst apart. One large part, spinning and jetting out flame like a welding torch, followed him through the net, and his thumb found the control and flipped the pistol to full automatic. A burst of fire, and the bullets, too, were exhausted...but at least the spinning, flaming hunk of metal was spinning off in a different direction. It skipped across the surface of the bulkhead, scattering smoldering shrapnel as it went.

Lorn thudded against the steel plates. He turned and grabbed a rung, then pulled himself toward Kiri and Shadow. He shoved the empty pistol into Shadow's holster as he reached her and, for the first time, got a good look at the flat black control device. It meant nothing more to him up close: random lights, as far as he could tell. "The key?" he said.

"More or less," she said absently. "Crew used them. I... collected them. For years. Tucked them away here and there. Used them to get into places I wasn't supposed to be able to get. We were lucky—there was one hidden away not far from where I left you. Wasn't sure it would still have power after all these years...but it does."

"What does it do?"

"Just about everything," she said. "If you know the codes. And I know the codes."

"And what are *you* doing?" Lorn said, not trying to hide his exasperation. He looked up at the net over their heads as more maintenance bots reached it. "It won't take them long to find the opening in the net. And we're out of ammo."

"What I'm doing," Shadow said with more than a little heat of her own, "is disabling a series of security devices and failsafes that, if left enabled, would kill us to prevent us from accessing what we need to access. And I'd do it faster if you'd shut up."

Lorn clenched his fist in frustration, then turned toward Kiri. "How are you?"

"Been better," she said between clenched teeth. "Think I cracked the humerus."

"Are you bleeding badly?" Lorn said. "I've got nothing to wrap it with."

"Just a scratch," Kiri said. "I'll live."

"Not if we don't get out of here," Lorn muttered, glancing up as a maintenance bot scuttled over their heads. A minute later, it was exploring the cut in the net. The cut was too small for it to get through...but that seemed unlikely to be much of a hindrance to something that carried its own laser cutter.

"That's it," Shadow said suddenly. "I hope."

"You hope?"

She ignored him. She touched the control device one last time, then let it drift on its cord.

At the centre of the bulkhead was a very large hatch, big enough to accommodate a giant maintenance bot like the one Shadow had crashed the cargo sled into. Surrounding it were a series of smaller, man-sized hatches, ladder rungs running from hatch to hatch and out from each hatch to the outer walls of the core. The hatch at the end of the line of rungs to which they clung suddenly slid open. "Let's go!"

Lorn didn't have to be told twice. "Grab hold," he told Kiri, and towing her again, he pulled himself along the ladder toward the open hatch.

Shadow disappeared through it. Lorn glanced back just before reaching it to see the maintenance bot dropping through the now-enlarged hole in the net and heading their way. It put on a burst of speed, scuttling along the ladder toward them. It was going to be a near thing.

Kiri cried out in pain as he grabbed her and stuffed her through the hatch. "Sorry," he said, but the bot was close now. He pulled himself headfirst through the hatch after her. "Close it!" he cried.

The hatch started closed. Lorn jerked his head back as a manipulator arm suddenly thrust through it, the whirling blade at its end just missing his head. He expected the hatch to open again as it encountered resistance, but instead, it ground inexorably closed. In a burst of sparks, the manipulator arm separated. The blade quit spinning. The hatch closed.

"I disabled all fail-safes," Shadow said. "Including the one that keeps hatches from crushing people. Something you might want to keep in mind next hatch we go through."

"Good advice," Lorn said. He took a deep breath—it seemed like he hadn't had one in a while—and looked around. They were in a silvery tube that led straight aft, lit by concentric circles of illumination at three-metre intervals.

"Welcome to the Aft Propulsion Module," Shadow said. "This next bit's easy...assuming I successfully disabled the security protocols, of course."

"If you didn't?"

She shrugged. "We'll probably never know."

"How do you plan to disable the ship from here?" Kiri said.

"You have to ask?"

"The reactor?" Kiri said.

Shadow nodded.

"You said it was inaccessible," Lorn said.

"Inaccessible to you," Shadow said. "With this," she held up the control device, "I can get at it."

"To shut it down?"

"Something like that."

Lorn looked at Kiri. "Better hang on to my foot again. Could be a bit of a wild ride."

"I don't mind," she gasped. "But I can't promise I won't get sick."

"That's how you know it's a good ride," Lorn said. He looked back at Shadow. "So go already."

Without a word, she turned and began pulling herself along the tube, straight toward the beating heart of the *Mayflower II*.

Chapter Seventeen

THE TUBE, only wide enough for one person at a time, made conversation difficult. But when Shadow called a halt at a six-way intersection—two tubes at right angles left and right, two at right angles up and down, and one carrying straight on—to consult the control device, which apparently also functioned as a map, Lorn had to ask, "Where the hell did that net come from? Not that I'm complaining, since I'm not currently a grease spot on the bulkhead, but..."

"Shh," Shadow said, concentrating on the control device, but to his surprise, Kiri answered.

"Acceleration net," she said. "Everything in the Core *should* be tied down during maneuvering. But just in case something isn't, or in case of emergency, you don't want stuff smashing into the aft bulkhead."

Lorn felt like an idiot. "Should have thought of that."

Shadow indicated the tunnel that was "right" from Lorn's current orientation. "This way."

The new tunnel, identical to the last, ended in a hatch: a rather forbidding hatch painted with red stripes and bearing a large sign in stark white letters on a black background: ACCESS FORBIDDEN WITHOUT COMMAND AUTHORIZATION ON PAIN OF SUMMARY EXECUTION. The hatch did not say what it accessed, but Lorn could guess. "Reactor control?"

Shadow nodded. "End of the road." She tapped her control device. "Now we'll find out if I *really* disabled the security or not..."

Lorn held his breath. The hatch slid open. A puff of air blew in his face. Nothing else happened.

He heard Shadow exhale her own breath and wondered just how uncertain she'd been.

"So far, so good." She released the key and pulled herself through the hatch with both hands.

Beyond was a short tunnel studded with unfriendly-looking protuberances. Lorn wondered how many pieces they would have been sliced into if the security protocols *hadn't* been disabled.

The hatch at the other end bore no dire warnings, probably because the designers assumed anyone who had made it that far alive had to have proper access. It *did* bear a sign, though: MAIN REACTOR SECONDARY CONTROL.

The hatch opened to Shadow's touch. Beyond...

Lorn had expected something spectacular: a giant globular room, maybe, with light burning at the center of it like a star caught from the heavens. Instead, he found himself in a white room with a blank black control panel stretching across its far side, equally blank gray vidscreens above.

"That's it?" he said.

"You were expecting to actually see into the reactor?" Shadow said. She snorted. "There's a *lot* of shielding between it and us. Be thankful. If you could actually see it, you'd already be blind and dead. Or at least dying."

"Just seems a bit...anticlimactic," Lorn said.

"The climax is still coming." Shadow lifted the control device, touched it.

The blank black expanse of the control panel suddenly sprang to life, a complex array of indicators, buttons, read-outs and...Lorn blinked as sound filled the air. "Isn't that Mozart?"

"My father's choice," Shadow said shortly. "I liked it when I was a kid. I can't stand it now." To the strains of the "Allegro" from *Eine Kleine Nachtmusik* she drifted to the control panel and put her hands on it.

The vidscreens lit up with a diagram of the entire ship. Shadow's hands moved, and the display zoomed in on the Aft Propulsion Module. "Damn," she said. "Most of them are gone."

"Most of what?" Lorn demanded, but Shadow didn't answer.

Lorn was getting tired of that.

Shadow's hands kept moving. The display zoomed in again. "There," she said, pointing.

Lorn crossed to get a better look. "Escape Pod 371A," he read.

"Lots of them seem to have failed. But that one shows green. You and Kiri get to it."

Lorn gave her a look. "And you?"

"I have work to do here."

"And then you'll follow?"

"I'm going a different way." Shadow turned back to the board. "You'd better get going. I've got the module's maintenance bots shut down at the moment, but up on the bridge, there are ways around that. I suspect they'll be moving soon."

"Then, we should wait. In case they try to interfere—"

"No," Shadow said. "You should go." Her hands had never stopped moving across the board. A view of the planet appeared, a red cross in Margaret's Land. "I've programmed the pod to land near *Falcon's Egg*. Up to you to figure out how to take it out now. This mission is a failure. We lost the missile warhead and Jedda, we can't access the bridge, and I can't deorbit the ship from here. All I can do is make sure it's not part of the equation going forward. Now move! I've programmed the lights to show you the way." She pointed to a hatch in the "floor" of the control room relative to the control console. It slid open, revealing another tube, this one curving so that its end was hidden. "One more thing," she added. "These pods have docbots built into them, on the theory workers evacuating the ship were likely to suffer injuries. It might be able to get that nanotracker out of you...and do something about Kiri's arm."

Lorn nodded. "Good luck," he said. "See you on the surface." He glanced around at Kiri. "Ready?"

"Ready," she whispered. She took hold of his foot again. Lorn hoped she could hang on. *Well, if she can't, I'll carry her,* he thought fiercely and launched himself into the tube.

The hatch closed behind them, hiding the control room and Shadow.

For the first ten minutes, they journeyed uneventfully along the curving corridors, twice changing direction to follow the lights. Then, suddenly, Lorn heard Shadow's voice, apparently originating from thin air.

"Better hurry, Lorn. The bots have woken up. Shouldn't be any in your area. But they're heading for me. I'll delay as long as I can before I have to take action."

"What action?" he asked.

But Shadow's voice continued as if she hadn't heard him, which she likely hadn't. "I can give you another seven or eight minutes. No more."

"No more before *what?*" Lorn said, but Shadow didn't speak again.

He glanced back at Kiri. She gave him a weak smile. He looked forward and resumed pulling himself along the endless line of rungs.

Another minute, and the end of the corridor came into sight: another hatch. It slid open automatically as they approached.

The escape pod was smaller than Lorn had anticipated, with acceleration couches for only six...and, in a rather alarming alcove lined with devices uncomfortably similar to the manipulating arms of the bots that had been chasing them, a bed. That, presumably, was the docbot.

Time enough to check it out later. For now, he helped Kiri into the co-pilot's seat and buckled himself into the pilot's. As he did so, Shadow's voice spoke from the control panel. "Sensors say you're in the escape pod."

"Sensors are correct," Lorn said.

"It's programmed and ready to go," Shadow said. "Ready to—"

"Cynthia, is that you?" a voice cut in.

Dead silence for a moment, then, "Father," Shadow said.

"What the hell are you doing down there?" Captain Nikos growled. "I can't believe you came back—"

"I can't believe you never left."

"Whatever you're up to, you won't get away with it. Crew are on their way and a dozen military robots. They'll shoot to kill. You have no choice but to surrender."

"Surrender, father?" There was scorn in Shadow's voice. "Didn't you try this once before, when I took the bridge of your precious ship? I didn't surrender then. Why would I surrender now?"

"Whatever you think you're doing, it won't work," the Captain snarled. "We don't even *need* the main reactor to power our new weapons or to maneuver around the planet."

Silence for a moment. "You really don't get it, do you, Father," Shadow said. "You really don't understand how much I hate you."

"I'm your father!"

"*That's why I hate you!*" Lorn's eyes widened at the naked pain in Shadow's voice. He'd never heard her sound so exposed. "I loved you. I loved you as much as any little girl could ever love her Daddy. And you betrayed me. You betrayed all of us. You lied. You would have kept us from ever finding a planet. You would have killed millions. Just to keep your precious power. I loved you, *and you weren't worthy of it!*"

Lorn shot Kiri a look; she was staring at him, wide-eyed.

"Cynthia…" Now Shadow's pain had an echo in her father's voice. "It wasn't for me. It was for you. I wanted you to take my place. I wanted you to—"

"To become a tyrant? What kind of dream is *that* for a father to have for his daughter?"

"But it's all different now, Cynthia," Nikos said. "Earth has found us again. We can go home—"

"Earth isn't my home, Father, it's yours. It's never been my home. *Peregrine* is my world now. And you're on the wrong side—again. Just like you were on *Mayflower II*. The Loyalists plan to use your precious ship to enforce their control over Peregrine and to fight the rebels when they arrive. Millions will die because of you. And you don't care. Again. You don't care about anyone except yourself. Especially me."

"Cynthia!" The word sounded half-strangled. "The strike force is almost there. You have to surrender. You have to surrender, or they'll kill you. They're Loyalists. *I can't stop them.*"

"I can, Father," Shadow said. "I can stop them—and I can stop you." A pause, then, "Sorry for the interruption, Lorn. Launching."

Acceleration slammed Lorn into his seat, making Kiri

groan, choking off his voice just as he started to say, "Wait, Shadow…"

The blank screens in front of them lit. The curving horizon of Peregrine's blue, green, and white sphere filled one. The other showed *Mayflower II*, dwindling behind them.

Lorn found his breath again as the acceleration eased. "Shadow!" he cried. "Get out of there!"

"I'm not going anywhere," Shadow said. Already her transmission crackled with increasing distance. "I promised I'd take *Mayflower II* out of the equation. It won't be supporting the robot attacks below. It won't be supporting *Falcon's Egg* when the Loyalist forces arrive."

"But your father said disabling the reactor won't accomplish anything!" Lorn said.

"It wouldn't. But disabling it was never my plan." A pause. "The strike force is outside," she said. "Time to end this. Goodbye, Lorn."

"Shadow—" Lorn began—and then gasped and flung a hand over his eyes as *Mayflower II*, shrunk to the size of a toy in the vidscreen, vanished in an eye-searing blaze of light. The vidscreen darkened automatically, and Lorn lowered his arm to see, where the giant starship had been a moment before, a sphere of expanding gas and debris, a star-bright glowing ball at its centre, dwindling behind them.

Chapter Eighteen

THE ACCELERATION STOPPED, leaving them weightless again. Lorn stared at the viewscreen as, over the next few minutes, the burning heart of Mayflower II fell below the limb of the planet. Shadow had just killed hundreds of people, with no warning, with no opportunity to escape. She'd killed herself. She'd killed her father. She'd killed Art Stoddard's parents, and who knew how many others who had only stayed aboard *Mayflower II* because they thought they were too old to start a new life on a new world.

More killing, all in a good cause. Always in a good cause.

His eyes burning from more than the light of the explosion, he looked at Kiri. Her face was pale. "I never thought—" she whispered.

"I should have," Lorn said. He heard his voice shaking, but he couldn't seem to stop it. "I should have known the minute the original plan fell through. She came within seconds of launching the matter/antimatter missiles at Peregrine seven years ago when it looked like the Skywatchers would attack. She shot Art Stoddard when he tried to stop her. She's been singleminded in her defense of the refugees in the Annex. You heard her talking to Art back in the cabin. She was close to starting a terror campaign in Bagnell. She's always known what she wants to accomplish, and she's always been willing to kill." He looked down at his trembling hands and clenched them into fists. "God help me, I used to admire her for it. I blamed her for shooting Art, but I looked up to her. I wanted to be like her." The image of the pregnant woman he'd shot flickered through his mind. *And I guess I got there. Killing without thought...just like my hero.* "But look what she's just done...and for what?" He glanced at Kiri again. "Has she accomplished anything?"

"It's a huge blow to Captain Almaida," Kiri said. "But as long as *Falcon's Egg* remains intact, it won't stop her from seizing the planet with her robots. She'll do anything to take control and use Peregrine in her fight against ELF. She'll fight to the death."

"Then it's still up to us to put an end to the killing," Lorn said. "If we can."

Kiri swallowed. "I don't know...how much help I can be."

Lorn suddenly remembered the docbot. "Let's find out." He slipped out of the pilot's chair, floated over to Kiri, and helped free her from her own seat, then guided her back to the alcove he'd seen as they entered. There was a friendly green button on the bulkhead beside it: he pressed it.

"Welcome to the Emergency Automated Medical Treatment Device," said a male voice. "Please remove all clothing from the patient and place the patient in the examination compartment."

Kiri gave him a weak smile. "You just want to see me naked again."

"As often as possible," Lorn said, and then, gently as he could, helped her strip. The wound on her arm was long but not deep and at least partially closed, although fresh blood welled up as he helped her into the docbot's compartment.

"Microgravity conditions detected," said the voice. "Please secure patient to bed using a restraint that will not interfere with the treatment of any wounds."

That was easy: Lorn put a belly strap across her.

"To activate examination and treatment, pull down hatch," the voice said.

Lorn reached up and tugged the gull-wing door of the alcove closed. Green lights flashed.

"Multiple muscle strains and minor bruising detected. No treatment required. Minor fracture of the left humerus detected. Forearm laceration detected. No immediate treatment available for humerus fracture. Recommend immobilizing limb for six weeks. Administering pain medication. Cleaning laceration. Sealing skin. Treatment complete."

And just like that, the docbot opened.

The wound on Kiri's arm was now a long pink scar, glistening with some kind of wound-glue. Behind it, the flesh was mottled green and blue from bruising. "Pain medication is a wonderful thing," Kiri said. "I feel almost human again." She shivered. "A cold human. Help me get dressed."

Together, they managed to get her back into her clothes, though she cut off the sleeves, leaving her arms bare: one sleeve because it was bloody, she explained, and the other because otherwise, "I'd look like a dork."

When she was done, she gave Lorn a bright smile. "Your turn. Get naked for me."

Sighing, Lorn stripped and slipped inside the docbot. Kiri closed the hatch.

"Multiple muscle strains and minor bruising detected. No treatment required," the docbot said promptly, as it had for

Kiri. Then, "Foreign body detected in left buttock. Recommend removal. Proceed?"

Left buttock?

"Proceed," he heard Kiri say from outside the docbot. It sounded suspiciously like she was laughing.

"Please rotate to present buttocks to manipulator arms," said the docbot, and Lorn complied, though it did cross his mind that if there was one phrase he could have gone a lifetime without hearing, it was that one.

Something cold sprayed his left butt cheek. "Local anesthetic applied." He felt pressure that didn't quite rise to the level of pain, then there was another hiss, something slapped his rear, and that was that. "Object removed."

The door opened, and he pulled himself out gingerly. He tried to turn to see his own rear, but of course, that didn't work. Kiri was not quite smirking at him. "Oh, shut up," he said, and got dressed.

Together they returned to the pilot's and copilot's seats. Kiri gasped once as she strapped herself in one-handed. "Good painkillers," she said when he glanced at her. Her face had paled again. "But nothing's perfect."

There was nothing Lorn could do to help her, so he turned his attention to the control panel. "We're on a pre-set course to a landing somewhere near *Falcon's Egg*," he said, pointing to a display that showed their ultimate destination in Margaret's Land. "There's no way we'll be sneaking up on them. They'll be waiting for us."

Kiri nodded. "Maybe we can use that. How long do we have?"

Lorn studied the readouts, trying to make sense of them. "Looks like...maybe three-quarters of an hour? We're already descending."

"Good thing, considering there's a giant debris field we'd smack right into if we stayed in the same orbit," Kiri said. "Go to the back and check the lockers. This vessel may be ancient, but if this is like every other escape pod I've ever seen, they'll be there."

"What will?"

"Bailout suits. In case the pod is too damaged to land safely."

"Bailout...oh!" Lorn slipped up out of his seat, then pulled himself to the back and opened each of the eight lockers he found there in turn. "You're right," he called. "They're here." He returned to his seat. "You'll have a hell of a time using one of those with that arm," he said doubtfully.

"Completely impossible," she agreed. "So I'm staying on board, and *you're* bailing out."

He frowned. "Kiri—"

"They don't know how many of us are on board," Kiri said. "And I know their sensor protocols. They're not going to detect a single man in a bailout suit, at least not unless someone actually sees the chute. Their attention will be focused on the big vehicle landing close to the compound. When the door opens, they'll find me...and I already have a history with *Falcon's Egg*. They'll know *Mayflower II* has exploded—couldn't exactly miss that—and figure I had something to do with it. They'll take me to the ship."

"As a prisoner," Lorn said.

"That's where you come in. You have to rescue me. Then together we'll take out the main computer. That'll kill the ship and the robot army. When ELF *finally* arrives," a hint of bitterness touched her voice, "Almaida will have no choice but to surrender."

"Take out the main computer *how*, exactly?"

Kiri touched her chest. "Computer expert, remember?"

"And precisely how am I going to rescue you without a working firearm between us?" Lorn demanded.

"Can't do anything about ammo," Kiri said, "but you should have full laser power again by now. So should I."

"What?" Lorn snatched out his sidearm and stared at it. Sure enough, the power indicator glowed green. "I thought we'd have to change the battery packs."

"No battery packs. Radioisotope generator," Kiri said. "We have made a *few* improvements in the centuries since your SSIN sidearms were designed. They couldn't keep up with the draw we were putting on them while we fought our way through the Core, but they've had plenty of time to recharge since. With both yours and mine, you should have enough fire-power for what is, need I remind you, a stealth attack, not a frontal assault." She took a deep, shaking breath. Lorn wondered if the painkillers were already wearing off. *They're probably decades old*, he thought. *It's a wonder they worked at all.* "You'd better get suited up," she continued. "If these suits work like most, once you're in it and it's powered up, you'll have the option to jump anytime within a set window. Wait too long, and you're stuck. So don't delay too long—but still, put it off as long as possible. The lower you are when you jump, the less risk there is you'll be spotted from the ground."

Lorn looked up at the screen showing the planet. He recognized the ocean below. The terminator was halfway across it. "One bit of luck," he said. "We're coming down in the dark."

"Good. We need all the luck we can get."

Lorn hesitated, then leaned over and gave her a kiss, long and hard. "That's for even more luck," he said as he drew back. *And love?* he wondered. It seemed too much to hope for. He could barely live with himself. How could he hope that anyone else would want to live with him? Especially not someone like Kiri. Even though she'd returned the kiss enthusiastically enough, he couldn't bring himself to believe that they had any future together. Once the mission was over, she'd be heading off on her next, and he'd be left behind, with only his memories for company...a horrifying thought.

Well, look at the bright side, he thought. *There's a good chance you won't survive the next few hours.*

"Hold on," she said. "We're about to start decelerating."

Rockets fired, and they were pressed down into the seats. For the next few minutes, the ship shook like it wanted to tear itself apart. Lorn held on and hoped whatever the ancient pod used as a heatshield didn't have any holes in it.

Apparently, it didn't. The flight smoothed out. Deceleration eased. They were flying, and he had weight again.

"Go," Kiri said. "Suit up. See you at *Falcon's Egg*."

He nodded. "First things first," he said and put his hands at her belt.

"I don't think I'm up for *that*," she said, her mouth twitching.

Lorn laughed and undid her belt. He drew it off of her, readjusted the holstered gun, and then buckled it onto his own waist so that a sidearm hung at each hip. He kissed her again, almost desperately, wishing he could read her mind to find out how she really felt about him, then moved to the back of the pod.

He climbed into the bailout suit, a full-pressure suit like a spacesuit, only less bulky. It had a kind of utility belt with pouches on it—survival supplies, he supposed. *Might be useful,* he thought. He remembered the jungle of Margaret's Land. *Will* definitely *be useful if I land too far away,* he amended. The chute was built into the back of the suit. A red handle dangled on the front of the suit, bearing a tag that read EMERGENCY CHUTE RELEASE.

As he sealed the helmet, a female voice spoke to him. For a

second, he thought it was Kiri on the radio. "Welcome to the Sub-Orbital Life Preserver Mark II," it said. "Please tell me your name."

"Um...Lorn," Lorn said.

"Welcome, Umlorn," said the voice. Lorn opened his mouth to protest, then closed it again. He wasn't going to get into an argument with a talking pressure suit.

"According to vehicle sensors, the current altitude is 45,124 metres. The bailout window is between 40,000 and 1,000 metres. Rate of descent is currently 52.6 metres per second. Please select an altitude for bailout."

"One thousand metres," Lorn said.

The voice was computer-generated, of course, but he still thought he detected a hint of disapproval as it said, "Please confirm, Umlorn. Minimum-altitude bailouts are inherently more dangerous than mid-altitude bailouts. Recommended range for bailouts is between 20,000 and 3,000 metres."

"One thousand metres," Lorn said again.

"One thousand metres confirmed, Umlorn." said the voice. He almost expected a resigned sigh. "Current altitude 43,523 metres. Rate of descent is currently 51.2 metres per second. Please enter the belly escape hatch and lie face down, Umlorn."

Lorn turned his head and looked to where Kiri still sat in her acceleration couch. She had twisted her own head around to see him. He gave her a wave and a thumbs-up. She smiled weakly. Then he knelt and opened the escape hatch in the floor, revealing a space disturbingly coffin-sized. He prostrated himself inside it. The hatch closed automatically above him. "Inner hatch sealed," said the voice. "Awaiting designated altitude."

The minutes crawled by, the computer counting down the altitude and the rate of descent, which remained at around 50 metres per second until they were under 10,000 metres. Then it slowed. That just dragged out the rest of the wait. Lorn listened to the computer's voice, the rasp of his own breath, and the thudding of his heart. His faceplate pressed into foam padding, he could see nothing.

The end, when it came, was sudden. "Fifteen hundred metres," said the voice. "Stand by for bailout. Fourteen hundred...thirteen hundred...twelve hundred...eleven hundred...bailout!"

The outside hatch exploded outward, and Lorn dropped into darkness, tumbling as the wind caught him, catching a glimpse overhead of the glowing form of the stubby delta-winged escape pod as it glided on toward its preprogrammed landing spot.

The suit stabilized. Off to his left, the descending shuttle suddenly appeared again, lit up by powerful searchlights from the ground. He wasn't far from the *Falcon's Egg* compound, then. He took note of the direction: a little north of west. Once he was on the ground, there'd be no landmarks.

Not that he'd need any if he were nothing but a small and exceedingly messy crater on the jungle floor. Where the hell was the chute?

He flinched as an alarm squealed in the helmet. "Suit malfunction!" shouted the voice. "Initiate manual chute release!"

"Shit!" Lorn said. He scrabbled with his gloved hands for the red metal handle he'd seen earlier. He couldn't grab it.

"Approaching minimum safe chute release," said the voice. "Initiate manual chute release immediately!"

Finally, he had it. He pulled. It was stuck.

"Minimum chute release altitude!" said the voice, and he pulled as hard as he could.

He felt the chute burst from his backpack, stream upward. A mighty jerk tore the breath from his body.

Five seconds later, he slammed into the jungle canopy.

Branches splintered, would have shredded him to hamburger if not for the bailout suit. One limb smacked his helmet so hard his ears rang and the faceplate starred, but it didn't break.

And then he thudded into soft ground. A moment later, the folds of the chute dropped onto him.

Feeling like a bacterium fighting a white blood cell, he struggled free of the material and finally staggered to his feet. He ached in several places, but nothing seemed to be broken...something of a miracle, he thought, looking up at the patch of sky overhead. He blinked as a bright burning light crossed it. The core of *Mayflower II*, it had to be. He wondered how long it would continue to burn. *She called herself Shadow,* he thought, *but she went out in a blaze of light.*

A blaze of light and an orgy of death.

The point of light vanished, and Lorn turned his attention back to the tasks at hand. He stripped out of the pressure suit, then went through the pouches of its utility belt. A thin, strong rope. A knife, an axe. A pocket tent, a water-purifying bottle, a lighter, a compass. About what he'd expect. The belt couldn't be tightened enough to stay on his waist when he wasn't wearing the suit; instead, he slung it crossways over one shoulder.

He kept the compass in his hand. Its internal computer had presumably already calculated the local magnetic field and correlated it to the planet's poles. He sure hoped it had because otherwise he could be setting off in a completely random direction...and Kiri would be waiting a very long time for her rescue.

"That way," he said out loud. He peered into the darkness.

He could see nothing. "I hope," he added under his breath, and plunged ahead.

The jungles of Margaret's Land, he remembered very well, merely dangerous by day, could be deadly at night, when the really big predators hunted beneath the trees. But tonight, the jungle seemed strangely silent. *The screaming descent of the escape pod must have driven the animals into hiding,* he thought.

That was one possibility: the other was that the top predators among these tangled and twisted trees were no longer dragonbears and spidertigers, but the killer robots of *Falcon's Egg.* *At least I'm not still carrying that damn nanotracker,* he thought, and reflexively rubbed his left buttock. It didn't ache so much as itch.

For whatever reason, no ravening monsters immediately burst out of the undergrowth to savage him. Even better, no killer robots sliced him in half, stitched him full of bloody holes, or blew him into red mist. *So far, so good,* he thought.

An hour after he landed, light glimmered ahead of him through the thinning trees. Pocketing the compass, he slowed his approach, eventually dropping to his hands and knees and finally crawling on his belly to peer over the top of the ridge overlooking the *Falcon's Egg* landing site.

There stood the fat black ovoid of the starship as before. But far fewer robots bustled around it than before. *Busy elsewhere,* he thought. Some of them were probably on the far side of the planet, wreaking what havoc he could only guess at. And others...

There. Just coming into the clearing. Half a dozen killerbots, escorting a small contingent of actual humans, carrying a stretcher. *Kiri!*

He studied the terrain between him and the ship. Enough trees dotted the downward slope that he could descend it without being seen. But beyond those trees, a good two hundred metres of open space gaped between the bottom of the ridge and *Falcon's Egg* itself: open space into which the robots that had escorted the humans into and out of the forest now spread out to patrol.

The ship's main hatch remained open. An empty automated cargo sled rumbled out of it and rolled toward one of the outbuildings, even as a second sled appeared from the building and rolled toward the ship. Boxes and barrels burdened the second sled. *They're stocking up*, he thought. *Loading water and biomass. They're planning to launch soon.*

Well, *he* was biomass. And he thought he'd just discovered a way to get on the ship.

He headed down the slope.

It took him another hour to reach the closest cover to the outbuilding. The cargo sleds continued entering and emerging from it at regular intervals. Dull brown siding that looked to be made of compressed plant materials covered the two-story structure. It had big doors on three sides, two of which were closed: the sleds rolled in and out of the third, on the side opposite him. Facing the forest—and him—two ordinary human-sized doors, painted red, glowed beneath lights.

He took a deep breath, then dashed across the open space, choosing the rightmost door at random and pressing his back to the wall beside it, outside the pool of illumination from the light above it. He looked left and right. Nothing moved. He stepped into the light, feeling horribly exposed, and tried the door: it wasn't locked. He ducked inside.

He'd thought it would be a warehouse of some kind. Instead, it looked more like the head of a mineshaft. He stood in shadow on a walkway that encircled the building, interrupted by the doors. A ladder to his right led up to a second walkway, higher up, which ran around the building above the doors and from which cranes extended. They didn't seem to be in use.

The main floor of the building, brightly lit, was taken up by two elevator platforms, one currently level with the building floor, one out of sight somewhere down the shaft, in which he could see nothing but metal walls and the beginning of a string of lights. An empty cargo sled skirted the open shaft and rolled onto the raised platform, which immediately started sinking. As it did so, the other platform rose up through the exposed shaft, bearing a loaded sled. The moment the platform reached the top of the shaft, the sled rolled away.

He'd known much of the infrastructure of the compound was underground: he and Kiri had entered the ship from down there. Apparently, the Loyalists had even built their warehouses beneath the surface. But he saw no humans: if any were supervising the loading, they were on the lower level.

He stayed in the shadows of the walkway until the next loaded sled had almost reached the surface. Then he leaped over the side and dashed across the brightly lit floor.

There wasn't room for him among the tightly packed bits of cargo, but with a grunt, he pushed a barrel off the sled. It thumped to the floor, toppled, and rolled away. He crouched in the space it had left as the sled began to move. The people below—if there were people below—would, he hoped, simply think the barrel had been stowed badly and put it on the next sled.

He still didn't know what the barrel had contained. Water? Oil? Dill pickles? The crates, too, were unlabeled. Food seemed the most likely, but he didn't know why it was coming up from underground.

It didn't matter. What mattered was finding Kiri...and disabling *Falcon's Egg*'s computer, cutting off the head of the killer robot horde.

As for why the ship was preparing to launch, that no doubt related to the destruction of *Mayflower II*. Without the ancient starship available to provide orbital support, Captain Almaida must have decided to risk her flagship instead. She needed to control the high ground: Peregrine had enough of an in-system space presence to pose a threat to her automated armies otherwise. And once the local defenses were overwhelmed, she could set down her seedship somewhere closer to civilization and resume churning out robots.

The sled had left the outbuilding, and Lorn suddenly felt horribly exposed. He scrunched down in the space left by the barrel, his back to a stack of crates that hid him from the starship itself—but not from the robots patrolling the clearing.

None were close, but he could see two off in the distance—and the moment he emerged into the open, they started toward the sled. Either they had really good pattern recognition algorithms and knew he was neither barrel- nor box-shaped, or they inspected all sleds as a matter of course. Either way...

He pulled the pistol from his right hip, checked the power meter. Still fully charged. But the ground was uneven and the distance too great. He couldn't hope to hit either robot at that distance.

He wasn't sure they couldn't hit *him*.

But they didn't fire. Perhaps there was a security protocol that prevented them from damaging cargo unless absolutely necessary, and they still weren't sure there was a problem. Or perhaps, like the first of their kind he, along with the unfortunate Ekwansi, had encountered on the ridge above *Falcon's Egg*, they were programmed to capture intruders, only firing if fired upon. Which, if true, made him doubly glad he hadn't risked a shot.

He couldn't see how close he was to the ship. And he had to presume the robots had at least warned someone on board

Falcon's Egg about something strange on the sled. He tensed. The sled would have to ride up the loading ramp to reach the hatch. He'd have to time it right...

The sled sloped up. He waited until his view of the ship's curving black hull, towering above him, was cut off by the top edge of the hatch...and then hurled himself to one side, rolling over onto his stomach, weapon out. He had one quick glimpse of the startled brown face of a crewman, then fired, the shot going wide but slicing across as he adjusted downward. The front of the man's tunic smoked as the laser sliced through his chest, and he fell with a horrible gurgling sound. Lorn was up and running an instant later, scanning the hold for any other humans, but there were only robots, which ignored him and the corpse, simply setting to work immediately unloading the sled, the barrels going into one elevator, the crates into another, all of them whisked away without any human intervention at all.

But that didn't mean humans weren't on the way. He remembered the Marines who had tried to stop *Ninshubur's* escape.

He had to find Kiri. And free her. And not get either of them killed in the process.

He remembered Kiri using a stolen ID card to move around the ship before. He searched the body of the young man he'd killed, whose dead eyes stared up at him. For a long moment, Lorn stared back. He'd killed again, without thinking, acting by instinct, acting as he'd been programmed to do by the SSIN...

Acting like a robot.

Was he really any different?

I don't have time for this. But he still delayed long enough to close the dead man's eyelids before pulling the ID card from the lanyard around his neck. He dashed to the personnel elevator, likely the same one he and Kiri had been in before. He swiped the card on the reader by the door as he remembered her doing, and the door slid obediently open.

But where to go?

How smart was the elevator?

"Deck guide please," he said.

"Please restate query," said the elevator.

"Um...please tell me what is located on each deck of the ship."

"Decks 25 through 20 are cargo holds and handling facilities," the elevator said. "Deck 19, power systems and engine room access. Deck 18, brig and sickbay. Deck 17—'

"Stop," Lorn said. "Deck 18, please."

"Ascending," said the elevator.

The ride lasted just long enough that Lorn expected at every instant it would be cut short as someone realized they had an intruder—and where he was. He held the sidearm ready. But the elevator halted, and the door opened without incident.

It revealed a circular room with three men and a woman in it, engaged in intense conversation. "She's lying," the woman was saying. "ELF isn't coming, or its ships would be here by now."

"What if she's not?" a man responded. "Without *Mayflower II*, we can't—"

"Hands up," Lorn shouted, stepping into the room.

All four were armed. All went for their weapons. All died as Lorn sliced his laser through them, filling the room with gray smoke and the smell of burnt meat. Swallowing hard, hands shaking, he stepped over the corpses. He'd think about what he'd just done later. He had to find Kiri.

She wasn't in one of the brig cells surrounding the central desk. She lay in the sickbay, down a short corridor through another door, strapped to a bed, still wearing what she'd worn on the shuttle. Her sleeveless left arm had been properly bandaged and splinted, and as Lorn entered, a man wearing a pale green lab coat leaned toward her, a hypospray in his right hand, as she struggled against the restraints. "It's just a painkiller and sedative," he was saying soothingly. "It will help you sleep..."

Lorn clubbed him with the hilt of his pistol. He dropped bonelessly to the ground. "So will that," Lorn growled. He undid the restraints and helped Kiri sit up. "Easier to find you than I thought," he said. "Where *is* everybody?"

"Just a skeleton crew here, preparing for launch," Kiri said. She sounded almost like herself again. "The rest are across the sea in shuttles, supervising the attack. I heard them talking. There's fighting in Bagnell. Some other city I'd never heard of has already been taken...Fortuna, I think. They said something about heavy casualties."

Lorn felt sick. "It's a port city. I know people there." More death. More destruction. "This has to stop. *We* have to stop it."

"We will." Kiri got to her feet. She swayed a little, grabbing Lorn's arm for support for an instant, then straightening. "I'm all right," she insisted in response to his concerned look. "But I need my shoes." She pointed to a locker next to the door. "They're in there."

Lorn got them, brought them to her. Rather than putting them on, she held them up and turned them over. "Marines could be here any minute—" Lorn warned.

"This is important." Kiri tugged at the tip of one of her shoelaces. It pulled free. She held it up. "Detonator," she said and stuck it firmly into a small opening in the heel. She tapped the black rubbery material with her finger. "Explosive." She did the same with the other boot. Only then did she tug on the footwear.

Lorn stared at her. "You're kidding me. You wear *shoe-bombs?*"

She nodded. "ELF field operatives wear these as a matter of course. It's a deep, dark secret, of course. The explosive is completely inert—and undetectable—until the detonator is inserted. Even then, they can't be set off by accident. It takes a sharp shock."

"How sharp?" Lorn said.

She smiled a little. "Well, I can't just click my heels together," she said. "We're talking a hammer blow or a gunshot. Or high heat: a laser would do it. You can set off both together a little easier: smashing them together as hard as I can would probably do it."

Lorn stared at her. "They're a suicide weapon?"

"Not if I can help it," Kiri said fervently. "But I definitely plan to 'boot' the main computer."

Lorn winced. "I can't believe you said that."

Kiri laughed. "I can't either. Now let's go. *Not* the way you came."

"No," Lorn said, remembering the corpses he had left behind. "Not that way." He didn't want Kiri to see what he had done.

Kiri raised an eyebrow at that but didn't ask any questions. She bent down and pulled the ID card from the unconscious medic, then led Lorn to the far side of the sickbay, empty of other patients, to a second elevator. She swiped the stolen card across its touchplate. It opened.

"Deck 2," she said, then glanced at Lorn. "Computer core. And it's unlikely to be empty. Got my gun?"

He handed it to her.

"Here goes nothing," she said, and together they turned to await the opening of the elevator door.

Chapter Nineteen

LORN HAD HALF A SECOND, staring at the empty corridor the elevator door revealed once they'd stopped rising, to think, *That was easier than I thought*, before Kiri began firing. Sparks and drops of molten metal spattered as her laser sliced through the walls in six precisely spaced points. Then she stepped out of the elevator. He followed, and the door closed behind them.

He stared at the holes she'd drilled. "Security systems?"

She nodded. "Cameras...and lasers."

"You trained for this."

"Among other scenarios, yes," Kiri said. "Needing to attack the main computer core has always been one of the higher-probability scenarios. But that was the easy part. Come on."

She led him down the smoke-shrouded corridor to the next, still tightly sealed, door. "Right about now," she said, taking a position to one side of the door and motioning him to take up a matching position on the other, "someone in there is realizing that all of their security cams just went dead in the hallway. Which means—"

The door opened. An annoyed looking woman stepped into

the hallway. Her eyes just had time to widen as she took in the drifting smoke before Kiri had grabbed her arm and thrown her hard against the wall. As she fell, Kiri was already through the hatch, Lorn right behind her.

The room beyond, circular, with a dome-like ceiling and strange pearlescent walls broken only by the door they'd come through and another opposite it, was unoccupied. No killing, Lorn thought with relief.

"Lucked out," Kiri said. She went back into the hall, where the woman was just rolling over, groaning. Kiri grabbed her and hauled her to her feet.

The woman, short and rather heavyset, blinked unfocused eyes at her. "Kiri Ishida? I don't—I heard you—"

"Couldn't stay away, Meredith," Kiri said. "Sorry about throwing you into the wall." She took the woman by the hand and led her into the room beyond.

Lorn closed the door behind them. "This is the main computer control?" he said, staring around the empty room, with its shimmering white curving roof.

"It's a holographic interface," Kiri said. "Oddly enough, my access has been cancelled. Fortunately, we're taking a more brute-force approach." She pulled Meredith across to the door on the far side of the room. "We still need to get through this door, though. Hold out your hand, Merry."

Meredith still seemed stunned. A trickle of blood had run down the side of her head from beneath her hair; she'd hit the wall harder than Lorn had thought. "What...? No, I'll..."

But Kiri had already pushed her palm against the plate to the right of the door. The door slid open...

...and at the same instant, so did the outer one.

Lorn didn't consciously recognize the sound, but his subconscious, on high alert, threw him to one side and brought him rolling up with his weapon ready. His laser sliced through the throat of the lone Marine in the doorway, but the Marine's slug-thrower had already erupted in a burst of flame and thunder.

As the Marine crumpled, Lorn scrambled up and turned toward the inner door. Meredith lay crumpled in a spreading pool of scarlet, her back a bloody ruin, the door trying to close on her body, opening and half-closing over and over and over.

"Kiri!" Lorn cried. He leaped over the corpse into the room beyond.

It wasn't much to look at: perfectly square, with four silvery pillars stretching from floor to ceiling set in a quadrangle in the middle. In the center of those rose a round column about a metre tall, whose flat top contained a glass panel, glowing green. Kiri sat with her back against it, face white, clutching her side, blood oozing between her fingers and pooling on the white metal floor. Lorn dropped to his knees beside her. "How bad is it?"

"Bad," Kiri said weakly.

He was already pulling the survival belt off his shoulder, opening the first aid compartment. The packaging was strange, and who knew how old the product was, but he found what he expected to find: sealed pouches containing quick-coagulation dressings. He ripped one open, pressed it to the wound. "We'll find the infirmary," Lorn said. "That doctor that treated you before...I'll make him..."

"No time," Kiri said. "More Marines will be here any second. You have to get out of here."

"No," Lorn said. "I'm not going to leave you."

"Yes, you are," Kiri said. "Or you'll die, too."

"They can only get in here one at a time. I can—"

"That's not what I mean." Kiri locked eyes on his. "Lorn, I lied. The explosives *are* a suicide weapon. They always have been. You were right. The only way to kill this ship is to blow myself up. But not you. You have to get out of here."

He stared at her. "No," he said.

"Lorn, it's the only way—"

"No!" the word burst out of him with the force of a bullet. "Too many people have died. I won't let you be one of them."

"You have to!" Kiri said. "Lorn, if I don't do this, then everything else that has happened has been for nothing. All the people who have already died...not just here, but across the galaxy. *Including my brother.* If Peregrine falls to the Loyalists, if they can secure it, use it to strike back...Lorn, my life doesn't mean anything with stakes like that. You have to let me—"

"Your life means something to *me*," Lorn said. "It means everything to me."

"More than your whole planet?" Kiri said. "More than your parents? Your little sister?"

"I'm not making that choice," Lorn said. "I'm not." He turned suddenly, sitting on her legs, pulling off her boots.

"Lorn, no!" She struck at him with her one good arm, but he hardly felt it. He had the boots off now. He got up then and spun toward her, holding them. "You have to let me do this!" she cried.

"No, I don't," Lorn said. "You're so willing to die for the cause, Kiri. Maybe too willing." He looked down at the boots. "These...these are *crazy*. And I know crazy. You brought me back from the edge of crazy on the journey to Earth. You told me I needed to live to save my planet. And you were right. But guess what? You need to live, too. You need to live to save *me*." His voice broke. "Kiri, you've been running your whole life, running from what happened on your planet, running from what happened to your brother, running away from all that... and running toward death, trying to be a hero. But you don't have to. There's got to be another way."

Kiri's face was contorted with fury and pain. "There is no other way," she snarled. "You fucking idiot, you're condemning your whole planet to destruction. And why? Because you fancy yourself in love with me? *What makes you think I love you?* I've had a dozen men. You're just one more."

Lorn let the barb slide past. "Find another way, Kiri," he said.

"The explosives can't be detonated by remote control," she said. "They need a sharp shock."

"Or a laser," Lorn said in sudden inspiration. He looked down at the boots. "*Or a laser*, Kiri."

"So fucking what?" she said. "How does that help?"

"The hallway had lasers in the walls, you said." He looked around the walls of the small chamber. "What about in here? If we'd broken through that door without using Meredith's palm-print...?"

"We would have been sliced apart," Kiri said. Then her eyes widened. "Oh!"

"The lasers react to movement?"

She nodded.

"Then I think I know how to do it," Lorn said. "But first I've got to get you out of here."

He moved her as gently as he could, but even so, she was white and trembling with shock when at last, he had her in the outer room. "Prop me up against the wall," she said weakly. "With a view of the door. In case another Marine shows up."

He nodded and left her there, sidearm in hand, while he went back into the main computer control.

His idea was simple. Once they sealed the door, the security systems would activate. After that, any movement would draw laser fire. So he tied the laces of the explosive-laden boots together and laid them across the top of the control console. Then he took a length of cord from one of the survival pouches, and after testing it to make sure it would burn satisfactorily, tied it in with the laces as a kind of fuse. He dangled the end down the side of the console. It would burn up to the laces, burn them through, and drop the boots, waking the security system. And when the lasers hit those boots...

He went to the door. "No visitors?" he asked Kiri.

"No," she said faintly. "They haven't twigged to what's going on yet."

"Then we've got a chance." He pulled her to her feet, slung her arm over his shoulder. "Ready?"

"This is crazy," she murmured. "You should have let me..." Her eyes fluttered.

"Hey!" he said sharply. "No fainting, or we're both dead."

She gulped and nodded. "I'll do my best."

"All I can ask," he said. He turned to the open door. "Here we go." He drew his laser, fired. He deliberately undershot, since overshooting it would be way worse, and traced the bright light of the laser mark up the console until the end of the cord suddenly flared with a flame that began climbing toward the shoes. Then he slapped the panel with his highly unauthorized palm, causing the door to slam shut, turned, and headed for the exit, Kiri dragging on him but managing to keep her feet moving.

They made it into the elevator, the ID from the doctor still letting them order it down. They reached the cargo bay. The door opened.

Four killerbots waited at the entrance to the cargo bay. They spun toward Kiri and Lorn, weapons barrels lifting...

From somewhere above and behind them came a muffled WHUMP. Air exploded out of the elevator shaft with enough force to drive both of them forward a few stumbling steps. When they straightened and faced the robots again, Lorn saw they no longer had anything to fear from them: they were frozen in place, inert lumps of metal.

The same couldn't be said for the Marines presumably rushing to the site of the explosion high above. They had to get out of there.

Together they stumbled into the clearing. The compound was devoid of humans, and all the robots were frozen in place. But it seemed to take forever at their halting pace to cross the open space. Kiri was barely conscious, her wound bleeding again, red soaking through her torn uniform. Halfway across, he stopped, picked her up, and, cradling her like a child, her blood spreading warm against his skin through his shirt, staggered the rest of the way.

A little way in among the trees stood an outcropping of rock: he rounded it, and then dropped to his knees, panting. Only then did he turn to look behind him, peering around the corner of the rocks. Marines had appeared in the door of the cargo bay. Binoculars glinted; men pointed. They must have seen him and Kiri enter the forest. They'd have them in minutes, and he could go no farther—not carrying Kiri, and there was no way he was leaving her. Not then, not ever.

The ship looked the same as always: the explosion that had destroyed the central computer had had no visible effect. No smoke rose from it; no holes had been blown in its sleek hull. *It still has its weapons,* he thought uneasily. *They could still launch, still destroy Bagnell...*

The formation of spaceplanes appeared overhead with no warning, outrunning the trailing shriek of their engines, which followed seconds later. Thick white energy beams reached down from them, raced across the compound, turned the running Marines into flailing human torches, and then sliced through the black hull of the seed ship.

Lorn guessed what was coming and threw himself to the

ground behind the rocks, pressing Kiri into the ground beneath him.

An enormous blast tore through the forest, uprooting trees, showering him with dirt. A massive chunk of metal the size of an aircar slammed to the ground not twenty metres away. The sound of falling debris pattered through the forest for several more seconds, but nothing else fell as close. Gasping, Lorn crawled to the edge of the rocks and looked back into the compound.

Falcon's Egg was a shattered hulk, smoke and flame pouring from the wreckage. The buildings of the compound had been flattened. Nothing living moved. Nothing living could have survived. Every human being that had been in *Falcon's Egg* was dead. The ship had become a funeral pyre.

So much killing, Lorn thought. *So many people have died.* The thought was a knot in his stomach.

But then he looked down at Kiri, and the knot loosened. *But not you.*

The spaceplanes had returned. They roared triumphantly as they set down in the clearing. Lorn took a deep breath, then staggered to his feet and ran to get help.

Epilogue

LORN STOOD with his hands on the handles of Kiri's wheel-chair, looking out the window of a posh boardroom atop one of the multi-story towers encircling the Bagnell spaceport at the bustle far below. There were more vessels down there than the field had ever seen, sleek spacecraft from the ELF fleet that had arrived in orbit even as he and Kiri had been fighting their way into *Falcon's Egg*.

Everything we did...breaking into Falcon's Egg, *destroying the computer core...it was all unnecessary,* he thought. Killing the computer had allowed them time to escape, but that was all it had done. The ELF spaceplanes would have killed it just as dead minutes later.

What *Shadow* had done, though...they'd learned, since returning to Bagnell, that *Mayflower II* had been fully opera-tional except for its drive systems. It would have been an impregnable orbital defense station, able to withstand anything the ELF force had brought to the system. Had it not been destroyed, Peregrine would have fallen to Almaida's robot army.

As it was, smoke still rose here and there around the city, where ruins smoldered. Preliminary estimates put the world-wide death toll at just under 20,000.

So much death. So much killing, Lorn thought again. He leaned down and kissed the top of Kiri's head. She reached up and patted his hand. "I feel silly rolling around in this thing," she said. "I can walk perfectly well."

"Doctor's orders," said a voice behind them.

Lorn's hands tightened on the grips of the wheelchair. "Here we go," he murmured, and turned Kiri around to face the board room table...and General Vermani, who had entered through the big double doors on the other side of it.

"I'm very glad to see you," Vermani said. He wasn't talking to Lorn; he had eyes only for Kiri. "I did not think I would."

"You fired at us, Atash," Kiri said. "You fired at *me.*" Lorn thought there was more pain in her voice than when she had been lying wounded in the computer room. "How could you do that?"

"It was my duty," Vermani said. His own voice revealed no strain at all. "I have always done my duty, Kiri. I had thought you would always do it, as well. I was horrified and heartbroken when you took *Ninshubur* against orders." His eyes flicked to Lorn, then back to Kiri. "However, I have spoken to the President. She is prepared to offer you a full pardon in light of your actions on Peregrine, which helped in the destruction of the *Mayflower II*, undoubtedly saving many ELF lives. You may return to full duty as soon as your convalescence is complete."

"No," Kiri said.

For the first time, Vermani looked uncertain. "No? Kiri—"

Lorn stepped out from behind the wheelchair. "She's not going with you, General," he said. "We've discussed it." He put his hand on Kiri's shoulder; she covered it with her own. "She's staying with me."

Vermani looked from him to Kiri. "I understand," he said after a moment. "And I'm happy for you, Kiri."

Funny, you don't look happy, Lorn thought.

"But the two things are not incompatible." He turned his dark eyes on Lorn. "I have also been authorized to offer you a commission in the ELF Field Intelligence Service."

Kiri's hand tightened on his. He stared at Vermani in disbelief. "What?"

"There are other seedships out there," Vermani said. "Other rogue commanders. Hell, there could be an entire Earth fleet hiding in some long-forgotten system, biding its time. Other worlds could be threatened as Peregrine was. The Loyalists could still try to retake Earth. The fight isn't over. It may not be over for years...or decades." He leaned forward on the boardroom table. "You could operate as a team," he said. "If there's one thing you've proven, it's that you work together well. You could serve the cause..."

Lorn looked down at Kiri. She smiled slightly. He turned back to Vermani. "No," he said. "The liberation of Earth is *your* cause. Not mine." He squeezed Kiri's shoulder. "And not hers anymore, either."

Vermani straightened. His jaw clenched. "Let her answer for herself," he snapped.

"I already have," Kiri said. Her voice trembled slightly, and Lorn squeezed harder, trying to give her strength. "My loyalty was never to the *cause*, Atash. My loyalty was to *you*. And you proved what that was worth when you fired on me." She pushed Lorn's hand gently away, then, and stood up, wavering a little. She stepped to the table and leaned on it. "I've been running away from my past, and the only thing I've been running toward is death," she said. "I almost caught it, aboard *Falcon's Egg*. But Lorn refused to let me. He saved me. Not because I could serve his cause or anyone's cause. But because he loves me." She drew herself to her full height. "As I love him."

Lorn knew a cue when he heard one. He stepped forward and put his arm around her waist. She leaned against him slightly, letting him bear a little of her weight. "General Vermani," she said then, "I hereby formally tender my resignation from the *Egalité, Liberté, Fraternité* Field Intelligence Service, and from ELF in general. It is my intention to become a citizen of Peregrine. It is our intention," she glanced up at Lorn and smiled, "to get married." She looked back at him. "You are welcome to attend, of course."

Vermani opened his mouth, then closed it again. "Kiri," he said. "Are you sure you...?"

"I'm sure," Kiri said. She put her hand around Lorn's waist, holding him as he held her. "We both are."

Vermani fists clenched. He stared at them for a long moment. And then, convulsively, his hands relaxed. His eyes suddenly turned bright. "Your parents," he said roughly, "would be proud of you." He took a deep breath. "As am I."

He stood at attention, then, and saluted them both. And then he turned sharply on his heel and left the room.

Kiri let out her own shuddering breath, and Lorn hurriedly helped her lower herself down into her wheelchair again. "That's that," she said. "I'm not Lieutenant Commander Ishida anymore. I've just taken myself out of the fight."

"There are other fights," Lorn said. He turned the wheelchair around and rolled it to the window. "You brought me back from the brink of a breakdown by reminding me what I was supposed to be fighting for," he said. He gestured out at the city. "This. Peregrine. My world. Where my parents and sister live. Where my friends Art Stoddard and Avara Morali and their little girl live. It's been saved twice. I've killed a lot of people trying to make it safe. A lot more people have died for the same reason." He knelt down beside her, took her hand in his. She looked at him with wide, bright eyes. "I'm tired of killing, Kiri," he said softly. "I'm tired of death and destruction. It's time for both of us to try living and building. I want to fight to make Peregrine a better world. I want Javik's sacrifice to mean something, and Shadow's. The rest of the galaxy...can look after itself."

Kiri smiled at him. "I thought you wanted to be a hero."

"Not anymore. I just want to be an ordinary human being."

"All heroes are ordinary human beings," Kiri said. "They just do extraordinary things. You've done your share of them, Lorn Kymbal. And I believe you'll do more."

"With you, Kiri Ishida," Lorn said, "I'm sure of it."

And this time, when they kissed, he felt no doubt at all.

———

Be sure to read Right to Know, *Book 1 in the* Peregrine Rising *duology*.

EDWARD WILLETT is the author of more than sixty books of science fiction, fantasy, and nonfiction for readers of all ages. *Marseguro* (DAW Books) won the Aurora Award (honouring Canadian science fiction and fantasy) for Best Long-Form Work in English in 2009. His young adult fantasy *Spirit Singer* (recently rereleased by Shadowpaw Press) won the Regina Book Award for best book by a Regina author at the 2002 Saskatchewan Book Awards. Several other of his books have been shortlisted for those and other awards.

Ed's most recent novels are *Worldshaper, Master of the World,* and *The Moonlit World,* the first three books in the *Worldshapers* series (DAW Books). Other recent titles include *The Cityborn* and the *Masks of Aygrima* trilogy (written as E.C. Blake), also from DAW; and the five-book *Shards of Excalibur* young-adult fantasy series, originally published by Coteau Books and just re-released by Shadowpaw Press. His nonfiction runs the gamut from science books to biographies to history. He hosts *The Worldshapers* podcast (theworldshapers.com), winner of the Aurora Award for Best Fan Related

Work, in which he talks to other science fiction and fantasy authors about their creative process.

Born in Silver City, New Mexico, Ed moved to Saskatchewan from Texas at the age of eight, and grew up in Weyburn, where his father taught at Western Christian College. He earned a BA in journalism from Harding University in Searcy, Arkansas, and returned to Weyburn to begin his career at the weekly *Weyburn Review*, first as a reporter/photographer/columnist/cartoonist, and eventually as news editor. He moved to Regina in 1988 as communications officer for the then-fledgling Saskatchewan Science Centre. He began writing full-time in 1993.

In addition to being a writer, Ed is a professional actor and singer who has performed in numerous plays, musicals, and operas, and sung in several auditioned choirs, including the Canadian Chamber Choir. He lives in Regina, Saskatchewan, with his wife, Margaret Anne Hodges, P. Eng., a past president of the Association of Professional Engineers and Geoscientists of Saskatchewan. They have one daughter, Alice, and a black Siberian cat, Shadowpaw.

You can find Ed online at www.edwardwillett.com.

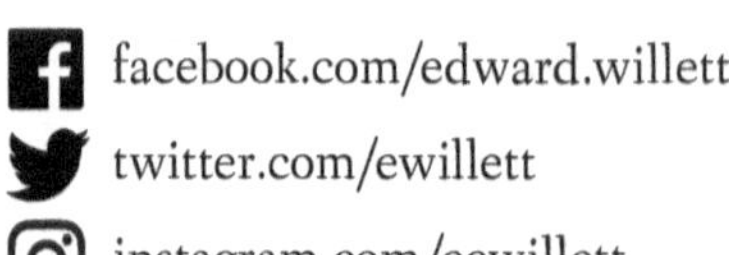

From Shadowpaw Press

Paths to the Stars

Spirit Singer

From the Street to the Stars

Blue Fire

THE SHARDS OF EXCALIBUR

Song of the Sword

Twist of the Blade

Lake in the Clouds

Cave Beneath the Sea

Door into Faerie

———

From Your Nickel's Worth Publishing

I Tumble through the Diamond Dust:

A Collection of Fantastical Poems